The Healer

Alterealm Series

Book 8

By J. Risk

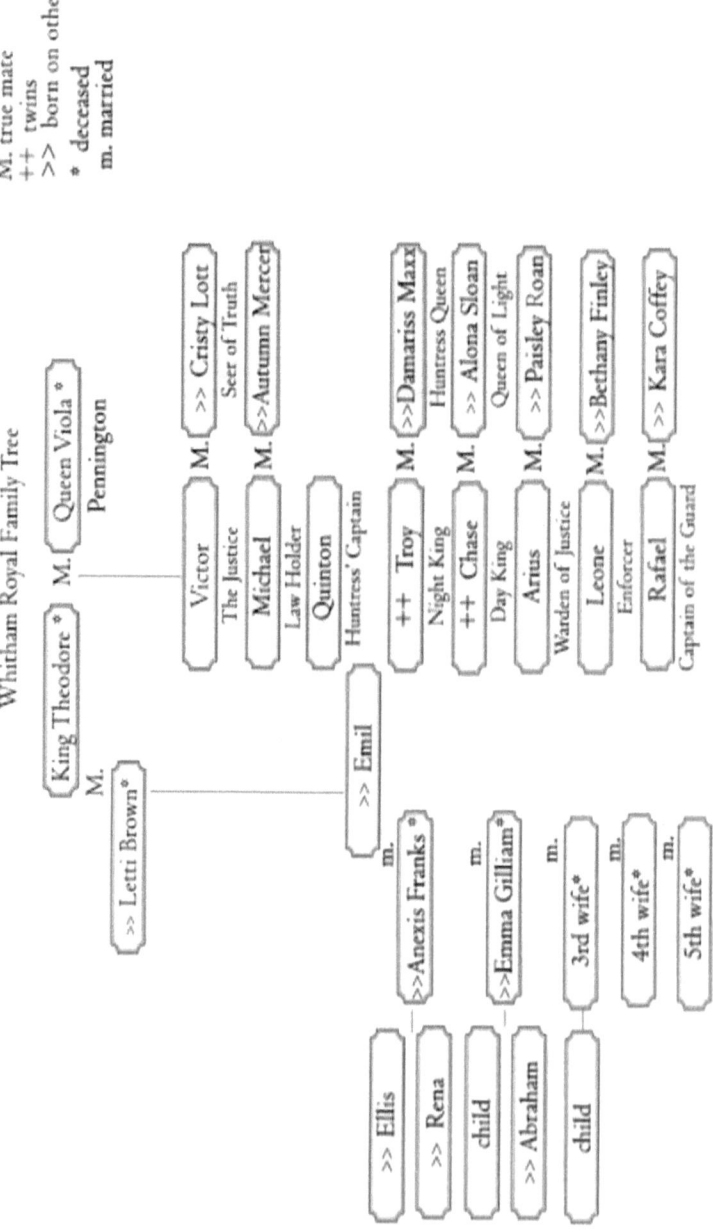

Whitham Royal Family Tree

M. true mate
++ twins
>> born on other side
* deceased
m. married

King Theodore * M. Queen Viola *
Pennington

Victor — The Justice — M. >> Cristy Lott — Seer of Truth
Michael — Law Holder — M. >>Autumn Mercer
Quinton — Huntress' Captain

++ Troy — Night King — M. >>Damariss Maxx — Huntress Queen
++ Chase — Day King — M. >> Alona Sloan — Queen of Light
Arius — Warden of Justice — M. >> Paisley Roan
Leone — Enforcer — M. >>Bethany Finley
Rafael — Captain of the Guard — M. >> Kara Coffey

King Theodore * M. >> Letti Brown *

>> Emil

m. >>Anexis Franks *
m. >>Emma Gilliam*
m. 3rd wife*
m. 4th wife*
m. 5th wife*

>> Ellis
>> Rena
child
>> Abraham
child

"Reagan. Where are you?" It was Paisley.

I looked around in the dim light. "I don't know."

"Is Quinton there?" That was Rafael.

"Quinton?" I rolled onto my hands and knees and tried to focus.

"Where are you?" Daxx told me.

I heard grunting and sounds of a struggle. Pushing to my feet, I took a deep breath and then regretted it. The taste of mildew filled my mouth. "I think we're in the basement." The grunts and sounds of struggle continued, followed by the sound of metal banging together. "Quinton?" I said as loud as I could. "Oh, it better be you." I mumbled. Finally standing, I focused to walk toward the sound, feeling for the pouch on my side at the same time. Stopping, I opened it and felt inside it, then I remembered I had just pulled it out when I ended up here. My foot connected with something, I leaned down and felt around. It was a pipe. "It's so dark in here."

"Use the flashlight on your phone. Access it the same way as when you check your battery." Paisley told me.

Nodding, to myself in the dark, I got the phone out of my pocket and turned on the light. Parts of the walls and other items were scattered all over and it looked worse than it smelled. "I think I liked it better dark." With one hand on my forehead, I held the phone up. "What happened?" The sounds I'd heard had stopped.

"Rea, I'm going to call Quinton's phone, listen for it." Leone said.

"Okay." I stopped where I was and closed my eyes, listening. The faint sound of music echoed. "I hear it." I listened as I started walking. Reaching a door, I looked in. "Keep it ringing. There are halls and doors down here." The music continued. I went in the direction it was coming from and then it stopped.

"Hang on." Leone said.

The ringing started again, I moved faster this time navigating through the rubble and other debris lying on the floor. It was louder when I stuck my head in a door. I shone the light ahead of me and saw him on the floor. "I've got him." I announced to all and hurried to him.

THE ALTEREALM SERIES

1 *The Huntress*
2 *The Seer*
3 *The Empath*
4 *The Witch*
5 *The Chronos*
6 *The Warrior*
7 *The Telepath*
8 *The Healer*
9 *The Kinetic* (coming soon)

Writing As: Jacqueline Paige

Dreams
Three steamy stories that started with a dream
Curses
Two tales of curses.

After the Silence
Volume 1 Bree

ANIMAL SENSES
1 *Heart*
2 *Scent*
3 *Passion*

MAGIC SEASONS ROMANCE
1 *Beltane Magic*
2 *Solstice Heat*
3 *Harvest Dreams*
4 *Autumn Dance*
5 *Winter Mist*

SINGLE TITLES
Solitary Witchling
Salvation

Published by FRP
Copyright © 2020 Roxane Kerr
Edited by Gaele L. Hince
Cover art by: Off the Wall Creations

ISBN: (Print) 978-1-7774682-5-5
ISBN: (Digital) 978-1-7774682-4-8

DEDICATION

For Bec – Sometimes courage can be found in places one would never think to look. When I look at you, I see courage and strength. I know you don't feel it, but it's there for the rest of us to see.

xox

Prologue

She stood in the shadow of the trees, blood dripping from her hand. With cautious steps, she moved into the light toward the small, silent shack. Even though there hadn't been trouble in years, she was taking no chances. She looked around once more before opening the door and stepping inside.

"Rea?"

Rea rushed over and helped her mother sit up. "Slowly, Momma." Keeping a hand on her shoulder, she knelt in front of her.

Her mother reached out to lay a gentle hand on her face. "I was worried, you were gone a long while."

Rea motioned to the table where she'd dropped her kill. "Rabbits are getting scarce here." She pulled the blanket up and tucked it around her mother's shoulders. "We may have to move to a new area soon." Rea moved over to stir the coals in the fireplace. "It's getting too populated here." Her mother's cough had her turning back. It was getting worse by the day. Quickly she moved to ladle out a cup of water from the bucket and bring it to her mother.

Sipping the water, her mother took a few breaths, waiting for the spasm to clear before speaking. "I'm not going to be making any more moves, love."

Rea looked at the tattered gloves on her hands. "We could go into town with people—or, or I could go into town and get an elixir. If you'd let me help…"

"No, Rea. You've been doing that for too many years now." She shook her head. "I'm tired. I've lived lifetimes more than most."

Unwilling to let her mother see the tears in her eyes, Rea turned away. "Do you regret it?" She glanced over to see her mother sitting on the cot, that faraway look on her face again. She sat down at the table.

"Staying?' Her voice was shaky, "no, not for a second."

Her mother's health had been declining for the last ten years. When she was young, before her ability developed, they'd stayed around people so her mother could feed. Once they realized Rea couldn't touch people… their lives became a blur, always on the move, never staying anywhere too long. She paused skinning the rabbit to look around the small shack. As dismal as it was, they'd lived in worse places. "Tell me about it again, Momma." She knew the story by heart, but it always lifted her mother's spirit to tell her about where she came from, and how she met her father.

"I'd never been to this side before." She exhaled a loud breath, "we were advised to delay coming over until after the war. We knew we shouldn't come, but then we would have forfeited our turn and would have to wait for the selection, hoping that our names were drawn again."

Rea didn't interrupt when her mother paused, she knew she was reliving the emotions of the past.

"They made certain we'd come out in a safe area…" she made a noise of exasperation, "or as safe as any place could be. Kin fighting kin, it was madness. You know all of this, Rea…"

Rea pulled off her blood-soaked gloves and pulled on clean cotton ones, then got up to add some wood to the fire. "I know it, but I could hear it every day and never tire of it, Momma." She straightened up and looked at her. "Do you think your friends went back over?" Her mother's memory didn't always work lately, so anything Rea could do to help, she did.

Her mother blew out a breath. "I imagine they did." She shook her head. "I cursed myself for a week when we were separated."

Rea went back to the table and began to slice the flesh from her kill. "Would you truly have been arrested if someone had seen your devices?"

"Our porters? Yes. The light bulb didn't exist over here, not for fifteen years after we came over. Technology like our porters would have created chaos and worries of conspiracy…"

"I heard talk they have electricity in the city now."

Her mother smiled. "*That* is something I have missed."

"I hope to see it someday." Read admitted.

"You will, daughter. You're going to live long enough to see many amazing changes in this world. Rea—I want you to do what you have to in order to survive and keep going. *Never look back.*"

Rea picked up the pan, full of cleaned rabbit, and placed it on the fire to brown the meat. She couldn't listen to her mother speak of when she was no longer there. "Do you think I'll live as long as you have?"

"You could live *much* longer than I. Your father was quite a relic when we met." She chuckled softly, "his words, not mine. I'm not sure how old he was, precisely."

The sizzling of the meat was the only sound in the small space for a few moments.

"All three of us gave our porters to Synova to keep in her clutch. I hadn't thought to bring one, or you wouldn't exist." She made a soft noise, "I'm glad I forgot." Another pause. "My only regret was I never did get to see the new kings. Your grandmother said they were blond and beautiful. The whole realm was alight with the promise of the prophecy being realized."

Using a cloth, Rea took the pan off the heat and set it on

the table. Opening the cupboard, she hoped there were enough potatoes to turn the meal into a stew. "Do you think my father is still alive?" Rea knew anything was possible.

Her mother made a soft sound. "I don't know. Our love was forbidden since time began. When they found out we were together, they took him away. He would have loved you with all of his heart."

Rea looked over to see her mother laying back down.

"Don't go near any with eyes as dark as coal, Rea, you are the result of a love that shouldn't have been." Her mother closed her eyes. "I don't know what would happen to you if they found out."

Rea watched her breathing settle. "I won't, Momma." She whispered.

Waiting a few more minutes, until her breathing was the steady rhythm of sleep, Rea pulled the gloves from her hands and went over to her mother. Kneeling down, she placed her hand on her mothers' neck, as she did each time she slept. Rea knew it wasn't what her mother wanted, but she wasn't ready to face the world without her. "I'm sorry, Momma," she whispered under her breath, "I need you too much to let you go."

Chapter One

Hugging the bag gently against my chest, I ran up the last few stairs and pulled the door open. Loud voices had me crouching down behind the steel barrier. Why were they up here? No one came up here anymore.

With my chin hovering close to the dirty cement, I looked around to see if I could see where they were. This parking garage was rarely used. Maybe the first level once in a while, not the top two. People in this neighborhood couldn't afford cars. It was barricaded off for a reason.

Taking off my backpack, I opened it and worked the bag into it. My bread was going to be smushed now, and if the juice carton was punctured, I'd have a backpack of soggy fruit punch flavored bread. Doing up the zip, I put the backpack on, making sure the straps were tight. I wasn't impressed. At all. It had taken me two days of helping at the clinic to make the money to buy this food and a new pair of gloves. I looked at my new leather gloves. They were almost as important as food to me.

Sighing, I peeked around the barrier again. There was a group of men, a trace of black all around them, so bad men. They were herding six others into the corner of the garage. The same corner I needed to use to get where I lived. The six people were scared, rightly so, judging by the size of a few of those men. Three women, a young girl, a little boy, and a man stood in the corner huddled together. What kind of shake-down was this? Over a dozen douche bags against a few scared people.

I looked the men over, they weren't from any gang I recognized. There were no colors, logos or symbols showing, and they were carrying barbaric weapons. Seriously, carrying swords in this day and age? It was like a role play group gone wrong. I looked back at the door wondering if I could get out without being spotted? I could just wait it out in the stairwell and sit at the top until they left.

I closed my eyes berated myself—because turning the other cheek and pretending life was sweetly full of roses and pretty rainbows was *so* not in my DNA. I moved to the other end of the barrier and tried to find somewhere better to hide without being seen. I had no idea of what I could do against that many men, but I hadn't done anything stupidly heroic in a few months, so why not think about it? YOLO, right? You only live once. As far as I knew, that was true.

If I could move without making a sound, I could get to the large pillar and move into the dark corner behind the stairwell. *If*, was the key negative word pretending to be hopeful. It always led to thinking things were possible. Rolling my eyes at my own ridiculousness, I held the small pouch at my side, so the chain didn't jingle. As long as they kept griping at each other, I shouldn't be heard.

I watched and waited for the best opportunity, mentally psyching myself up to succeed. When the focus turned to the big guy in the middle, I hunched down and hurried toward the pillar. I probably looked like a waddling duck, but I was going to pretend I was moving gracefully and undetected across the floor.

Reaching the pillar, I braced against it before bending down to look around it. No one was looking at me. Good job, Rea. I touched my shoulder and gave it a pat. Another quick look and I made a split-second decision to rush to the dark corner.

As soon as I reached the dark, I ducked down, just about to lean back against the wall before I remembered my bread in my pack. I rested my arm against the wall instead.

A very unhappy looking man waved his hands around.

"Why here?" He demanded.

"In case it has escaped your notice, we're running out of concealed locations." The man in the middle replied tersely. "This place is hidden in plain sight."

The first man snorted, "well, if it's going to be a regular drop off location, we need to have chairs while we wait."

"Yes, your comfort will be our top priority. I'll bring it up at the next meeting." Was the sarcastic response.

"I think we should call, Nathas, they're late." Another man said while holding up his phone.

Nathas, the man in the center of the men, nodded, "message them first, it might be poor timing for a call." He turned to a man leaning against a pillar, his arms crossed over his chest. "You're sure about this bunch?"

The man nodded, then turned and looked over the scared people in the corner. "It's faint, but they have the right genes somewhere in their history."

Nathas smiled briefly. "Good."

I looked back at the man watching their captives. His eyes were as dark as coal. I debated about getting out of here, Momma's warning in my mind. Even if it put me at risk, I knew I couldn't do it. My shoulders slumped as I sighed silently.

I didn't know what genes had to do with anything. I did know I was outnumbered, more bad dudes were on the way, and I could see no way I could get all six people away from these men. I didn't *know* if they were a family, but there was no harm in romanticizing that it was a family huddled together—the family were about three feet away from my bungee. If I could get through the large men to them, I could grab one child, get over the railing and bungee down to my place. Probably. Hopefully. That half-baked plan left the other five with them and the role-playing failures would know where I lived.

Time for a new plan I shook my head. I had no other plan. I pulled out a chain from my pack, slowly to let it pool soundlessly beside me. My wannabe surujin wasn't going to be enough to get through all six men. I could probably trip up two, maybe three, but then what? Aside from cussing and sticking out my tongue. I had no other skills. I was purely a defensive 'run away' type of person, entirely self-taught.

I clenched my teeth together, growling inside my head. All I wanted was a jam sandwich and a glass of juice. Now, I going to be eating squished, misshapen bread and had to skulk around in this corner until they left as I watched them abduct the family/nonfamily they held captive.

The little girl was crying. Dammit.

Noise from loud footfalls coming up the ramp jerked my head around to watch. Their friends had arrived. A blonde woman charged at one of them, growling out a battle cry. Okay. Not friends. I watched for a moment as several more people appeared. They were also carrying barbaric weapons, but they were using them against the original creeps, so I decided that was a better option.

"Nathas Roan, you're a traitorous bastard." A large redheaded man bellowed.

Two of the women skidded to a stop and turned to see who the redhead was looking at. The one with the black hair rushed toward him. "I've got his feet." She told the other woman. She stopped a few feet from him and held out her hand toward him.

The blonde woman beside her snarled. "I've got his face." She did this little jump in the air and spun around and kicked him in the face. He went down, just catching himself before his face hit the floor.

"*What the Hell?*" I whispered, in awe of what she'd done. I needed to learn *that*.

A tiny redheaded woman came out of the shadows, with bright orange sparks coming off her hands. I looked at my gloved hand, deciding I was in no place to judge. I watched her toss a flaming ball at the one they called Nathas, and he hit the floor.

"Leone." The tiny redhead said.

"Trying." One of the new arrivals grunted as he blocked the swing of a sword with his own much larger sword.

"I got him." The blonde woman that had rushed into the group ran toward Nathas, still being beat on. She slid toward him holding a box in her hand. I thought she was going to shock him, but instead he vanished.

Vanished.

Gone without a trace.

I swallowed. Okay that was a bit freakier than I was comfortable with, and freaky was my very existence.

The women spun toward those fighting.

I noticed two other women standing in front of the abducted family. One was flicking nun-chucks back and forth, the other squatted down with a large blade in her hand. A man rushed for them, sword in hand when an arrow came out of nowhere and hit him. He crumpled to the floor.

I leaned around the corner and looked up. Standing up and leaning over the railing was a woman with a bow. Swords, bows, knives, nun-chucks and flying balls of fire. *What* the actual *F* was going on? Usually I was the only oddity in the room.

"Quinton!"

I turned back to see one of the good barbarians crumple to the floor. He was holding his side.

"I'm fine." He growled. "Get that bastard."

The man with black hair, nodded and turned to the man holding a blood-soaked sword.

I bit my lip and told myself absolutely not. They had this. It was probably just a small flesh wound. I moved out of the dark to one of the pillars, I saw a man running across the cement toward the one laying on the ground. The injured man shifted, trying to pick up his sword as he held his side.

Without debate, I ran out from my cover, swinging the surujin as I went. When I was close enough, I flung it toward the attacker that was about to impale the injured man. It wrapped around his ankle, I jerked and he fell face-first onto the hard surface. Letting go of the chain's handle, I ran past him to the injured man.

Jerking my gloves off, I grabbed the leather and tried to pull it away from his bloodied body. "You'll be fine." I told him, pulling the knife from its sheath at his side I used it to rip the leather of his vest apart.

He had a large slice in his side. I put both hands on it and pushed. "You'll be fine." I told him again, then glanced to his face. Brown eyes stared at me, with fear. "It's okay." I nodded. The brown hair hanging in my face started to turn to grey, I jerked my head, flipping it out of the way. I felt the draw, it was strong. Maybe I'd underestimated how bad his injury was. It must have been life-threatening to take this much energy for me to heal it.

"Stop." He told me, terror in his eyes.

I offered him a brief look, I didn't want him to see my eyes turning black. The blood stopped flowing out between my fingers. "It's slowing, you'll be fine."

"Stop." He growled and grabbed my wrists, trying to pull my hands free of him.

"Rafael, blueish-grey hair." Someone screeched.

"Victor, no." A blond man slid beside me and put his arm in front of me. "I had a vision of her."

A pain went through my chest. I couldn't heal him further. Pulling my hands away, I grabbed my gloves and stood up. I stumbled a few steps. I'd used far too much energy on him. Brushing past the woman kneeling down beside the injured man, I ran for the corner, hoping I had enough energy to get there.

"Stop her!" Someone yelled.

I grabbed the bungee and swung my leg over the railing. Holding on with all I had, I jumped over the edge. I misjudged and released too soon, then fell to my back on the roof below. So much for my bread and juice surviving.

"Where did she go?" I could hear them above me.

Opening my eyes, I saw a few of them looking down over the railing.

I rolled to my knees and stood; my head was spinning. I looked at the small shack at the back of the roof and stumbled toward it. Once I got inside, they wouldn't be able to follow me.

I was almost there when a man with messy black hair appeared in front of me. His eyes were as dark as coal...

He smiled. "I have so many questions for you."

I tried to stand without swaying. "Please, just..."

He held up a hand and looked behind me. "Leave her unharmed. I need to know how she came to be."

"We're not going to harm her, Bastian, we're getting her to medical."

I turned to see the man I'd healed standing there. He was on his feet, leaning against another man, but I'd helped him. He would be fine. They blurred, I took a deep breath trying to stay conscious, but my hair was now white and covered my eyes.

Damn, was my last thought, I wasn't getting that sandwich.

Everything went black.

Chapter Two

I lay there with my eyes closed, taking an inventory of how badly I'd drained myself this time. I hadn't over done it in fifty years, maybe more. I didn't feel ill or dizzy, so maybe not as bad as I thought. A faint beep registered, what the heck was that? Opening my eyes, I brushed my hair off my face, noting it was slightly grey still. Jolting, I sat up fast. I looked at the monitor beside me and then to the I.V. pole, then to the needle stuck in my arm. A hospital.

OMG. I couldn't be in a hospital.

Taking a deep breath, I focused to try and make the beeping slow back down. I looked around. No windows. Crap. Okay, so I was in a hospital hooked up to an I.V. and heart monitor, all bad news for me. If the nurses came in to check on me and saw that my hair had changed color… I was in for the rest of my life, with tests and prodding. I wasn't feeling that at all. I stared at the thin bracelet around my wrist and wondered what that monitored. I took it off slowly and watched the monitors. Nothing happened. I dropped it beside me on the bed.

Shifting, I swung my legs over the side of the bed. I still had my clothes on, so that was a plus. Nothing was more awkward then trying to escape with your butt hanging out of a hospital gown. I stopped all movement when I spotted the table. On it sat my surujin, gloves and what I was pretty sure was a jam sandwich and glass of juice. My backpack was on the floor beside it.

WTH??

I stood up, making sure the monitor and I.V. didn't disconnect and alert the staff. The door was open a few inches. I'd have to move fast once I pulled out this needle and took the pads off my chest. I glanced back at the table— and the sandwich. Shaking my head, I decided that nourishment would have to wait.

Voices in the hall had me freeze where I stood, like a statue.

"How's she doing?" A man's gruff voice asked.

Shivers went down my spine. I didn't know how I knew this, but I was positive it was the man I'd healed.

"Everything seems normal." A woman answered.

"Alona, I watched her hair turn to white. That is *not* normal." He scoffed.

"Well, aside from that and her eyes darkening, everything checks out." She sounded pleasant. "How are you doing?"

He made an annoyed sound. "I'm fine. Wasn't as bad as I'd thought."

"How's Quinton's savior doing?" A man asked.

"She's not my savior." Quinton growled.

"She's still resting but seems to be fine." The soft-spoken woman said.

"And the family, how are they, duchess?"

Duchess? My nurse was royalty? That was—odd.

"They're doing as well as can be expected. Liza has them at one of the safe houses until we can find out why Willis Hubert wanted them."

Someone snorted. "I think we know *why* he wanted them."

"Bastian said they have Alterealm DNA. It's faint but there." Another male answered.

Alterealm? Was it possible? I hadn't heard that name spoken in one hundred and twenty years. Not since my mother had passed away. So that left me wondering if they were the people my mother had warned me about. One had dark eyes. I held my breath trying to decide if I should bolt out the door and make a run for it. Logic predicted I wouldn't get far with the number of voices outside the door.

"Ah, and how long can we expect Bastian's company, brother?" A jovial male asked.

"He's not budging until he speaks to our mystery guest. Says he needs to know how she came to be."

"What does that mean?" A woman asked.

"We're not entirely sure."

"Michael and Arius guarding Nathas?" She sounded amused.

"Yes. Keeping Autumn and Paisley off him is quite the task I'm told."

"Never a dull moment, my newfound family." Yet another male's voice.

Someone snorted. "Happy to keep you entertained, Emil."

"Everyone stay out here, we don't need everyone hovering when she wakes up." One of the first voices said.

Eyes wide, I realized they were coming in. I backed up to stand behind the head of the bed putting as much distance as possible between the door and whomever was coming in.

Two very tall, and handsome men stepped into the small room. They had pale blond hair and were identical, except for one having a goatee. Their eyes were not dark. They looked familiar, then I realized why. I'd heard them described for many years. I knew who they were. My mouth dropped open and it felt like my heart flipped inside my chest. "Blond and beautiful." I whispered. Stepping out from the bed, I bent at the waist and bowed my head. "Your Majesties." I held the position as my mother had told me I must do until they acknowledge me.

"We're famous." The one said. "And beautiful."

A hand touched my head lightly. "Rise." The other one said without a trace of amusement in his voice.

I straightened up and looked at them, biting my lip so nothing inappropriate would fly out of my mouth. I was standing in front of Alterealm's twin kings.

"How do you know who we are?" The one without the goatee asked.

"My-my mother told me all about you and Alterealm." I decided to stick to the truth. Did kings still behead people? Yeah, the truth was best.

"I see. Where is your mother?"

I looked from one to the other, wishing the one looking amused was asking the questions instead. "She died a long time ago." I whispered.

"I'm sorry to hear that." His tone was softer.

"Was she a resident of Alterealm?" The other one asked.

"Yes, your majesty." I nodded.

"Have you ever been here before?"

I looked around the room. "We're *in* Alterealm?" I heard the beeping speed up. Reaching down, I pulled the pads off my chest so it would stop monitoring me. I stepped over and flipped the machine off.

I was in Alterealm. Finally. Safe from my father's people. I spun around and pointed to the device I'd taken off. "Is that a porter? Mother described them, but it looks nothing like that." I rolled my eyes. "Of course, your technology has probably advanced times ten by now." They were both giving me an odd look.

"It's actually a stabilizer." The one with the goatee held up his arm, "this is a porter."

I nodded. "Of course. You'd want to make sure I didn't die when you brought me over." I stopped and looked from one to the other. "Thank you, and so you know, I spent thirty years trying to ferret out someone from here to bring me over." I smirked. "Your people are very discreet, and I never found one."

"That's good to know." The serious one gave me a serious look. "That we're hard to detect over there."

I nodded again. I looked at the I.V. and then pulled it out and hung it over the bag. "So, now what? Do I have to pass a test or something to be a full citizen?" I heaved out a loud breath. "I can't believe I'm finally safe."

"Safe from whom?" The one with the goatee asked.

I wished I could remember which one was King Troy and which one was King Chase. I blew out a breath, not sure how to explain anything. "From my father's people." I decided again the truth was probably best. "My mother told me to avoid them."

"Who is your father?" The stoic one asked.

I opened my mouth and closed it. "I-I don't know. They took him before I was born." I was getting identical looks from them.

The serious one nodded, then looked at me. "Let's start with your name." He motioned to his twin. "This is Chase and I'm Troy."

I felt honored and bowed my head slightly again. "I'm Reagan. Well, actually my given name is Rea, but I changed it about a fifty years ago to blend in with more modern trends."

He glanced to Chase, then back to me, "and your last name? So we can locate any relatives if they're still living."

I opened my mouth, then snapped it shut. "I don't know. Mother and I used Hayden, but I think she made that up."

He pulled his phone out of his pocket and started typing something.

A man pushed between them and came in. It was the one I'd helped. I paused for a moment to look at him, now that he wasn't bleeding all over the place. He was just as beautiful as his kings were. His brown hair had auburn highlights in it, as it fell across his forehead. For some strange reason I wanted to go touch it. His eyes were brown with lighter flecks in them. They were very pretty eyes, although I'm sure he'd scowl at me even more than he already was if I were to voice that.

"And this is our brother, Quinton." The one said with a smirk.

I rushed toward him and reached out, then saw my bare hand. Turning I grabbed my gloves and put them on quickly. "How are you doing?" I went over and pulled his shirt up. "I didn't realize how deep it went or I would have just closed it so you didn't bleed out..." There was no mark on his side. Had I done that? No wonder I was drained. It wasn't the first time I'd healed with too much oomph when my adrenaline was pumping.

He stepped back out of my reach.

I looked up to see his dark brown eyes looking at me like I was the strangest thing he'd ever seen.

"You did that?" Chase looked at Quinton, then back to me. "You healed him with your hands?"

I reluctantly looked away from Quinton and nodded. "Yes." I shrugged. "Don't ask me to explain it, I don't understand it."

"Did your mother have the ability?" Troy asked. "A skill such as that would be easy to trace back to your family"

Family. Could it be possible I had relatives? I shook my head. "No. She said she was unlucky with no special talents."

"Perhaps your father did?" Chase asked.

I shrugged. "Not that I know of. I don't know a lot about him, just..." Surely it was safe to tell them. "My mother said if I encountered anyone like my father, with eyes as dark as coal—to get away from them and never look back."

They gave each other a quick look.

"Interesting." Troy said.

"Why did your hair go white?" Quinton blurted out.

I touched my hair, that was almost back to brown now. "Oh, I didn't realize how bad your injury was and expended too much energy."

He studied me with a hard expression. "Don't touch me again." He spun on his heels and stomped out of the room.

"Well," Chase looked at the door, then back to me, "I apologize for my brother's abruptness." He smiled at me, "thank you for helping him." He inclined his head to me.

"Your brother," I remembered the royal family my mother had talked about. I made an o with my lips, "you have many brothers." I smiled.

"Too many some days." Troy said and rubbed the back of his neck.

"Excuse me," a man with black hair stepped into the room, "I have to go help Rena pack up." He didn't look pleased with this. "I probably won't be back until after breakfast." He stopped and looked at me. "Emil." He bowed his head briefly, "thank you for assisting my brother."

Another brother. That explained why he was so nice to look at. "Reagan." I took a short breath. At some point it was going to sink in that I was in Alterealm. *The* Alterealm. There was no guarantee my reaction would be pretty. I would probably be more like a screaming fangirl.

He gave me an abrupt nod, then glanced to his brothers and left the room.

"What's with Quint? He just lit out of here like his butt was on fire." A tiny redheaded woman came in.

Chase grinned, "He didn't seem receptive to the idea that Reagan healed him with just a touch."

"Just add that to the list of his strangeness lately." She smiled at me. "Hi, I'm Bethany."

I smiled back.

"What strangeness?" Troy asked her.

She gave him an exaggerated look. "You haven't noticed that we see him less and less lately? Or that we never see him unless we're eating, fighting," she shrugged, "or planning?"

Troy looked over her head to Chase then back down at her. "I hadn't noticed."

"Big shocker there." A blonde woman came in. "I can't stall Bastian much longer." She glanced to me, gave me a quick once over then looked up at Troy.

Troy heaved a sigh. "We'll deal with Bastian," he motioned to me, "Rea's mother was one of ours." He looked at the woman again, "we're going to need to call a meeting to discuss her intriguing history and appease the Solrelm Prince."

Solrelm? Maybe it was part of Alterealm and mother had never mentioned it.

She nodded. "At the meeting room?"

Troy nodded. "See if you can get Autumn and Paisley to leave the cells too, Daxx, and then Michael and Arius can attend."

Daxx grinned. "I'll see what I can do."

The kings turned and walked out of the room in unison.

"This is Daxx. Troy's mate." Bethany told me.

"Oh," I bowed my head, "your majesty." When I straightened, Daxx was scowling at me and Bethany was grinning.

"That will be enough of *that*." Daxx mumbled.

"We're very informal most of the time." Bethany told me.

I filed that information away. "Who is the Solrelm Prince?"

"Bastian." Daxx answered as she went over and picked up my surujin. She looked over her shoulder at me. "That was something, when you used this."

I shrugged. "Run away is my method of battle. Anything to postpone a fight."

She smirked. "You're going to get along with Crissy really well then."

A tall blond man rushed through the door. He stopped abruptly and looked at me. "Your hair was blueish-grey."

I nodded slowly.

"I've been seeing you for weeks."

I opened my mouth, then closed it and looked at Daxx, she shrugged. "Okay."

A woman came in. "He has visions."

Which explained it, but not at the same time.

"I'm Kara," she motioned to the man, "this is my mate, Rafael."

Rafael. I knew that name. I bowed at the waist quickly.

"Uh, stop doing that." Daxx said.

I straightened.

"So it's true." Rafael crossed his arms over his chest and grinned down at me. "You are one of ours."

I went over and picked up my backpack and put it on. "My mother was."

"Which means you are." Kara smiled at me.

Daxx pulled her phone out of her pocket then sighed. "We have to get to the meeting room, Bastian is getting impatient." She handed me my surujin. "Have you ever ported before?"

I took it and quickly dropped it into the pouch at my side. "No."

"It sucks." Bethany said then vanished.

Eyes wide I stood there looking where she had been. "Where did she go?"

"Meeting room." Daxx held out her hand. "Close your eyes, take a deep breath, and hang on."

Chapter Three

I opened my eyes to see we were standing in a completely different room. I let go of Daxx and looked around. I wanted to jump up and down but managed to suppress it. Barely. "That was a ride." I couldn't help grin. I'd ported!

"Uh," Bethany looked over her shoulder at me. "Figures you'd think that." She looked up at a tall redheaded man, "am I the only one that will never get used to it?"

He gave her an understanding smile, "it just takes some longer, love."

"Maybe it's your magic stuff making it harder for you." The blonde woman that had drop-kicked that Nathas man came in. She stopped in front of me and looked me up and down. "Nice use of the surujin."

I smiled at her. "Nice kick you dropped that guy with."

Her smile left. "Yeah, well, dear old dad deserved that."

I had no words to offer her. He was her father?

"He deserves a lot more than that, Autumn." The woman with the short black hair came through the doorway. "If I have my way, I'm going to stop time around him for the rest of his life."

King Chase walked in. "When did Sarg become so dark?"

A man with long black hair and grey eyes walked in behind her. "Don't even go there, Chase or I might have to deck you."

Emil came in. "I see I've missed more mayhem."

Chase looked at him. "I thought you went to help Rena?"

Emil shook his head, a hard look on his face. "She kicked me out." He turned to look at Autumn. "How long does her—emotional flux last?"

Autumn shrugged. "Like I'd know." She went and sat down.

"When my sister was carrying our kings, she actually stabbed your father with a salad fork in the middle of dinner." A petite redheaded woman came in carrying a tray of sandwiches.

Emil sat down beside Autumn. "Let's hope this isn't a sign she's carrying twins."

Autumn's head snapped around to the man with the black hair and scar on his face. "There could be two." She said softly.

He closed his eyes for a second, then opened them and gave Emil a hard look.

"She has an ultrasound scheduled next week after she's over here." The woman that had been swinging the nun-chucks said as she walked in gracefully.

Autumn nodded. "Two, three, whatever, as long as everyone is healthy, right?" She turned back to Emil.

"Yes." His look softened. "That's the main thing."

I turned and looked around. Then stopped and gaped at the smooth, carved thrones sitting at the end of the room. I walked over slowly, in awe. "OMG." I whispered under my breath. I was really in Alterealm.

"Are you okay?" A short woman with sandy blonde hair stepped up beside me.

I nodded slowly. "I can't believe I'm here."

She bobbed her head. "I'm glad you are." She looked at my hair, "and that your hair turns grey." She leaned closer and looked at my eyes, "and that your eyes go black." She

22

nodded, "you are *very* important." Giving me another smile, she turned and walked away.

"What Crissy means is, she's being seeing someone with grey hair for a few weeks and couldn't figure out the connection." Kara said with a knowing look. "Would you like anything to …"

"I don't know *why* I had to sit in the acclimation chambers." The man with the dark eyes said in an annoyed tone as he came into the room with King Troy. "It's not like I've never been to this realm."

"We prefer to take caution with a man from a royal family." Troy told him, "There was nothing you could do until the Doctor finished."

I studied him. His eyes were dark as coal. He was one of those my mother had warned me to avoid. So Solrelm was not part of Alterealm.

The prince from Solrelm waved his hand around. "How is the woman?"

I realized he didn't recognize me. My hair was brown again. I continued to stand beside the thrones, unmoving. I studied the two kings. Would they protect me if this prince of my father's people wanted to take me?

"She fares well." King Chase said, without looking at me.

"The resident we're holding in the cells from your realm, is not a happy man." A tall redheaded man came in through a different doorway. His expression and posture said not to mess with him. Usually someone like him would have black all around them, but oddly he didn't.

"Ah, yes." The Prince crossed his arms over his chest. "He'll be accompanying me back home."

"I'd like to know a few things before he goes." Rafael came through behind the scary man.

"Like?" The prince asked.

"If there are more of yours helping Willis Hubert." The man with the scar on his face crossed his arms and leaned back against the wall. "It would explain how they're able to find so many with Alterealm blood in their veins."

The prince frowned. "It would. We can see even the slightest trace from generations ago." He gave the other man an abrupt nod. "Rest assured we'll get all information for you."

Seeing a person's bloodline? "You can see things like that?" I blurted out before my mouth remembered I was trying to be unseen.

"There you are." The prince came rushing over to me. "Your hair…" He looked at me with great scrutiny. "I didn't even notice you hiding beside the thrones."

"Bastian…" Troy came over.

Bastian waved his hand at him. "I'm not going to steal her away—I just need to know how it is she exists."

He wasn't taking me. "I-I don't know what you mean." I looked at Troy than back to him.

Bastian got right in my face, his dark, serious eyes inches from mine. "I need to know how you came to be."

Someone snorted. Daxx came over. "Probably the same way everyone else did. Unless you think she was hatched, and her mother was a chicken."

Crissy came over quickly. "Creatures can be hatched that aren't birds. Like fish…" She stopped when everyone looked at her.

"No, no, no, little one." Bastian said in a quiet tone. "Can you not *see* it? This mix. How is she this mix? It's impossible." He grasped her shoulders and turned her to look at me. "Look. Tell me what you see."

A low growl emanated from across the room.

Bastian dropped his hands from her and stepped back. He looked at the scary redheaded man. "Sorry, Justice, I forgot protocol and all that…" He waved his hand around. He turned back to Crissy. "What do you see?"

"Um," Crissy looked at me, then above my head, "that she's good. All good." She nodded her head quickly.

"No, no, no." Bastian hissed out a breath in exasperation.

"Bastian. Why don't you tell us what *you* see and try to shed some light on what you're talking about?" Chase said wandering over slowly, an amused look on his face.

"Yes. Fine." Bastian gave him a hard look then turned to me. Placing his hands on his hips, he stood there continuing to stare at me. Then around me.

I felt like I wanted to be somewhere else. Every pair of eyes on the room were on me.

"She's half Alterealm." He finally said.

"We know that. She already told us her mother was from Alterealm." Bethany said sitting on the corner of the platform the thrones were on.

"Right." Bastian looked animated then looked back at me. "And-and that means her father…" He frowned, "no that's impossible."

"What is impossible?" Daxx threw her hands up as she stomped over.

Now I wanted to crawl *under* the thrones as they all stood there staring at me now.

"Her father was one of mine." He said with disbelief in his tone. "There's basically no human in her at all. I thought it was the lighting at the garage…"

"Wait. What? What do you mean I'm not human?" Eyes-wide I stared him down.

"On the outside, you appear to be, but not really." Bastian said softly. "Which means I've been—*my* people have been lied to for too many millenniums to count." He scowled.

Daxx huffed out a loud breath and went to the nearest chair and sat down. She motioned to the table. "Sit. Explain."

Bastian put his hands on his hips and turned back to me. "I can't sit. Now is not the time to *sit*. I need answers."

He wasn't the only one.

He pointed to me. "Your parents. You knew them?"

I shook my head slowly. "My mother only."

He nodded, but his expression said that wasn't all he wanted to know.

"They took my father before I was born." I told him.

"They?" He raised both eyebrows and watched me.

"His people. That's all I know." I glanced away from him to see the room was filled with more people and they were all crowding closer.

"My people found out about him and your mother and took him?" Bastian clarified.

"Yes. That's what she told me."

He ran his hand through his messy hair and looked at the floor. "There would have to be a record then…" he mumbled quietly. With a fierce look he snapped his head back up to look at me. "When were you born?"

Clasping my gloved hands in front of me, I tried not to look as panicked as I felt. "After the war."

"First?" King Troy asked.

"Second?" Rafael inquired.

I shook my head. "Civil."

"You were born after the civil war?" Bethany asked. "The one that ended in *eighteen* sixty-five?" She was standing beside me now.

I nodded.

"Cool." She turned to the woman with the long black hair. "She's way older than you, Alona."

Alona smiled, "and yet looks younger."

King Chase turned to look at her. "There's not a woman in any realm to rival your beauty and grace, my beloved."

"Everyone, out of Reagan's face. *Now.*"

I turned to see Quinton leaning inside the door. I didn't even know he'd arrived.

"Quinton's right. Everyone sit down." The small red-headed lady came in. She was carrying a plate and glass. "Come, love. The contents of your backpack didn't survive the fall, so I've made you something to eat." She set it on the table and turned around. She tsked and looked at the men around me, "You should be ashamed of yourselves, hounding her after she gave so much to help your brother."

The large bodies started to back away.

"That goes for you too, Prince Bastian. I know your mother quite well. She wouldn't stand for this sort of harassment—against a *woman* with Solrelm blood."

Bastian jolted like she'd smacked him. He stepped back. "You are so right, I completely lost my mind and forgot." He looked back to me and bowed slightly motioning to the table. "Please, sit and eat."

I moved around him to where the lady had set the plate.

"I'm Mitz, by the way, dear. If you need anything, you let me know." She gave me a gentle smile that reminded me of my mother.

"Th-thank you." I sat down.

"All of you sit and behave like the royalty you're supposed to be." She ordered before walking from the room.

Chapter Four

Chairs scraped across the floor as everyone sat down.

"I can't recall the last time Mitz was that brusque." The man with the scar said to Autumn as they sat down.

"Yeah, it's not her normal tone." Rafael agreed, "unless bloody weapons on the table are involved."

I looked at the sandwich in front of me, then lifted the top piece of bread. It was jam. The others passed the tray of sandwiches around and started eating. Picking up the glass I took a sip. It was fruit punch. She must have seen what I'd had in my backpack I decided.

Bastian sat there, not eating, just staring at his clasped hands resting on the table.

Quinton also wasn't eating. He sat across from me, just looking at me. "Did any of you introduce yourselves to, Reagan?" He turned and looked at the scary redheaded man, "before you got in her face?"

"Uh," Daxx looked around, "I think some of us did at medical?"

Several heads turned and looked at me. I set the glass down.

"I'm Crissy." The short woman with sandy blonde hair said as she looked up from her notebook to nod at me, with a smile. Turning to the scary redheaded man, she huffed out a

28

breath. "I can't find anything for Reagan." She stabbed the notebook with her finger. "For all the others there was something." She frowned and just sat there unmoving for several seconds. "Strange fog," she whispered.

He gave her an affectionate look, "I'm sure you'll find something, heart."

She nodded and looked at me again. "Do you have any tattoos?"

I shook my head, not even wanting to guess why she'd ask that.

"Okay." Standing up quickly, she turned to the door. "I need to go to my corner." She nodded, then paused in step and looked at me. "I'm glad you're here." With that she walked out of the room.

Her corner?

"You'll get used to Crissy moments." The woman with the short dark hair said. "I'm Paisley." She gave me a pleasant and real smile. "This is my mate, Arius." She put her hand on the shoulder of the man with the long black hair.

"Prince Arius?" My mother had told stories about him. I looked at him. He didn't seem as terrifying as my mother had said.

Arius looked surprised. "Your mother explained a lot about Alterealm."

It wasn't a question, but I still nodded. "Yes. She would talk about it for hours. I loved how happy she looked when she talked about it."

"I'm sorry you lost her." The woman with long black hair said. "I'm Alona, Chase's mate."

I started to get up.

"Please don't." Daxx said.

I sat down and looked back to Alona. "I'm not required to show respect?"

Alona smiled, almost smirked. "We are very informal outside official moments."

I nodded. "Okay." I looked around the table, glancing briefly at the pendants each person wore. "Can I guess who the rest of you are?" I felt silly. "For thirty years I listened to every detail my mother told me."

King Chase smirked. "Give it your best shot."

I inhaled and exhaled slowly and looked around the table slowly. "Okay. King Troy and Queen…" My mouth went wide when I looked at Daxx. "You are the Huntress."

Daxx gave her mate a hard look. "When I'm allowed to do my job."

I grinned. I had no idea what that meant. "My mother often wondered if the prophecy was more fable."

She lifted her hands. "All true."

I nodded, then looked to the scary man. Bastian had called him Justice. His amulet had the scales of justice on it. "Prince…Victor *the* Justice of Alterealm." I said hesitantly.

He inclined his head. "I am. Mate to Princess Cristy."

Cristy. Crissy. "She's lovely." If not a little confusing. I decided keeping that part to myself. I looked to the woman beside him, then to the man seated next to her. His amulet had a shield and sword on it. "Captain of the guard?" I studied him. "with a playful light in his eyes." I smiled. "Rafael. You weren't the Captain when my mother was still here."

Rafael grinned. "No, but she's taught you the sigils well."

"Yes." I nodded. "She wanted me to escape here and know how to show proper respect." I looked at his tattooed arm then to Kara's. My mother had told me the tattoos were identical in design. "You're mate to the Captain." I said looking at her.

"I am." Her cheeks heated.

I took that to mean they hadn't been mated long. Autumn was next. I grinned at her. "And you—you need to teach me that kick."

Autumn snorted. "Always willing to help a girl learn to defend herself."

"I'm more suited for healing than fighting, but you never know when it could come in handy." I studied her pendant, a book and a sword, then looked to the man with the scar on his face. I inclined my head as I'd seen them do often. "Prince Michael, the Law Holder of the realm."

He bowed his head for a second. "Yes."

I smiled, feeling somewhat like a schoolgirl that had gotten the highest score. Taking a short breath, I looked at the couple seated next. I frowned, it was the marking for the enforcer, which made no sense. Prince Quinton was the enforcer, or so my mother had told me. "You're the enforcer?" I glanced at Quinton. He sat there with his arms crossed over his chest, an unreadable expression on his face.

Bethany leaned forward. "Yes, Leone is the enforcer and my mate."

Daxx sat upright. "Quinton is one of my Captains now."

I exhaled. "Of course, the huntress would have need of her own Captains." I smiled at Quinton and received no sign of pleasantry back. Clearing my throat, I turned to the last man sitting there. Emil. I did the math in my head quickly and came up with nine brothers. He was clearly a brother, as he looked too much like Arius to be otherwise. My jaw dropped. "The prophecy was—is true." I whispered more to myself than the rest of the room.

Emil tilted his head to the side. "I'm feeling left out here." He glanced to King Troy, "I spent three hundred years seeking answers and a woman that has never been here knows of my existence."

Troy lifted his hands, then dropped them. "Her mother was well versed in the realms' prophecies." He frowned and turned toward me. "Did she have an official position here?"

I opened my mouth, then closed it. "Not that I know of…" Her necklace. I stood up quickly. "I have to go back over." I stepped around the chair. "Her necklace. It's over there."

Emil held up his hand. "We will get it." He motioned to the chair. "Please sit, allow us to catch our breath."

"It was my mother's family emblem. The pendant. I have to get it."

"Her family's emblem." King Chase looked to his twin. "An emblem makes finding her family much simpler."

"It does, brother." King Troy looked at me. "We will take you back to get it tomorrow."

"We have many things on our to-do list right now." Paisley said, giving her mate a stern look.

I wanted to object, but this was the royal family Of course they had more important things to do. "Thank you." I sat back down.

"You've arrived at a very busy juncture in this war of good and evil, I'm afraid." King Chase told me.

"War?" I'd seen enough wars in my life.

Bethany nodded. "What you witnessed in the garage was a part of what we're fighting."

"Taking people?" I remember the child crying.

"That and more. Specifically, people with Alterealm DNA. Especially women." She said softly.

I could only think of a few reasons why someone would abduct women. None of them good. "Why with Alterealm DNA?"

"Because the man behind it wants to breed his own kingdom of followers."

"Excuse me?" I wasn't sure I'd heard Autumn correctly.

"I said breed." Her tone held no emotion.

"That—that's…" I looked around at the others. "But you're stopping them, like you did tonight?"

"We don't always get there in time." Alona said, remorse showing on her face.

I glanced at Prince Bastian, then around the table. "But—now you know how they're doing it…"

"I'm afraid there is much more to it, Reagan." Victor's tone was somber.

"Worse than using abducted women like cattle?" That was hard to believe.

"Much worse." Bethany whispered.

I sat there for several seconds, attempting to figure out what was worse, and honestly couldn't come up with anything. The fact that they'd agreed to take me back to get the necklace was amazing enough if they were dealing with all of this. I nodded to my own thoughts. "Would you like me to leave so you can discuss realm business?"

Daxx looked at Alona, who glanced to Paisley then to her mate.

"I feel like," Alona studied me for a second, "she's meant to be here." She motioned to Bethany, "she abducted Leone," then she smiled at Kara, "she shot Rafael…"

"Arius saved me." Paisley added.

"Michael me." Autumn nodded.

"I saved the idiots that took you." Michael told her with a smirk.

"Cristy did see her." Victor straightened and rested his hands on the table.

"As did Rafael." King Troy looked at Rafael. "Don't think we aren't going to talk about that."

Rafael sighed, then glanced to his mate. "I figured we would be."

"You can stay." Daxx gave me a brief smile.

I just sat there trying to take in everything they'd said. Abductions, shooting… I realized they were all looking at me. "Okay, but FYI, I know nothing of realm business—stuff."

Daxx snorted. "You know way more about Alterealm then all of us did."

"Myself included." Emil sat back and crossed his arms.

"Your very existence has already given us one answer we couldn't dream of." King Chase waved his hand around. "We've been crunching numbers, figuring out puzzles and all we needed was to find Solrelm traitors." He stood up. "I need coffee." He walked toward the table with a coffee maker on it. "Beloved, can you make this thing brew some caffeine for me?"

Alona smirked and got up.

"On that note of miraculous revelations," Bastian motioned to me, "I'll collect my traitor and take him home to get you answers about any others."

"All details are welcome." Michael told him.

"Wait." I stood up. "I still don't know why you said I wasn't human."

He paused and looked around at the others. "None of the ladies are now. Not with the mates' bond." He tilted his head and grinned at me. "You'll blend in perfectly."

I looked at a few of the women. They all looked human to me, if not gobsmacked hearing what he'd said. "My father…" I turned back to him, "is there a chance he's still alive?"

"Oh, not to worry there, I plan on finding out every detail on that front." He smiled, then looked at the kings, one at a time. "Your majesties." He bowed his head, "you will be hearing from me soon."

"I'll take him to the cells." Arius got up. He leaned down and kissed the top of Paisley's head. "You can catch me up when I get back, babe." He started for the door.

"You can't keep me away from him forever." She called to him.

Arius glanced over his shoulder. "Only until I have backup…and you agree to wear an inhibitor. For his safety." He walked out quickly.

Autumn turned to Michael. "Don't even think of restricting me when I meet *dad*."

I glanced from Paisley to Autumn. "So that Nathas man is your father—and he's helping abduct people?"

"It's worse than that." Kara said. "They thought he was dead—they didn't know they had a sister and Autumn ended up on the street when she was six."

My jaw dropped. I looked at Autumn. "I'll heal him as many times as needed, so you can hurt him all over again."

Autumn smacked her hand on the table, then turned to Michael. "I like her. She stays."

Quinton got up. "I'm going to check on Detrick and Gudrun."

"Let us know if they're up for a talk." King Troy told him.

Quinton nodded. "Last I checked, all that we rescued from the asylum would need days of rest and proper medical care." Rubbing a hand across his forehead he turned to Michael. "Still nothing at the market. We found two marks like that though, so it has to be some sort of signal." He stood there for a moment and looked at me, "the doctor will be checking you over tomorrow. I want to make sure healing me had no long-term effect on you." He turned to Michael. "Get her a phone and programmed porter." With that he tuned and left the room.

I turned slowly to Autumn.

She shrugged. "Tests couldn't hurt."

Michael gave king Troy an odd look. "He's a bigger ass than normal."

"When are we contacting that woman that gave me the note?" Kara sked. "I'd like to know what she's doing working there."

Daxx glanced at me. "They were holding residents from Alterealm in an asylum for years."

"Oh. How did they all end up in the same place?"

"That's what we're going to find out." Rafael said with an unpleasant expression on his face.

"Considering Gudrun has been missing for over two hundred years, and is a great warrior, I need to know all of the details of his detainment." Victor's tone was even, but the expression on his face was—lethal.

"Let me know if any need my help." I held up my gloved hands and wiggled my fingers. "It's what I do." I paused. "I'm not sure how well I can help with mental health issues or trauma like that, but at the very least I could make them feel more at peace."

"Good to know." King Troy said.

His twin came back over with a cup of coffee. "You don't need to wear the gloves among us." He turned to Alona, "I wonder if her ability would help those that have lost a mate."

I looked at the gloves on my hands. I'd worn gloves almost all the time since mother and I discovered what touching someone could do. I didn't have to hide that here, but they were a part of who I was now.

"What repercussions do you suffer from healing others?" Kara asked me.

"It weakens me, sometimes just my hair lightens, other times if I help too much it renders me unconscious."

"You seemed pretty weak after helping Quinton." Bethany said.

I winced. "Sometimes in the heat of the moment I overdo it. I didn't realize the extent of his injuries at the time."

"We are grateful for your help." Victor inclined his head to me.

Arius came back into the room grinning. "That poor sap almost wet himself out when he saw one of his princes collecting him to go home."

"I can't blame him there." Emil shook his head. "Bastian is a bit on the strange and scary side."

I covered my mouth as I yawned.

"I think," Emil turned to King Troy, "we should all go get some rest and come up with strategies tomorrow."

King Troy rubbed the back of his neck. "I can't argue with that. I don't remember the last time I slept."

"We can take first watch." Alona motioned to her mate. "I think we were the last to nap."

Daxx slumped forward onto the table. "We'd get more rest if we just slept with our heads down on this table."

Victor stood up. "I'm entirely too old to sleep on the table." He bowed his head. "I'm going to go retrieve Cristy and hopefully persuade her to rest." He walked out unceremoniously.

Kara looked at Alona. "Reagan could take my old room."

Alona nodded. "Yes. I'm sure a soak and some sleep in a quiet room would be welcome."

"I'll take her up on my way to my bed." Emil said standing up. "This has been a long day, or night." He shrugged.

OMG, I was going to sleep in a palace. It was the only thing that registered in my mind.

As we walked past tall pillars and molded arches, I had to focus to keep my mouth closed and not sound like some fangirl by squealing. I was walking though the palace in Alterealm. I couldn't help wishing my mother was alive so I could tell her. She'd talked about the palace on top of a mountain—and I was *in* it. I looked at Emil, who gave me an odd look.

"You haven't heard a word I've said."

I stopped. "I'm so sorry. I'm just-just," I waved my hand around, "walking in the palace in Alterealm."

He chuckled, "yes you are," he looked around. "Alona has been refurnishing it. I'm told it hasn't been used in…"

"Since the twin kings were born." I nodded.

Motioning to the stairs, he started for them. "You have more knowledge of here than I did weeks after finding out I had eight brothers."

I walked slow up them, wanting to drag out walking through the palace as long as I could. "I often wished I had a sibling."

"I used to." Emil smirked. "I can't even describe what it has been like for me."

I gave him a side glance, "probably better than hiding."

He hissed out a breath. "Yes, it is. Trying not to be found out for two hundred and fifty years was a challenge."

I grinned. "Took you fifty years to figure out you were different?"

Chuckling, he motioned in the direction to turn at the top. "No, I knew that early on. Took fifty years to figure out I wasn't dying any day soon and what to do about it."

"I guess I was lucky and had my mother to clue me in." I stopped and looked at a portrait on the wall. "He looks like you."

"Or I, him." Emil studied it. "I think Quinton said that's my great-great grandfather, but I could be off on some greats."

"They're not all decked out and covered in sparkling jewels." I noted out loud.

He shook his head. "This royal family, I believe has always ruled modestly."

"All realms need more of that." I glanced at him, "the rich to tone it down and live like the rest of us."

"I agree." He motioned down the hall. "I'm not trying to hurry you; I just need to lay down soon or fall over." He smirked, "the last few—weeks, at least, I've lost track—have been hectic."

"How serious is the rest of this? They didn't explain."

"Thousands, possibly hundreds of thousands at risk in more than one realm."

I stopped walking and looked at him. "That Willis guy wants to take over the realms?"

"Something like that." He pointed to the door beside me. "That's your room." He looked at the door across from it, "I think that room is empty, but if you go up to the next level," he pointed to a staircase, "I'm the first door at the top." He inclined his head. "Help yourself to anything in there, I'm sure by now Mitz has the closet filled with anything you could want in your size." He smirked.

"Thank you, Prince…"

He held up his hand. "Just Emil. Titles are for special meetings and balls." He grinned. "I haven't known I was a prince long, so hearing it is still—peculiar." He turned to leave then stopped. "Oh, if you feel like going for a stroll, best take someone with you. Kara has a mountain lion cub as a pet."

My eyes widened. "Seriously?"

"Long story, I'm sure the girls will fill you in." He smiled, then turned and went to the stairs.

I stood there for a second. Mountain lion cub! I'd never had a pet. I couldn't wait to see it. Turning around I opened the door and went in. It wasn't elaborately fabulous, then again, I lived in a one room shack on top of a roof. I flipped the light switch and closed the door. I just stood there after I did that. I was in Alterealm. *In Alterealm.* I'd finally be safe from anyone finding out about me.

I was suddenly exhausted. I'd been running on adrenaline for the last few hours, but still needed to recover fully from healing Prince—just, Quinton. I looked at the huge bed. Quick wash and I was falling into that inviting dream.

At least that's what I thought until I saw the bathroom. It would be a crime to not bathe in that large tub, and I was all for committing no crimes.

Chapter Five

Standing outside the room, I looked around. I wasn't sure if I should try to find my way back downstairs or wait to be retrieved. I walked out of the small hallway and looked at the stairs. What was the protocol be for this? I snorted out loud. I was in a palace in a realm few knew of. Being here was something I never thought I'd be doing. Heading toward the stairs, I noticed a huge room through the windows that lined the hall. I looked through the glass. It was empty aside from some crates. The other side was lined windows as well. The door was open, so I didn't think it would be off limits. I went in and walked slowly to large doors on the far side.

It opened to a huge balcony. Glancing over my shoulder, I opened the door and went out. Leaving it open, I stepped to the railing. I know my jaw dropped open as I looked over the vast countryside. The palace was really on top of a mountain. I could see for miles and miles. Small villages, open fields. A lump formed in my throat as I thought of my mother. She'd talked about the palace, always wanted to see the views from the palace.

"I found her."

I startled and turned to see Autumn standing there in the door.

She smiled and motioned to the view. "It's crazy isn't it?" She came out. "I stand outside our room all the time and think there had to be some kind of mistake for me to be here."

"Nonsense." Michael came out onto the balcony.

"I had to take a look." I said quietly and looked back over the country. "My mother talked of the palace on the mountain often. It's a bit—astonishing for me to be here."

Michael came over and stood looking out. "I missed living here." He turned and smiled at Autumn, "I'd still be in the underground chambers if it hadn't been for Autumn."

She snorted. "I wasn't living underground."

I had nothing I could say to that. I'd had my times of living in tunnels and odd places.

Michael held out a phone. "This is yours. All of our numbers are programmed into it."

I looked at the phone. I'd never had one. I'd looked at them in stores, but who was I going to call?

"This is an earbud. It makes things easier if we're not all together but need to communicate."

I looked at it, then tucked it in my pocket. "I'm sure there won't be any need for me to be…"

"I thought that too. Trust me if we're deep in a fight, then it makes things easier." Autumn nodded and crossed her arms over her chest. She shrugged, "and hearing the guys razz each other is fun."

I opened my mouth, then cleared my throat and nodded instead.

Michael held out a watch-like device. "This is your porter. Should anything undesirable happen, it's chipped for easy location."

I took it, turning it over to look.

Autumn waved her hand around oddly. "Never leave home without it. Trust me on that."

I gave them an awkward smile. I was given my own porter. I put it on my wrist, then stood there dumbfounded.

Michael reached over and popped it open. "Top button will bring you here to the courtyard." He pointed down to the ground. "Bottom one will take you to the girls' office." He dropped his hand away. "We're just on our way to…"

I couldn't *not* do this. I pushed the second button. Just like that I was standing in a room with desks and other furniture. I laughed out loud.

Michael appeared beside me. His expression didn't give anything away.

"Sorry. I had to." I closed the porter and clasped my gloved hands in front of me.

He pulled his phone out of his pocket. "She's at the cave." He shook his head. "You will wait for me. I'll be right there." He put the phone in his pocket. "We need to go. Autumn and Paisley are being allowed to see their—Nathas."

I nodded. "Oh, I'm to go?"

He huffed out a breath. "You may as well, or you'll be wandering the halls for hours down here." He motioned to the door.

"We're in the underground chambers now?" I started walking.

"Yes. I believe the girls made the map on your phone, to help you find your way around."

I had to walk fast to keep up with him. Even with my height of five foot seven, there was no keeping up with his long strides. "So are all men in this realm so tall?"

He didn't even glance at me. "Mostly." His blue eyes connected with me for a second. "We were created to keep the balance between our realm and—the side you were on." He shrugged, "I suppose they thought being a bit larger would better enable us."

I could only nod to that. Mother had talked about the purpose, but until now, with this war, I hadn't realized it was a serious thing. We went past more doors, then he turned, I followed, not even trying to remember the way.

When he finally stopped, we were in front of two large metal doors. He motioned for me to go through. I did and then followed him into a room right inside. It looked like a large control room of sorts.

Many of the others were here. All were looking at a row of monitors.

Autumn turned and looked at Michael. "Arius won't let us go until after he deals with some issues."

"Issues with?" Michael went over and looked at the monitors, then stepped over and did something on the board below them. "Nelson." He said quietly. "Stay here." He turned and went back out the door.

I moved over and looked at the monitor he'd adjusted. Arius and Quinton were in a clear cell with another man. The other man was waving his hands around. Arius stood there, his hands on his hips watching him. Quinton leaned against the wall, his arms crossed over his chest.

Bethany turned and looked at me. "Nelson is one of Willis' Generals." She looked back at the monitor. "He also wanted to kill Crissy, but Autumn took the blade for her."

Shocked I looked from her to Autumn.

Autumn shrugged and crossed her arms over her chest and glared at the monitor.

Arius jerked his head and looked right at the camera.

"Sending your beast a message?" Daxx asked with a smirk.

"Mhmm, my feelings of irritation and anger." Paisley said looking unhappy.

Arius motioned to Quinton, then they turned and walked out of the cell that held Nelson.

"Guess it worked." Bethany said then looked at the door at the moment Arius came in.

"What does Nelson have to say?" Daxx inquired.

Quinton heaved a big sigh. "Says he'll give us information if we let him see Leila."

"Is he lying?" Bethany asked.

Arius waved his phone, "just messaged Raf to bring Kara, so she can find out."

"What if Leila doesn't want to see him?" Crissy asked.

I turned, I hadn't even seen her sitting in the corner beside a cabinet. She had the ability to not be seen. I envied her that, I knew how hard it really was.

"I guess we'll deal with that after we find out if he's actually has real information." Arius said while looking at his phone. With a hesitant look, he turned to Paisley. "Troy wants us to wait for him before you go in to see Nathas."

Paisley sighed. "I figured he would want to see what he could find in his head while we *visited*."

Autumn crossed her arms over her chest and then shrugged. "They're not going to let us in the cell *with* him."

"You are correct." Victor came into the room. His eyes immediately connected with Crissy, before he looked to the rest of us. "Troy and Chase are currently dealing with Elder Roan. He's not being allowed into the cells until after Troy and Kara see, or hear, the truth."

"See or hear the truth?" I looked from Victor to Arius. I couldn't comprehend how they did that.

Bethany nodded. "Yes. Troy can see in a person's mind and Kara hears their thoughts."

I opened my mouth, then closed it. "Oh." I glanced at my hands. "I'm feeling normal for the first time in — ever." I said softly.

Autumn grinned.

"We have quite the eclectic mix here." Victor said while watching the monitors.

Quinton came in. "Raf and Kara can't get here for a few minutes, they're in the medical ward checking on those we recovered from the asylum."

"She's listening in?" Daxx asked.

"That was my take on it," Quinton watched me as he spoke, "while Raf talks to them."

Chase navigated past Quinton blocking the door, giving him a curious look. With a grin he glanced at Michael, then Arius. "Ready to meet your father-in-law?"

Michael cringed and looked at Autumn. "Yes and no."

She crossed her arms over her chest.

Michael cleared his throat and turned to Arius. "Can we get him moved to the observation cell?"

Arius nodded while studying Paisley. With a more abrupt nod, he turned on his heel and walked out of the room.

With a quick glance at me, Quinton followed him.

Autumn crossed her arms over her chest and looked at the floor. "I've waited my whole life for answers."

"And you shall have them, Princess Autumn."

Everyone turned.

An older man stood in the door. He wore a black robe and somber expression.

"Elder Roan." Michael went over to him.

"I won't interfere, but I wish to be present." He looked to Paisley, then Autumn. "My granddaughters' answers take priority of course."

Michael inclined his head and motioned to the door. "Shall we."

"Oh boy." Daxx said as we filed out the door.

Leone stood in the hallway beside Quinton. They watched Autumn walk by.

"I wouldn't want to be Autumn's sparring partner after this."

Quinton gave Leone a quick glance. "You never do anyway."

Leone grinned. "Because I'm a smart man."

Bethany chuckled as she moved by them.

I stood there off to the side, not sure if I was supposed to be following. I knew nothing about any of this.

Quinton just stood there, looking at me. I didn't know what the expression on his face meant. It looked like he wanted to say something, but he didn't.

Leone cleared his throat and gave his brother a strange look. Quinton scowled at him, then walked down the hallway. Watching him for a few seconds, he glanced at me. "You coming?"

"I wasn't sure I was supposed to."

Leone shrugged. "I don't do all the meant-to-be and fate signals thing, but the girls say you are part of this," he shrugged, "so your part of it." He motioned for me to go down the hall. "This might get messy." He said as he walked beside me, "the guys say Autumn and Paisley aren't going in the cell with Nathas," he smirked, "but they're going to lose that battle."

"I don't know how I'd feel if I were to meet my father." I frowned, wondering if that may still happen some day. "But my circumstances are quite different."

He nodded. "Yeah." He made a strangled sound in the back of his throat. "if you're able to project calm or anything, now would be the time to do it."

We turned a corner and walked into a larger space between the clear walls. I stopped just outside it, still unsure if I should be here. The area was filled with the royal family. Even Rafael and Kara were there now.

Michael and Arius were having a very face-to-face, up close and personal discussions with Paisley and Autumn. I glanced to see Leone look at me and smirk.

Emil came up beside me. "This is going to be interesting."

With long strides, Troy came down the hallway, his expression said he was in charge and no one had better doubt it. He gave Emil a quick nod. "You, Raf and Leone can keep things under control out here."

Emil straightened and stepped further into the room of people.

Troy went over to Victor and said something. Victor nodded and walked out the other side of the space.

I noted Arius's and Michael's expressions were hard. I had to wonder if the women had won the argument to be in the cell with their father. Alona stood toward the far side, by herself. She spotted me and gave me a small smile. Moving around the tall bodies, I went over to her.

She gave me a soft look. "This may be the safest place to stand."

I watched as Arius and Michael left the room with Troy and Chase. Leone and Quinton moved over and stood in front of the exit they'd used. Autumn and Paisley stood there with them. I didn't know the details of what was going to happen next, but the tension in the room was so thick even I was having to work harder to draw breath.

"You ready, honey?" Rafael turned to look at Kara.

Moving to stand right beside the wall she nodded.

"If you can't keep your thoughts under control, step out of this area so Kara can focus." Rafael looked around the room at the rest of us.

No one moved.

"Here we go." Leone did something on a small pad beside the door.

Chapter Six

The reflection on the wall changed and then I could see inside the next room. Inside it, the kings, Michael and Arius stood with the man I recognized as the man from the garage. Victor stood in the doorway. All of their expressions should have been warning enough to anyone that doubted they were not to be messed with.

"You're going to stand there, Nathas. You move in any direction and I will shut you down." Arius said in a tone that made me want to run.

Nathas took a moment to look around him, then nodded.

Arius looked at Victor and nodded.

Victor walked out of sight.

Quinton took a deep breath and then stepped aside to let Autumn and Paisley leave.

Seconds later they walked into the room with Nathas. They stopped a few feet inside the room and stood there, side by side, the exact same expression on their faces. Quinton and Victor came in behind them and stood there.

I held my breath as the silence dragged on. I couldn't decide who to watch. Autumn and Paisley were silent and unmoving, studying the man that stood in front of them. Nathas had a puzzled look on his face, the kind you get when you realize something, but are having a hard time believing it.

"Paisley?" He said in a hesitant tone. He looked at Autumn. "Aubree, how is this possible?"

Autumn snorted. "That's what we want to know." She looked at Paisley. "And the name's Autumn now." She shrugged and crossed her arms over her chest.

The expression on Nathas face was clear shock. He paled. "I thought," he looked at Troy then back to the women, "I thought…"

"I don't want to know what you thought." Paisley said quietly. "I want to know why my sister was on the street at six."

"The street." He said in a hollow tone. "My wife, Peyton—your mother," he shook his head, "she was attacked. I found her," he took a deep breath, then exhaled quickly, "she was in the morgue." He shook his head, "no one could find our," he looked at Autumn, "find you."

Paisley looked at Autumn, then back to him. "So you just disappear? Wife dead, one daughter missing and you abandon the other?"

Nathas frowned. "Peyton's mother agreed to look after you. She even took on my name so you would have it."

Arius stepped toward Paisley, she held up her hand and he stopped.

"You gave me your name? How generous." She scowled at him.

"Your wife was killed and you did nothing?" Michael scowled at him. "You had all of Alterealm's resources at your disposal and could have found your daughter…"

Nathas snorted. "I had nothing at my disposal." He looked from Michael to Troy, "not here."

I watched the Elder pace toward the door, then stop and look in at his son again. Shaking his head, he leaned closer to Leone and spoke quietly. Leone looked over his head to Emil at the other end.

"How—how are you both here?" Nathas' voice was quite a bit louder now. "Here in Alterealm?"

Autumn snorted and shoved up the sleeve of her hoodie, revealing the tattoo on her arm. She looked at Michael and then back to the shocked man.

Nathas' eyes went wide. "You're mate to Prince Michael?" He looked at her for a moment with his mouth hanging open. When he glanced to Paisley, she lifted the pendant resting on her breastbone and dangled it.

Nathas squinted, then straightened. He looked at Arius with fear on his face.

"That's right." Quinton smirked, "your son's-in-law are the law and warden of Alterealm. Your daughters are Princesses of Alterealm."

"I-I…" lifting his hands, Nathas rested his palms on either side of his head.

"What were you doing helping Willis Hubert?" Victor demanded in a cold tone.

"Does he have the tattoo?" Chase asked turning to Arius.

"I don't need to be magically persuaded to do something about changing the failed systems of this realm." Nathas said in a low tone.

"He's aware." The Elder made a sound of annoyance and walked out of the room.

"The systems are in place for a reason." Chase stared at him, hands on hips. "Most are not meant for this realm. If they were, they wouldn't die when they cross over." He gave him an exasperated look. "You know all of this. Your father is on the Elder's council."

"Right." Nathas gave him a bored look. "Peyton wasn't my mate. I wouldn't have been approved to bring her over…"

"Had you come to us when your wife was pregnant, we would have made accommodations to allow her and your children here." Elder Roan pushed his way past Quinton and Victor and now stood between Autumn and Paisley. "You didn't though, you just vanished and never returned." He gave his son a loathsome look, "leaving your incredible daughters out there on their own."

Nathas looked livid now, "I didn't vanish, old man…" He stopped and his eyes went wide.

Paisley had her hand held in the air. "Do not disrespect your elders." She ground out between clenched teeth.

Arius placed his hand on her shoulder. "Release him, babe."

Inhaling deeply, she dropped her hand and looked at Nathas.

The man just stood there, eyes wide, shock and fear on his face. Then his expression started to change.

"Say one peep against my sister and I will lay you out on the floor so fast you might swallow a few of your teeth." Autumn glared at him.

"I think we've had enough family reunion for today." Chase stepped in front of Paisley.

Michael put his hand on Autumn's shoulder. She nodded, then turned toward the door.

As they filed back into the room, Kara held her hand up. No one spoke for at least a minute. Kara nodded, then did something on the pad beside her. Taking a deep breath, she turned around.

"I didn't get much." She said looking at Troy. "His thoughts were all over the place as soon as he saw the girls."

Troy nodded. "We may get some information from him, after he's had some time to settle." He looked over at Victor, "Willis and Nelson are in his head a lot."

"My son is one of his generals and has been helping orchestrate this entire thing." The Elder said in a sad tone.

"This started long before Nathas disappeared." Rafael stated.

Chase nodded. "About a century before he did, or more."

The Elder didn't look placated. "It doesn't change his involvement or behavior prior."

Paisley stepped over to Troy and pointed her finger in his face. "I don't care if you have to tear him apart from the inside out, you find out what he knows. All of it."

Arius moved over to her quickly. She shook her head and paced away.

It didn't take a genius to see how she was hurting. It wasn't a physical injury, but I knew in some cases my touch could soothe. I pulled off one of my gloves and went over to her. I touched her hand. "I can't imagine the pain you're feeling." I said softly.

She took a shaky breath and nodded. "You have your own pain." Taking another deep breath, she took a much deeper breath in then breathed it out.

Quinton came over and frowned at me. Without a word, he reached down and pulled my hand from hers. His eyes were moving over my hair as he did.

I didn't need to look to know it had lightened slightly.

"Oh, Reagan." Paisley gave me a teary-eyed look. "Thank you."

Arius was beside her in a second, pulling her into his arms.

Autumn crossed her arms over her chest. "I'm ready to move on."

Paisley gave her a small smile. "Same. We're here and happy, the past has no hold on us now."

Arius kissed the top of her head.

Stepping back from me, Quinton gave me an odd look.

Rafael glanced to Kara briefly. "While Nathas *settles*, I say we move on and figure out what we're doing with that woman from the asylum."

Quinton crossed his arms over his chest. "I was hoping we could get some more information from the residents we pulled out of there." He looked over at Victor, "make sure we're not walking into a trap."

Victor inclined his head. "I was thinking the same." He motioned around the room, "locking the royal family in that place would go far to ensure Willis' plan is successful."

"Were you able to find out anything, Kara?" Daxx crossed her arms over her chest and leaned back against the wall.

Kara shrugged. "Not really. They're still out of it."

"Doctor has most of them on tranquilizers until their over-all health has improved." Rafael looked at Quinton. "Detrick is the most coherent today."

Quinton nodded. "He asked to not be drugged."

Troy rubbed his hand against the back of his neck. "I still want to look in a few heads that have been brought in most recently," he exhaled and looked to Quinton, "can you and Emil take Reagan over to get her belongings?"

"I'll come too." Autumn stated. "I need some fresh air."

Michael gave her a quick appraisal and nodded to Quinton. "Take two guards with you."

Quinton nodded. "Right after we get the doc to check out Reagan and make sure there's nothing lingering from yesterday."

I opened my mouth, then closed it, deciding that knowing might not be so bad.

"I'm going to go look around the market again and see if I can spot any more of those symbols." Leone looked to Michael.

Michael kissed the top of Autumn's head. "I'll come with you."

"Take guards." Victor stated.

"You really think we'd be attacked at the market, here, in Alterealm?" Leone waved his hand when Victor straightened. "Never mind, we'll take guards."

"I'm going to rest." Alona announced.

Troy blew out a breath. "Anyone that doesn't have something critical to be doing should rest when they can."

"Rest is good." Crissy jumped up from the corner she'd been sitting in. "The climax is almost here." She grinned, nodding her head quickly. "I'm going to my tower." Without waiting, she turned and left the area.

"The climax?" Daxx looked to Troy. "I don't like the sound of that."

Victor nodded his head slowly while looking where Crissy had gone. "She's been going with very little sleep—less than normal." Pulling out his phone, he started typing on it. "I'm going to go see if she can explain any more."

"Please share if you do." Bethany said.

"Yeah," Daxx nodded, "like if the climax is in our favor— or bring bigger weapons..."

"Any details are welcome." Emil rubbed his hand over his face. "Let me know when you're going over." He looked at Quinton. "I'm going to go see if Rena is in a better mood today."

"Good luck." Quinton said, then his brown eyes locked on me. "Let's go see the doc." He waved his big hand toward the door.

Chapter Seven

As we went through the endless hallways, I tried to think of something to say to break the silence. I had no problems with the strong silent type, but Quinton seemed to take it further than most. Each time I glanced up at him, his brown eyes locked on me for a second before he looked away.

"You don't like me." I stated.

He looked down at me. "Did I say that?"

I shook my head and followed him around another corner. "No, but your body language does."

"You're an expert on body language?"

His tone revealed nothing. It wasn't cold or reflecting any real emotion. "No.

"Then don't make assumptions that you know me or my thoughts."

We walked up an incline in the hall toward a door.

He entered some numbers on a pad. Opening the door, he motioned for me to go through.

I did and found two large men standing on either side. They straightened, adding a few more inches to their already very tall height.

"We're going to the infirmary." Quinton told them.

They looked at me, then back to him.

"Is everything all right, Prince?" The one with the beard asked.

Quinton nodded. "Yeah." He started walking.

The men stood there looking at me. When I realized they were waiting for me, I hurried to catch up to him. We were walking across some sort of courtyard in the middle of buildings. At the door to each building were more guards. Seeing this made me realize two things. The Alterealm my mother had known had changed, and this war they were fighting was serious.

When we reached the door, the guard opened it. Quinton paused and looked at him. "Tell Ira I said to switch out to the six-hour rotations." He looked at the other guard, "I want the guards to be fresh."

The guard nodded. "Will do."

We went into the building. As soon as I stepped in, the shock must have shown. It didn't look like any hospital I'd been in. The lobby was decorated like a tasteful hotel, not sterile, white and reeking of sanitizing chemicals.

"We do things differently here." Quinton said quietly. He motioned for me to go to a door at the side.

I followed him into a room, then stopped. It was an office.

"Wait here. I'll go find the doctor." He stood there for a moment looking down at me. "I'll see you when you're finished." Taking a deep breath, like he had something to say, but then he turned and walked out the door again without speaking.

I walked back out of the office feeling much like I had for the last twenty-four hours, amazed. The doctor was nothing like any doctor I'd ever talked to. I always worked with the intake at the clinic and not the doctor. This doctor showed me nothing but respect, asking if each test was acceptable. I kept expecting to see Quinton giving him that dark stare in the corner, but he hadn't come back.

I stood there trying to decide if I was to go back out the way we'd come in or wait here for Quinton to come back. Wandering to the other end of the lobby, I looked down a hallway and didn't see anyone, so I went down it.

A nurse came out a door and smiled at me. "Can I help you?"

"I was looking for Prince Quinton."

She pointed, "he's just down there with the patients they brought back."

"Thank you." I went down the hall. There were two guards standing outside a door. I paused, not sure if I would be allowed in.

One of them put his hand in front of me, so I would stop. "What's your name?"

"Reagan." I said hesitantly. "I came here with Prince Quinton."

He dropped his hand and nodded.

I walked through quickly before he changed his mind. It was a ward of some kind, with curtains separating the beds. The people in the beds looked exhausted and malnourished. My guess was they were the people they had rescued. I grasped my own hands so I wouldn't pull off my gloves and run around touching these poor people. I couldn't imagine being held against my will. I'd spent my whole life avoiding that very thing.

As I reached the end, I paused when I heard Quinton speaking.

"I searched every inch of the wasteland for you. Damn near every day." There was pain in his voice.

"I'm staring again." A weak voice said. "But damn, your face Q."

"I know it's pretty, but that's not the point, Deet." Quinton didn't sound as light as his words implied.

"It's just—the huntress? *The* huntress fixed it?" He mumbled something. "I can't believe it finally came true."

Quinton cleared his throat and made some other noise I couldn't put an action to. "Well, unfortunately it means more than just a prophecy is true." Quinton said. "There's a whole shit show going on now."

"But your brothers are mated now?" The man sounded amazed, even in his weakened state.

"Yeah." Quinton chuckled. "You need to get back on your feet and see the women fate planned for them."

"Good? Bad?"

"They scare the hell out of me," Quinton said quietly, "in a good way, I suppose."

"I don't see a tattoo on your arm yet."

"Are you sure you don't want something? Every time you move you look like you're going to pass out." The curtain moved.

I jolted, not wanting to be caught eavesdropping. I peeked around the edge of the material. "I'm all done." I gave the man in the bed a quick smile, then looked to Quinton. "I have no idea where I'm supposed to go—or how to get there."

Quinton stood up and jammed his hands in his pockets. "Detrick, this is Reagan."

I looked at the man in the bed, he was a big man—or had been, but his malnourishment was clear. I could see the creases in his brow and the intense look in his eyes. I knew the look of pain. I pulled off my glove and stepped to the other side of the bed and held out my hand. "My pleasure." He placed a cold hand in mine. His hand was huge. I placed my other, gloved, hand over it and continued to hold on. "I overheard a bit as I was walking up." I glanced to Quinton then back to Detrick. "You guys know each other quite well?"

Detrick smiled briefly. "We grew up together." He cleared his throat.

I grinned. "Oh. You don't look your age at all."

Detrick chuckled, then he frowned.

"Dammit, Reagan." Quinton reached across and pulled our hands apart. His eyes burned into mine for a second before he pulled his hand away.

Detrick blew out a breath. "I don't know what you just did but thank you. My whole-body hurts or did. It's better now." He gave me a smile. "I thought I was hallucinating the hair though."

Putting my glove back on, I pulled my hair so I could see it. It was streaked with lighter colors now. Flipping it back, I shrugged. "No hallucinations."

Quinton cleared his throat. "We'll let you get some rest."

I stepped back to the end of the bed. "Feel better soon."

"Come back and visit anytime." Detrick said with a smile.

Quinton sighed loudly.

"What, you know I'm the social one." His friend offered.

"Yeah. I'll see you later." Quinton's tone was somber. He motioned for me to go.

He walked beside me until we were back in the lobby, then he grabbed my arm and stepped into the office he'd left me in. Before I could ask, he spun and glared at me.

"You can't just heal everyone you see." His pretty eyes bore through mine.

"I don't. That would be exhausting." I offered, not understanding why he was reacting this way.

"What did the doctor say?" He stepped back and put his hands on his hips, his gaze not leaving mine.

"He did some tests, to double check," I shrugged, "everything, but said I'm perfectly healthy."

He just stood there looking at me, his expression changing more than once. "Make sure you find out the results of those tests." Opening the door, he stomped out it. "Let's go get your stuff."

Chapter Eight

I took a deep breath trying to contain my excitement when I realized Quinton had ported us to the roof my shack was on. I grinned at Autumn, then looked at Emil. "I love that."

Autumn grinned, "yeah it's all fun until you do it accidentally." She nodded and pushed up her sleeves as she looked around. "Nice view."

I glanced around at the *view* I'd been looking at for a few years. "Quiet and safe was all I wanted."

Emil looked up where my bungee still hung down. "There wasn't a better way to get here?"

I shrugged and watched the guards walk to opposite sides of the roof and look down. "A few actually, but being predictable is a dangerous thing."

Both Autumn and Emil nodded. They understood.

Quinton just stood there, not speaking or looking at the view, his gaze was locked on me.

Emil walked by me and smirked. "It's not very big."

I shrugged. "It's dry and out of the weather."

Quinton crossed his arms over his chest, still staring at me.

"True enough." Autumn went over and looked down at the street.

"Are you okay?" I watched Quinton's expression.

"You don't even lock it up?" Emil sounded amused.

Eyes-wide I spun toward him. "Don't touch…"

There was crackling noise and the door sparked. Emil went flying backward. landing on his back a few feet away, still sliding across the gravel on the roof.

I ran over. "I am *so* sorry." I dropped to my knees beside him and pulled off my gloves and grabbed his hand to deal with the burns.

"Is my hair smoking?" He asked in a pained tone.

"No smoke." Autumn dropped down beside him. She shook her head and looked at me. "I did *not* see that coming."

"Me either." Emil dropped his head back down and closed his eyes.

"Let me see your other hand."

He held his hand in the air. I took it and put it between mine.

"Reagan," Quinton warned with an exasperated tone.

I looked at him as he moved closer. "Back off. I did this, so I'll fix it."

He didn't look pleased but stopped and stood there watching.

Emil opened his eyes. "I don't suppose we can forget this happened?" He looked at his brother.

Quinton smirked and shook his head. "Not a chance."

"I was afraid of that." He pulled his hand from mine and reached up to touch my hair. "I'm good. Thank you." Pushing up onto his elbows he blew out a breath and jerked his chin toward the shack. "I'll wait out here."

Autumn pulled me to my feet. "You good?"

I nodded. "Yeah, the burns weren't bad." I glanced at his feet. "His boots grounded him."

"I didn't feel very grounded." Emil mumbled, then sat up.

I went over to the door and pulled out a wire hidden beside the trim.

"Get all of it." Quinton said gruffly. "You won't be returning."

I came out a few minutes later with a duffle bag filled with everything that represented my long life. I took a deep breath and looked at Autumn. "I spent years looking for anyone from Alterealm, for people I knew I could trust." I blew out another breath. "I'd given up hope. But now…" A lump in my throat stopped me from saying anything else.

"I am glad you have found us." Emil looked at where he'd been lying, "with the exception of your security system." He gave me an exaggerated look. "I know what it's like trying to stay hidden in the shadows," he shrugged, "now I'm perfectly normal…"

Quinton made an amused sound. "I wouldn't go that far." He sobered and looked at me. "May I see your mother's pendant?" He gave me a soft look. "I might recognize it."

My hands shook as I pulled it out of my pocket and opened the cloth I kept it wrapped in. The very idea of having family had my emotions scrambled.

Quinton came over and touched my gloved hand, steadying it as I uncovered the pendant. Still holding my hand, he leaned closer.

"I'm not sure." He said softly. "It looks familiar, but I've seen a lot of emblems."

I nodded. "That's okay."

"Elder Nodin is a historian." Emil announced.

Quinton nodded, and straightened up. "He'll be able to tell you about your family." Quinton said quietly.

Words weren't always something you could count on, but eyes couldn't lie. The unspoken words I saw there meant the world to me. "Thank you."

"I don't know about you guys, but I need a nap—or something now." Emil looked at the necklace before I wrapped it back up.

"Showing your age a bit today?" Quinton asked as he waved the guards to come closer.

Emil snorted. "There's nothing wrong with my age, *big* brother, getting zapped is harder than it looks."

With a grin, Quinton reached over and put his hand on my shoulder. "Bring the guards back, *little* brother."

I had just enough time to hear Autumn laugh and we were standing in the glass room we'd walked by last night.

Quinton dropped his hand from my shoulder and stepped away. "Everyone will be here shortly to eat." He gave me a quick nod. "I'll be back in a few minutes." Then he vanished.

I looked around. If I went to find my room to put my bag away, there was no guarantee that I'd find my way back. I set my bag on the nearest chair. The room had large plants all around the edges, some the size of trees. Scattered throughout the room were glass tables trimmed with gold and plush white chairs. It was like a fancy restaurant...

"Oh, hello, love. I didn't know anyone was here yet." Mitz came down the steps carrying a tray.

"Quinton popped me here, then vanished again." I explained.

Setting the tray on the long table she shook her head. "Some of them are a bit short of manners." She smiled. "Do you want me to have your bag taken to your room?"

I looked at it, then to her. "I was going to take it, but was afraid I'd get lost—or distracted."

She nodded. "Yes, this is all new and confusing I'm sure."

I tilted my head and rolled my eyes. "Quite new."

"I was told you went to get your mother's pendant." She came over the stood in front of me. "What was her name, love? Maybe I knew her."

It took me a moment to answer. The very fact that I was going to meet people that knew my mother, for her true self, was heart wrenching. "Keiragan." I shrugged. "My given name is Rea, after mother passed, I combined them to become Reagan."

She gave me look that was full of warmth. "You can be Rea if you wish, or continue to honor your mother. No one will judge you here."

"Thank you." I pulled the cloth out of my pocket. "Quinton says an Elder Nodin may be able to trace my family with this." I opened it and held out my hand.

Mitz studied it and nodded. "It does look familiar." She smiled. "It's lovely, by the way."

I looked down at the silver pendant in my hand. It was so familiar to me, yet not at the same time. To me it was a reminder of my mother, but it held much more meaning now. It held the past and possibly the future. "The chain broke years ago."

"I'll see that you get a new one." She squeezed my hand enclosing the pendant in the cloth again. "Did your mother go over with anyone? Maybe we can find them as well." She smiled. "I'm sure they'd be thrilled to meet you."

"I, ah," I blinked, "I only remember one of their names." I took a shaky breath. "Synova." I nodded, "mother said she held everyone's porters because she was the only that took a purse with her."

"Synova?" Mitz nodded slowly. "I know of only one woman with that name."

"Elder Nodin will be here sometime before lunch is over." Autumn announced as she came into the room. She smiled at me. "Emil is feeling better."

"Oh, good."

"I need to contact Elder Landry, love. I'll be back shortly with the rest of lunch." Mitz went back up the steps.

"Need any help. Mitz?" Autumn asked.

Mitz paused and smiled at her. "No, but thank you, dear."

I looked over to find Chase studying me, again, as he had been every time I looked up from my plate. I wasn't used to the variety of food that Mitz had put out, and was trying to at least taste all of it.

Autumn leaned closer. "Ignore the king watching you." She pointed at Chase with her fork. "He'll be trying to—" she frowned, "grace you with some kind of nickname."

"The king has excellent hearing, dynamo." Chase grinned. He glanced at Bethany, then back to me. "Sparky is already taken but after today's events, you are worthy of being *dubbed* by myself."

"I'm so touched my suffering has inspired you, brother." Emil leaned back in his chair and motioned across the table to me. "Go ahead and go over and touch the door of Reagan's little shack." He smirked. "I dare you."

Chase scowled. "I'm sure electrocuting a king is frowned upon."

"No worries, brother king, I'll take the burden if something should happen to you." Troy lifted his cup and grinning at Chase.

"Touching, but no." He smiled at me. "It will come to me."

I couldn't help but grin. "I'm not sure if I should be touched or concerned that you're taking the time to think of me with everything else that is going on."

"I can compartmentalize, no worries there." He nodded, then turned back to eat.

"Excuse the intrusion. I was told I was needed."

A man with long, wavy grey hair stood on the steps.

"Elder Nodin, thanks for coming." Emil motioned him in.

"Prince." He inclined his head to Emil. "Your majesties." He glanced to Chase then Troy.

"Reagan's mother was from Alterealm." Quinton stood up. "She has a family pendant and we wondered if you could look into which family it belongs to." He nodded to me.

I stood up and took the pendant out of my pocket. "She said it has the family emblem in the center."

The man came over and inclined his head to me. "I would be pleased to assist you."

My hand visibly shook as I held it out to him. He paused and looked at the glove, then leaned closer to my hand. I'm not sure how long he looked at it, but there wasn't a sound in the room.

"Yes, it's from an old lineage," he glanced at Quinton, "Prince." He nodded and gently took the pendant from the cloth and held it closer to his face. "The marking around the edge is from your great-grandfathers' reign. Each reign has a different pattern..."

Troy came over and looked down at it. "I had no idea of the significance."

Elder Nodin nodded. "This bears the mark because this family served the royal family." He shrugged, "whether in a military capacity or..."

"Excuse me."

Everyone turned to see another man standing on the step. He wore a black cloak. Before I could study him more, a woman moved to stand beside him. If I had to describe her, I'd say she was very regal with her stiff stance and a pasted-on expression meant to be pleasant.

"Elder Landry?" Troy glanced to Victor, then at Michael.

"Excuse me for bypassing protocol and bringing someone that has not been cleared by Ira. Mitz called me and said it was of the utmost importance I bring her." He glanced at the woman. "This is my daughter, Synova."

Synova. My heart started beating faster. Synova inclined her head in a respectful way. "Your majesties." When she straightened, her expression turned to shock. Eyes-wide kind of shock.

"You look," she came down the steps slowly, pausing to give her father a quick glance, "just like her." Moving faster she came toward me. "Just like Keiragan." She shook her head. "How is this possible?"

I cleared my throat to find my voice. "She was my mother."

"Your..." she covered her mouth a second, "we looked for her for two days." There was pain in her eyes. "We had to get back before our passes expired." Her eyes teared up, "we reported her missing when we got back, but she was never found." She looked around, "is she..."

"She passed away over a hundred years ago."

Her expression changed to grief. "I am so sorry." Placing her hand against her throat, she shook her head. "I can't believe you are her daughter..." her eyes widened again, "she found her mate over there?"

I shrugged, "she had no tattoo—" I glanced to Quinton, "but she always said that may have been more because of who my father was." I frowned, "is." I knew it was making things more difficult for myself, thinking he may still be alive, but the last few days had shown me anything was possible.

Elder Landry came down the step and nodded to Elder Nodin. "Who was your father?"

Troy cleared his throat. "We'll be going over that in a meeting, as soon as we have more information."

The Elders looked at him for a moment, then nodded their heads in unison.

Elder Nodin looked at my pendant in his hand, then to Synova. "You know Keiragan's family?" He turned to me, "Miss Reagan's family?"

Giving me a hesitant look, she nodded before turning back to him, "yes."

"Don't keep us in suspense." Chase got up and wandered over. He waved his hand around, "Reagan has been waiting a hundred and fifty years to know."

"Dalston." She said softly. "Keiragan Dalston."

I know she said it and I did hear it, but I just continued to stand there. "So, so where did she get Hayden from?"

"Bastian is looking into that name." Michael stated. "When we had no record of it here, he said he'd check on it."

I nodded slowly.

"Dalston?" Victor came over, his serious look even harder than it usually seemed.

Synova nodded. "Yes."

Victor blew out a breath and looked at Quinton.

Quinton gave him a curious look.

He turned toward Michael, who pulled out his phone and started typing on it. "That is Gudrun's family name." Victor said then glanced to Troy.

"The guard we brought back?" Troy asked.

"Yes." Victor said no more. Crossing his arms over his chest, he stared at the floor, contemplating for a few moments. "I believe his family moved to the other side of the wasteland after he went missing." He looked to Rafael quickly, "having no more relatives serving in the guard, they moved to a less populated area." He sighed loud. "I'm afraid I haven't been keeping in touch with them as much as I should."

The words seemed to be floating around me instead of registering. I had family. Family that was living. I frowned, I should ask how this Gudrun was related. I wanted to, but I couldn't seem to find the words.

Someone touched my shoulder. I snapped back to the present.

"Are you all right?" Quinton looked down at me, his concern evident.

"I..." I blew out a breath, "I don't know." I looked at the floor for a second, then back to him. "Gudrun was rescued from that place?" He nodded. "Is he..." I couldn't bring myself to say it.

Lifting his hand away, he rubbed the back of his neck. "He spent a lot of time starving—he, uh..." His eyebrows drew together, "he's a..." clearing his throat, he gave his head a quick shake, "feeding was difficult for him in there, so he often was..."

He didn't have to say anymore. "I understand." My heart felt heavy with emotion I'd hoped to never feel again. "My mother, she—it became difficult for us to be around others when my," I lifted my hand and looked at the glove, "before we understood it, so she often went without for too long." Someone gasped, but I couldn't bring myself to deal with the sympathy or reactions right now. "How is he fairing?" I didn't even know what his relation was to me, but regardless of...

"You're not healing him." Quinton said in a tone that told me there was no room for negotiation. "After near starvation he's not in control of his hunger or coherent enough to prevent... he feeds by touching, Reagan, and I don't know if..."

I nodded slowly. "If my hand on him would be all it would take." I continued to nod. "I understand."

"How is he related?" Paisley came over, a sympathetic expression on her face. I hoped she wasn't going to hug me. I was struggling to contain my emotions.

"I'll know in a moment." Michael held his phone up, "I've just messaged the archives to check."

I nodded, even though none of this was registering. I had living relatives. For too many decades I'd tried to get here, to Alterealm, picturing my mother's family welcoming me with open arms. The more years that passed, the less I'd thought about it happening. Now, thoughts and wishes I hadn't even dreamed of in half a century had me feeling numb.

"I'm going to contact the rest of the family." Victor stated and turned to leave the room.

"Victor." Troy took a deep breath and exhaled as he glanced to me, "we'll need to have the entire family vetted, prior to meeting Reagan, or seeing Gudrun."

Victor's expression didn't change. "You think someone in their line is involved?"

"We won't know until Gudrun is more coherent, brother, and we're not taking any chances."

I looked from one to the other. "You think my family is involved in this war?"

Emil studied Troy for a moment, then turned to me. "There have been far too many misplaced family members involved."

I frowned, not understanding.

"My father." Alona said softly.

"Our—" Autumn turned and looked at Paisley, "Nathas." Her expression hardened as she spoke.

"My best friend." Bethany said with a sad expression on her face.

I just stood there, not knowing what to say.

"Magic was used to compel many to action." Quinton's gaze locked on mine as he explained, "They have no memory of it."

I took a shaky breath, then nodded, thinking for a few more seconds. "I suppose after more than a century, a few days will pass quickly." It wouldn't, but there was no reason to cause a scene. This was the royal family and causing a scene wouldn't buy me any favor.

Michael stepped over to Chase and showed him is phone.

"Ah," Chase tucked his hands in his pocket, "Gudrun is your uncle. Your mother was his sister." He held my look for several seconds, then turned to Alona, "perhaps you could stop in and see what the doctors have to say about a meeting?"

Alona gave me an understanding look, "I will before we go to rest."

Rafael stood up holding his phone. "There's another symbol at the market." He looked to Leone, "it wasn't there an hour ago."

Daxx turned to Autumn, "feel like shopping?"

Autumn grinned.

"Won't it be closing for the day shortly?" Paisley looked at Arius.

Arius shrugged, "best time to shop."

Emil noticed my confused expression. "Hubert has been using the markets here to communicate with those working on this side."

"Using symbols?" I didn't understand.

Bethany did something on her phone, then held it out. "This symbol."

I looked at it. "I think I've seen it." I sighed, "it was painted on the wall by the garage..." I looked at Quinton, "where we met."

Troy looked at Victor, "call Ira..."

"Don't." Daxx countered.

Troy gave her a hard look.

With a smile, Daxx shrugged, "bunch of kings and princes out shopping would draw all the attention."

Paisley nodded as she tucked her pendant under shirt. "Bunch of women," she shrugged, "will go unnoticed."

"I don't think it…"

Autumn turned to Michael, "careful iceman, sounds like you're going to use that word," She motioned to Daxx, "that sets off our Queen."

Daxx crossed her arms and looked at Troy, daring him to say the wrong thing.

"I could go as well." Quinton spun to face me, his expression said, 'not a chance'. I looked at my gloves and adjusted one, "unless you can see those that are rotten to their souls."

"You can see that?" Emil moved cautiously past Quinton.

I nodded. "Yeah. The traces around that lot in the garage were black AF." I looked at Autumn, not liking the glances the men were giving me, "it's how I knew who the good guys were or were not."

"Oh," Crissy jumped up from the plant she'd been sitting under, "I see auras." She frowned, "is that the same as a trace?"

I lifted my hands, then dropped them. "I have no idea."

Autumn gave an abrupt nod. "Reagan goes." She clapped her hands together once, "what's the fastest way there?"

Michael held his hand up, "hold up. We need to make…"

"No time for drawn out planning, Michael," Kara headed for the door, "for all we know the symbol means immediate action."

"Unfortunately, she's right." Rafael, glanced up from his phone, he was taping, "we'll get Kara set up somewhere she can observe with her bow," he looked to Chase for a second, "maybe put Alona and Crissy in her tower to watch the other direction…"

"Beth and Paisley can be crowd control if it gets chaotic." Leone looked at Bethany, who was fighting to contain a grin.

"I don't…"

71

Troy held up his hand, "careful, brother," he gave Michael a warning look, "I'm fairly certain that they are not asking our permission."

"We talked about this." Autumn held Michael's look. "Let me be me."

Michael looked from her to Troy, then to Rafael. "Get some guards out there dressed to fit in."

Rafael nodded, "Ira is sending people that will be delivering things around the market."

Daxx release a little squeal of joy, "Let's go, girls." She almost ran for the stairs.

"Wait." Quinton put his hand in front of me to stop me from following.

Everyone stopped.

I was trying to figure out what he was thinking. His expression was to hard read, like he had an internal conflict.

"Do you know how to use a knife?" He finally said.

I shrugged, "yes."

With an abrupt nod, he reached behind him, then held up a small knife in a case. "If anyone tries to grab you, use this. Then your port." He looked at my glove as I slowly took the knife. "And keep those damn gloves on."

Everyone was giving us strange looks.

I stepped back and bowed in slow motion. "Yes, Prince." With that I turned to follow Autumn.

"She pushes buttons, I like that." Chase said as we ran up the steps.

Chapter Nine

I adjusted the earpiece and pulled up my hood. It felt odd stuck in my ear, but the biggest adjustment was hearing the voices. In my entire life, I'd never had friends or anyone other than my mother, now I had the entire royal family in my ear.

"So how does it work?" Paisley's voice came through it. "Seeing a trace?"

My shopping partner was Autumn, I glanced at her and noticed she had as much knowledge of market shopping as I did, which was none. "I'm not sure." I said quietly, then stopped to touch a scarf hanging on a tall rack. "Not everyone has one, but if something is strong enough, it's there."

"So, if they're pure evil, you see it." It was Leone's voice.

"Yes."

"I see pure goodness, it's the brightest." Crissy chimed in.

I turned to see Autumn squatting down to tie her shoe, although she was looking all around and not really tying laces. "That sort of thing doesn't stand out for me, just health, and heart I suppose."

"Heart?" It was Emil's voice in my ear.

"Black heart, like evil or ill intentions." I clarified.

"That's very convenient for us." There was no mistaking Chase's voice.

"What do you mean health?" That was Quinton, and I tried not to dwell on the hard tone in his voice.

"If a person is in pain," I paused and looked down the next row of vendors, there was an odd green haze in the row. I stopped to concentrate, I'd seen that before, but always thought it was a pollution. "Like if they're injured or chronically ill." I inhaled, the air was fresh, not polluted. Shaking my head, I continued to move down the row.

"That makes sense." Bethany's soft voice was in my ear, "with your abilities, that you'd see things that are health related."

"I'm hoping she sees lots of black." Autumn turned and looked at me, "have you seen any black?"

I gave my head a slight shake. "Nothing yet." Gnawing on my lip, I decided I was going to see if there was a gas stove or reason for the green haze. I motioned in that direction to Autumn and without comment we went down the row.

"There's nothing happening in our area." Alona reported.

"Kinsley and I are going to the far end and working our way back toward you." Daxx reported.

"Eyes-wide, Miss Hinton." Troy said in a commanding tone.

"Always." A voice I didn't know said through the earpiece.

I paused and stood in the green haze, looking at the people in the area. No one would have use of gas or anything that would give off that sort of pollution.

"I don't *see* things," Autumn said quietly, "but my gut says something is," she glanced around unnoticed, as her hood hid the movement, "hinky in this area."

"Hinky?" Michael's voice wasn't soft. "What the hell is hinky?"

A female chuckle sounded through the earpiece. "Off, not right." Bethany explained. "We've been playing this word-a-day game on our phones."

"A point for Autumn." Paisley said quietly.

"Perhaps we can discuss the game later." Victor's tone was not amused. "What do you see, Autumn?"

She glanced to me as I held up a small bird carving. "Nothing off, it's just a feeling."

The hair on the back of my neck tingled. "I feel it too." I confessed. The vendor smiled at me, I took that time to really look. "Do you have any doves?" I asked him, "my mother's favorite bird." His expression changed. I didn't see anything bad in him. I taped the ornament as I set it down. "I'll have to think on this one." I turned to see Autumn was watching me. I gave her a slight shake of my head.

With her back to the stands, she looked around. "Reagan felt something, that's why we came this way."

"There's movement behind the next booth." Kara said quietly. "I can't see what's happening, but there are several people there."

"Left or right?" Autumn asked.

"To Reagan's right." She answered.

"Don't rush in." Michael cautioned.

"Got it." Autumn whispered.

I put my hand in my pocket where the small knife was.

"We're heading that way." Daxx said abruptly.

"Us too." Paisley said.

"Proceed with caution, ladies." Chases' tone warned.

"Rafael, walk the horses toward that small white building, and you should be able to see us." Kara said.

"We're moving that way." Emil said, "although with this ridiculous hat, I doubt I'll be able to see a thing."

Someone snorted, "you look like a gypsy." It was Quinton, "and Raf looks like a bum."

"Someone had to be down here, you and Arius darted for the tower like your asses were on fire." Rafael said in an unamused tone.

"Arius could have played this part with his hair…"

"Don't dis my man's hair, Emil." Paisley said sounded serious.

"I would never." Emil apologized quickly.

I glanced at Autumn, she smirked at me and shrugged. "We're going around the side of the building." She said without question.

I followed her. The green haze was thicker. I blinked, trying to see if it was just the time of day as the sun was starting to set. It was still there. "Do you see the haze?" I looked at Autumn, she looked around.

"No. It's almost dusk, but I don't see anything." She slowed, pushing her hood back.

"Haze?" Crissy asked, "or fog?" There was a slight pause. "There's a difference between them." Another pause. "I looked it up. Is it fog? I need to know."

I squinted and looked around. "I wouldn't call it fog, it's not thick, but it's…"

"Five people have gone into that small building." Rafael said.

"That shed isn't big enough to hold five people." Quinton stated.

"Tunnel?" Autumn's stance changed.

"There aren't any in this area." Victor said in a low tone.

"Not legal ones." Leone added.

"Any of the vendors pop on your radar, Reagan?" Alona asked.

"None I've seen so far." I followed Autumn, not sure what we were going to do once we reached this shed.

"Do not engage until we are there, Autumn." Michael's words sounded like an order, but his tone was pleading.

She snorted, but didn't comment.

"Two more went in." Kara said slowly.

"Keep the door in your sight." Rafael told her.

"Already done." She whispered. "I'm not sure my arrows will reach that far though."

"We're porting behind the shed."

"Be careful, Arius." Paisley said.

"Can you get close enough to stop the door from moving?" Quinton sounded out of breath.

"On it." Paisley whispered.

"There's no one around the front now, Autumn." Rafael told her.

Autumn nodded to me and moved cautiously around the side of the small building.

"Paize has the door." Daxx informed everyone.

We rounded the corner to see Paisley, Bethany, Daxx and another dark-haired woman standing there. Paisley held her hand in the air, pointing toward the door.

"Ready?" Autumn looked at Daxx, she nodded.

"Wait for us." Arius said.

"Now." Autumn said and then yanked the door open and stood there. "It's empty."

"What do you mean?" Chase asked.

"She means the shed is empty." Daxx said as she stuck her head in.

"Trap door in the floor?" Quinton was now standing beside her.

"Not unless it's made out of dirt." Daxx told him.

"Leone, get Clairee and Romulus here, now." Arius said in a low voice.

"Michael, have Ira find the market's director. I want every vendor in this row interviewed. Someone has to have seen something, even if they're not involved." Troy appeared beside Daxx.

She glared at him. "Were you cloaked?"

He gave her a cautious look. "There was no way you were walking through the market without a guard."

Daxx pointed to the other woman. "Guard."

"King." He countered.

"I don't mean to interrupt, but there is a small group of people running away from the market like the devil is chasing them." Kara said quickly.

Rafael tossed his frayed cloak to the ground. "Direction?"

"Uh, to your left, Raf." Kara told him.

Rafael nodded. "Leone…"

"Bronx and I are on the horses heading that way." Leone said quickly.

"There's nothing out that way." Quinton glanced to Rafael, "A few fields, then the wasteland."

"Maybe they're meeting someone out there." Alona's voice came through the earpiece.

"I think we caught them off guard." Emil said as he looked inside the shed. He stepped back out and looked at Bethany. "Can you sense magic or spells?"

She shook her head. "I'm not that skilled yet." She sighed, "I might be a natural witch, but learning how to use it is complicated."

He nodded. "Should we send the patrols to look?"

"No." Troy was typing on his phone, "it could be a ploy to pull them from an area. The patrols stay their course." He glanced to Arius, "I'm sending the ladies' guards out to search." He looked down at Daxx, "They're the only ones not currently occupied."

"Is there fog?" Crissy asked quietly.

Everyone looked around.

"Not here." Emil answered.

I looked around as well. The green haze was gone.

"Keep an eye out for foggy areas, Leone." Victor said abruptly.

"Fog. Got it." Leone's voice was choppy. I realized they were on running horses.

"Rafael, have the first years stay at the yard. I've been asked to call Prince Bastian." Chase said quickly.

I wondered if the prince had news of my father, but with everything happening thought it best to not ask right now.

Rafael nodded. "I'll send Kinsley back to keep a watch over them until the next shift gets there."

The woman I didn't know nodded. "I'll go now." She grinned. "I have my own porter set now for the castle and the yard."

Rafael tapped the screen on his phone and then putting it to his ear.

"This was a big let down." Daxx looked around, "I was hoping we'd get to kick some ass tonight."

"We may yet." Victor stated. "The vendors are being rounded up."

"Where are we meeting them?" Alona asked.

Troy looked at Quinton. "We'll wait at the meeting room until they're all gathered. Leone, stay on the line."

"Yeah." He sounded out of breath.

Autumn looked in the building once more. "Call if you find them. I need the workout."

"Will do." He sounded amused.

Chapter Ten

Daxx spun the cup in a circle on the table in front of her. "How much longer are we going to sit here?" She yawned. "I can't drink anymore coffee."

"I don't even know whose daytime it is." Bethany leaned back and closed her eyes.

"Why are we here again?" Kara asked.

"Yeah, I thought we were *all* waiting here." Daxx looked unimpressed.

Autumn paced away from the window. "Because our guards are out on the hunt and we've been benched."

"The vendors must have all checked out or Kara would have been called by now." Paisley put in her earbud and tapped the screen of her phone.

"Again." Alona agreed without looking up from the tablet. "On a good note, however, I think I've found the furniture for the sitting area on the second floor."

"*Thank goodness for that*, maybe we'll have a new place to sit and do nothing." Paisley snarked before leaning over and looking at the tablet. "Looks comfy."

"When they said *we'll* wait, I thought that meant them too." Bethany sighed, then looked over at Crissy where she sat beside the thrones. "Any more details on the climax vision?"

I didn't think Crissy was listening, but her head popped up and she looked right at Bethany.

"No." She lifted her shoulders, then let them drop again. "Yes. I don't know how they fit together." She looked at me for a second, "each time a girl has appeared, there was a connection to the rest," she shrugged, "mostly." Her solemn look turned to joy briefly, "even Victor can't help. We tried, I let him…"

Daxx jumped up, "no details."

"I was just going to…"

"TMI, sister." Paisley grinned.

"Oh. Okay." Crissy stared at her pencil for a moment, "there's fog, but it's not really foggy, I know that now," she nodded, "then there's—" she jumped up and pointed to me, "your necklace. It's your necklace." She nodded, a big smile on her face, then sat back down and dumped her pack on the floor. Grabbing a notebook out of the small pile of items, she began flipping through the pages. "I thought it might be a tattoo," she glanced up at me so briefly, I wasn't sure she really saw me, "but it's not. It's the pendant." Jumping up, she held the notebook open and stumbled in my direction.

Autumn had to catch her before she tripped and fell on her face.

Getting up, I took the book she held out and looked down. It was a sketch of the center portion of my mother's pendant.

"I saw that so long ago." She took a deep breath, then exhaled. "The fog has to do with you." She nodded. "And nothingness too," she frowned, "I don't know if it's nothingness, but it's a blank space." She turned to Daxx and grinned. "Each time one of us girls showed up, the visions were directly connected." Crissy laughed softly, "Victor and I figured that part out when Autumn came to join us."

Autumn snorted, "I wouldn't have minded a heads up before," she waved her hand around, "all that happened."

Crissy's expression became serious again, "we weren't one hundred percent certain," she shrugged, "Vic's words." Her expression became animated again, "but now I know *for certain.*" She hopped toward me and hugged me, crushing the notebook between us. "I have to tell Vic." She released me, then dashed over to her pack again, "you're the climax." She paused and looked back to me. "You are the key. You have the answers to end this." Standing up, she hugged her pack and then vanished.

The room was completely silent. I glanced around to see everyone looking at me.

"Does," I scowled, "does that come with more explanation?" I watched a few of the women shake their heads. "So," I motioned around the room, "what, what did she say exactly?"

Daxx rubbed her hands over her face. "Obviously there's some sort of fog or maybe…"

"Smoke?" Bethany was on her feet now too.

Daxx nodded, "could be." She pointed to me, "and somehow you have the knowledge or ability to help us get Hubert, or that other guy…"

"Arwan." Paisley nodded.

"Yeah him." Daxx mumbled.

I opened my mouth, then closed it.

"Basically, we have no idea, but it seems you are definitely meant to be here, now in this juncture in time." Alona stood up and stretched.

"I have no idea what any of that is about," Autumn grinned at me, "but if you can find either of those two, I will drop kick them so hard, their future will become history."

"Should we call the guys and tell them Crissy's latest?" Kara asked.

Daxx turned to look at Alona.

"I think not." Alona mused quietly. "Perhaps we can figure out how to put the pieces together while they're out grunting orders…"

"We're going to need our guards." Bethany nodded slowly.

"Who have been commandeered by our mates." Paisley sighed.

"Well," Kara glanced around at the others slowly, "we'll see how far we can get before we *need*, need them."

"Please." Alona crossed her arms over her stomach, "we are not feeble women by any means," she pointed to Autumn, then Paisley and Bethany, "you three can take out pretty much anything that comes at us," she smiled at me, "and now we don't have to call the boys when we have a mishap."

I stood there, trying to figure out what they were saying. I didn't understand any of this. "I'm not sure if I'm too tired, or…"

Alona chuckled, "I'd say let's break out the wine, but we could explain everything over a light snack instead." She touched her stomach, "I am feeling peckish."

"I could eat." Autumn nodded.

Loud music started playing. Autumn pulled her phone out of her hoodie pocket and smiled.

"Hey, Rena. Trouble sleeping?" She tapped the screen and continued talking, "I asked…"

"Autumn." A woman's breathless voice came out of the phone. "I fell. I didn't want to call dad, he'd…"

"I'll be right there." She clasped the phone in her hand and closed the distance between us and grabbed my arm. "Come on."

My adrenaline peaked and suddenly I was standing in a beautifully decorated room. Autumn let go of me and looked around, then darted forward. I followed her. A woman with hair almost the color of snow lay on the carpeting at the bottom of a few steps in a sitting room.

"We're here." I glanced behind me to see the other woman all standing where I had just been.

"Where's it hurt?" Autumn knelt over the woman.

"My leg." She grunted out a sound of pain as she shifted.

Autumn nodded, then pointed to the couch. "Someone grabs some pillows."

Bethany dashed past me and went to the couch.

"Rena, this is Reagan." Autumn looked over her shoulder at me, "she heals with her hands."

Rena leaned back against the pillows and looked over at me, pain clear on her face. "That's handy."

I went over and knelt down beside Autumn. I checked the angle of her leg, it seemed straight and in a somewhat normal position. "Can you move it?"

With a grimace on her face, she nodded. "I don't think anything is broken." She rolled her eyes, "I've experienced broken bones in my life." She slumped back and closed her eyes, "I just called because I need help to get off the floor."

"No cramping or anything? From the fall?" Alona was the only one keeping her distance as the rest gathered around.

Rena shook her head. "No. When my leg twisted, I fell on my hands." She held up her red-palmed hands. "A bit of carpet burn, but everything bends as it should."

Autumn turned to me, a question on her face. "Do you need anything to do this?"

I sat back on my heels and pulled off my gloves. "No. We'll see how bad it is as I go."

"Okay." Her expression was serious. "Just don't," she glanced to Daxx, "don't overdo it, yeah?"

"Maybe a bit at a time, so you don't collapse on us?" Kara sat down beside me.

I nodded, "Let's see how bad it is." I carefully pulled the pajama pant leg up to expose her skin. "If my hair starts to go completely grey, just lift my hands." I gave Kara a sideways glance, "sometimes my need to help drowns out my logic."

Kara nodded. "Got it."

I held my hands over Rena's leg, then looked up at her, "my eyes will go black, my hair will lighten, but it doesn't hurt me." I waited until she nodded hesitantly before placing my bare hands on her leg. I exhaled slowly, sensing the draw happening in my body. "It's not too serious." I said quietly and then closed my eyes.

"What the hell is going on?"

I heard metal clang together and opened my eyes to see Emil drop to his knees beside Rena. Two swords lay at his side.

"It's okay, Dad. I twisted my leg. Nothing is broken." Rena told him.

I closed my eyes again and focused on the draw I felt in my hands. It wasn't too strong, but if it had been left, it would have taken her a few weeks to recover fully.

"What—" I heard heavy footsteps, "Reagan." Hands grasped my shoulder and pulled me back.

I looked up to see Quinton looking very unhappy. Blowing out a breath, I pulled my hair forward and looked at it. It wasn't entirely grey yet, but it was lighter than I would have anticipated. "I'm fine." I said without looking at him. Ignoring his glare, I glanced down at Rena. "How does it feel?"

She moved her leg slowly, bending the knee and flexing her foot. "A little tender, but no real pain." Her eyes teared up. "Thank you."

I only smiled as a response. Turning I saw most of the royal brothers hovering around the sitting room space. They were dressed for battle in leather, holding large weapons covered in what looked like blood and dirt. I gave Daxx a hard look.

She frowned and turned to Troy. "I thought you guys were just out searching?"

Troy harnessed his swords on his back in a smooth motion. "We were. We found more than those that had taken off."

Bethany went over and brushed off Leone's face. "In a sand box?"

Leone looked unamused. "No. The wastelands."

"I still don't understand why they were just hanging out there." Rafael went over and pulled Kara to her feet.

"Chase, the carpet." Alona sighed.

Chase looked down at his dusty boots. "I'll send cleaners over first thing in the morning."

"Probably because we wouldn't think to look in the middle of nowhere." Michael clasped both swords in one hand, like they weighed nothing and came over to Autumn. "You should have called."

Autumn shook her head. "There was no time." She quietly ordered, "well, help her get to the couch."

Emil jolted and extended his hand to his daughter as she stood up. With slow movements, Rena got to her feet and tested her weight on the injured leg.

"Oh, Reagan, thank you." With careful steps she went over to the couch and sat down.

"I think we should get the doc over here to check her," Autumn got up, "and the baby." She looked at Michael. Without comment, he nodded and pulled out his phone.

"I'll go bring him over." Rafael disappeared.

I stumbled as I got up, "so if you didn't call, how did everyone end up here?" Quinton reached out and steadied me. "Thanks." I tried to give him a nonchalant look, but his annoyed facial expression didn't change. "I'm fine. Just a little lightheaded." I pushed my hair back from my face. "I'm just tired."

"You can't keep doing that." He said in a tone that expected most people would obey immediately. I was not most people.

"That's not your choice." I pulled my arm from his grasp and focused on putting my gloves back on. "If you think I'm going to ask permission after more than a hundred years of looking after myself," I glanced up at him, "royalty or not," I put the other glove on, "than you are a delusional prince." I bowed my head to him.

Someone snorted.

Quinton continued to stare down at me for several tense seconds. "I'll see everyone back at the dinning room." Then he vanished.

Alona came over and handed me a glass. She smirked, but didn't say a thing.

I took a sip, it was juice. "So," I looked at Troy, then Michael, "how did you guys know?"

"They can sense our emotions." Paisley paused and pulled out her phone. She put it to her ear. "I'm fine. Rena fell and twisted her leg. Yeah." She nodded and hung it up again.

"Arius has new guests or he'd have been the first one here." Leone told her.

"You sense emotions or just your mate's?" I looked at Emil.

He shrugged. "I think it's a royal family thing, because I don't have a mate, but I sensed the spike in emotions just as they did."

"We weren't sure if we were coming to fight, or what the situation was." Chase went over and hugged Alona. "After the last time we had to come here."

Alona cringed. "Don't remind me, those sops ruined my love of roses."

Bethany made a face of displeasure. "How did you know to come here?"

Leone rubbed the back of his neck. "Raf shouted to get to Alona's apartment. So here we are."

Everyone turned to look at Kara, she shrugged. "Aside from knowing my feelings, he can sometimes see what I see, if I focus."

"That's handy." Daxx commented.

Kara nodded. "Too bad we couldn't do it when I landed in the snow."

"Or when that spell trapped me in that dingy building." Paisley said.

Rafael and the doctor appeared near the door.

"All right, everyone, lets give Rena and the doctor some space." Troy said in that kingly tone.

"I'm going to stay." Autumn looked at Michael.

With an affectionate look, he inclined his head. "We'll be meeting in the chambers dining room."

"I'll be there." Autumn turned to help Rena to her feet.

Rena paused to look at Emil. "You don't need to stay. I'll call you as soon as we're finished."

Emil frowned, but nodded. He turned to the doctor, flashing him a stern look before disappearing.

The doctor looked over at me, "if you have a moment later, I have your test results."

I stood there trying to decipher if his expression. He had a poker face like no other, I couldn't tell a thing. "Okay, I'll come to see you in an hour?"

"Very good." He inclined his head then followed Rena and Autumn down the hallway.

Chapter Eleven

In less than twenty minutes the entire family was clean and seated in a large room gathered around a huge polished wooden table. There were a few portraits on the wall, so I spent most of the time picking out the resemblance to the brothers seated at the table.

Autumn had come back a few minutes ago and reported that both Rena and baby were in good health. I was still a bit tired, but happy to hear all was well.

The amount of food Mitz had put on the table was astonishing and it was disappearing at a rapid pace.

"Did you tell them?"

I looked up to see Crissy looking at me.

"Tell them?"

She nodded. "That you are the key to the climax." She knelt on her chair and looked around at the others. "Reagan has the answers we need."

I opened my mouth to say I had no answers when Rafael spoke first.

"Judging by her expression, little sister, I don't think she has them right now." He grinned at me.

"No." Crissy rolled her eyes. "I know she doesn't now, but she will, then the end will finally come."

"Uh, Criss, you really have to stop saying things like that." Daxx pushed her plate away. "The climax, the end." She turned and looked at her.

"I-I don't know how else to say it." Crissy looked to Victor.

Victor held her hand for a moment, then glanced around the table. "I believe what she is trying to relay is Reagan's arrival will give us the answers to ending this struggle."

"We found out about the Solrelm traitor when Reagan was there." Bethany nodded.

"And, if she hadn't been there, our brother's injury could have led to—" Chase paused and looked around the table, "where is Quinton?"

Rafael grabbed a platter and passed it to Leone, "said he'd catch us later and went out the back door with a plate of food."

Leone shrugged. "More eats for us, I say."

Troy looked at Bethany, she nodded. "Like I said, strange behavior."

With a serious look, Troy turned to Kara.

She froze with her fork halfway to her mouth. "Don't look at me, I can only know what's going on if he thinks it, I'm not psychic."

"Mmm," Troy turned to his twin, "I'll talk to him."

Chase grinned, "yes because that always goes well with our big brother."

Arius chuckled, "we could beat it out of him."

"Again," Chase waved his fork around, "that never goes as planned either." He grinned Daxx, "does it, Kitten?"

"Don't remind me." Daxx sat back and crossed her arms. "I need a nap." She looked at Michael, "what time is Bastian going to be here?"

Michael glanced at his phone. "Not for four hours yet." He yawned. "I think we all need some rest."

I wanted to ask why he was coming, but wasn't sure if I wanted to know if he'd found information about my father.

"Why are we meeting him?" Alona asked, giving me a quick glance.

Michael rubbed his hand over his jaw. "Follow up. He says he knows more of his are helping Willis."

"Any news of Reagan's dad?" Paisley asked giving me an understanding look.

"He didn't say." Michael motioned to Rafael, "we're going to set up a meeting with that woman from the asylum after we talk to Bastian though." He turned to look at Autumn. "Everyone get some rest, we're going to need to be our best."

"Where should we meet her?" Bethany asked.

"Somewhere we can control the situation." Leone told her.

"Which is?" Daxx leaned onto the table.

"We don't know yet." Leone answered.

"I have the ladies' guards scouting a few locations now." Victor informed all of us.

"Speaking of." Rafael stood up and motioned to the door behind me. "Perfect timing, Derian."

I turned to see a large man with a long, jet-black ponytail standing in the door. I didn't have to ask his profession, his whole aura screamed warrior.

"I was asked to arrange a personal guard for you, Reagan." Rafael came to the end of the table.

"For me?" I got up out of the chair. "I don't—" I glanced to Autumn, she shrugged.

"All of the ladies have one." Victor came to the end of the table.

"Derian has been on your side many times, he works with some of the people that live over there most of the year." Rafael explained, "I thought you'd be more comfortable with someone that has been on both sides."

The big man's pale green eyes assessed me briefly, then he bowed his head. "Miss."

"Uh," I glanced over my shoulder to see the woman all had the same look. A look that told me to go with it, because objecting wouldn't yield me a thing. "I don't know that I need a personal guard, but okay." I held out my hand, "Reagan."

He looked at my hand for a moment, didn't take it, but did smile. "Derian."

Clasping my hands together, I exhaled silently and then turned to Rafael. "Well, I need to go see the doctor to get my results…"

"I'll escort you." Derian stated and moved back from the doorway.

"Oh," I nodded, "okay." I turned to Rafael. "Do I come to this meeting with Bastian or is it just…"

"I'll come and get you." Autumn said as she stood up.

With an awkward smile, I nodded. "Okay. I'll see you then."

I turned the corner Derian motioned to.

"Are you all right?" He finally spoke after several minutes of uncomfortable silence.

I gave him a puzzled look.

"You're going to see the doctor."

I grinned. "As far as I know I'm all right." I paused as we passed a servant carrying a stack of linens. "I heal people," I paused not missing the fact that I could freely discuss this part of myself now, "with my hands." I held up my glove covered hands, "and Prince Quinton wanted the doctor to check my overall health after years of doing this."

"That's something." He looked at my hands and smiled. "Have you known the royal family long? Your connection wasn't explained to me."

"A few days."

"Oh, I got the impression you had known them longer." He gave me a sideways glance. "To be eating in their dinning room."

I chuckled. "I can't even explain it, Derian." I stopped and stared at the hall in front of us. "My mother was from Alterealm," I glanced up at him, "my father was—" I didn't know enough about that situation to go into detail, "not."

Looking back down the hall. "In the past few days, I've gone from surviving on the other side, to a palace in Alterealm." I huffed out a breath and looked at my gloved hand, "I'm not sure why I'm here," I gave him an exasperated look, "here helping the royal family, not here in Alterealm." He didn't move. "Never mind being told by Crissy that I'm the key in ending the war they've been fighting." I lifted both hands and let them drop. He still hadn't moved a muscle. "I don't understand most of what's going on." Deciding I'd said enough, I started walking again.

"Crissy?" He was beside me again.

"Victor's mate." I slowed down when we neared the door with the pin pad.

"Oh. If the seer of light has seen it, then I guess you must be." He paused to look at me before entering the number, "she hasn't ever been wrong, from what I've been told." He punched in numbers and opened the door. "She can even decipher the prophecies."

I stepped out the door, noting guards were there again.

Derian nodded at them and we started walking across the yard.

Halfway across I stopped and looked at him. "I'm sorry for being short with you." I blew out a breath and began to walk again. "I spent years looking for a way to get to Alterealm and gave up." The guards stood at attention as we got closer. "After being alone for the last century, I'm having a bit of a struggle getting used to so many people around me." I hadn't even realized it until I said it out loud.

The guards inclined their heads to us.

I waited until we went through the door, to look back out at them. "Everyone keeps doing that."

"Doing what?" He checked out the guards too.

"Bowing their heads to me." I headed toward the room Quinton had taken me before.

"Well, you are in tight with the royal family." Derian shrugged his large shoulders, "which means you're a VIP in some capacity." He smiled and motioned to the door I was heading toward. "You're even using the royal family's office here."

I frowned. "That's what it is?" I opened the door and went in. He stopped on the other side.

With a smile he stood there. "I'll be here when you're finished." He closed the door.

Sighing I looked around. There was no one here. I was going to knock on the door the doctor had come through before when I heard voices.

"My prince, I can't increase it anymore." It was the doctor's voice.

"What about that elixir stuff you used on Autumn?" It was Quinton.

"That—that is for injuries, not," there was a pause, "not your situation."

I frowned, wondering what was wrong.

"Keep looking." The door handle moved.

Like a naughty schoolgirl, I darted to the other side of the room and sat in the first chair I reached. The door opened and Quinton filled the frame.

"Reagan?"

I gave him a brief smile. "Hi. I'm here to get my results."

He stepped into the room, then looked behind him.

The doctor moved past him hesitantly, then nodded to me. "Miss Hayden," he went over to the small desk and picked up a folder. "I have your results right here." He opened it and looked inside, then nodded and looked back up at me. "I couldn't find a thing wrong with you." Shaking his head, he glanced briefly to Quinton, "in fact you may be the healthiest patient I've ever had."

I stood up. "I guess I have a good immune system." I clasped my hands in front of me. "I don't even recall ever having a cold in my life."

The doctor's expression was thoughtful for a moment. "That may be tied to your ability." He nodded slowly, "I'd have to speak to a few colleagues to confirm it, but if you're able to heal others it may be that you can't get sick like the rest of us."

"You mean her body just heals itself?" Quinton crossed his arms over his chest and stared at him.

"It may be something like that, but I have no way to know for certain without DNA testing, and someone more knowledgeable with her genes' and biology, perhaps…"

Quinton raised his hand and looked at me.

I looked from one to the other. "Pass. Hard pass." I nodded. "I'd prefer not to know the details." I held up my hands. "They heal and that's all I need to know."

Studying me for a moment Quinton then nodded his head and looked at the doctor. "No more tests then."

"As you wish." The doctor inclined his head for a moment, then turned and went back into the other room and closed the door.

Quinton looked at the door for a moment more. "Did I miss anything?"

"Everyone is going to rest before a meeting with Prince Bastian." I tried to look directly at him, but the traces around him stood out and distracted me. Not wanting to attempt to explain that, I adjusted my gloves.

"Did Raf find you a guard?"

"Yes." I looked at the door. "Derian is standing outside." Turning to him, I locked my gaze on his eyes, so I wouldn't look around him like I was dissecting him. "Do I really need a guard?"

He nodded without hesitation. "Yeah. You do." Stepping around me like I might bite him, he opened the door, then motioned to it. "I'll see you at the meeting."

I went over and stood in the doorway and watched him walk away. The haze around him wasn't red, but it wasn't clear either. It was there though. The same color I saw when people were ill. I'd seen it when he was hurt, bright red, but not since. I bit my lip and looked at Derian. "Healthy as ever." I smiled.

He inclined his head. "Are you going back to the chambers?"

I shook my head. "No. I'm going to rest."

Derian smiled. "Then, its to the palace." His smile widened. "I'm very excited I'm detailed to someone staying in the palace."

I laughed. "Well let's not take the long way then." I held up my wrist with my porter. Stepping closer he put his hand on my shoulder just as I pushed the button.

Chapter Twelve

Again, I was in a room with the entire royal family. This time there were several people in black robes and several large men standing around the room like statues. I glanced behind me to see Derian was there, looking like he was made of stone.

"They're our guards." Bethany leaned over and said quietly. She pointed to one on the other side of the room. "That's Mac, he's mine." Her expression grew serious. "I don't know what's happened, but they're not usually *in* the meetings with us."

"So that's bad?" I studied the men. If anyone was insane enough to go against one of them, then they deserved the trouncing they'd get.

"Yeah. It can't be good." She sighed and sat back. "I feel like we're going to be under house arrest, again."

Autumn snorted and sat down on the other side of me. "Like that ever works out for them."

Bethany laughed quietly. "They can try."

"All the elders are here." Autumn stated.

Daxx leaned forward on the table so we could see her around Autumn. "I'm hoping that's good for us." She shrugged, "maybe some news to share."

Ira came in the room and stopped inside the door.

Chairs scraped as people shifted to different seats as the others sat down.

"Here we go." Bethany said quietly.

I turned to ask Autumn something only to see Quinton had sat down beside me. Even sitting he was a large man.

Ira stepped aside. "Prince Bastian of Solrelm."

The dark-eyed prince stepped in the room and then stopped. "Gangs all here." He said quietly and then walked to an empty chair, "let's not get hung up on formal greetings," he sat down.

"We thought it best to include the elders in this." Victor said in a proper tone.

"That works for me." Bastian said in a low tone, then looked at the elder with a long white braid. "Did all you know that my people can, in fact, have offspring with people from other realms?" He leaned forward in his seat.

I glanced around the table to see surprised and shocked looks.

"Ah, there we have it. This lie—" he waved his hand around, "this deceit has been going on so long even your oldest didn't know." He turned to Troy.

"We're not Alterealm's oldest." Elder Nodin stated.

Bastian gave him a bored look. "Close enough. It's been going on for more than ten centuries at least."

"Twenty-six centuries." The woman with the braid said with a look of consternation. "Explain this." She looked back at him.

"Its simple, Elder…"

"Varus." She supplied for him.

"Varus," Bastian continued, "I have very recently discovered that an Alterealm resident had a child with one of my own people."

Elder Nodin leaned forward. "You have proof of this?"

Bastian made a strange noise then pointed to me. "She's right there."

I wanted to slide off my chair and sit under the table as all eyes turned to me.

"Miss Hayden, is this true?" Elder Landry sat up straighter.

I cleared my throat. "I have no proof, other than what my mother told me." I glanced at Quinton to see he wasn't happy Bastian had singled me out either, "when-when my father's people found out about him and my mother, they took him." I looked at Bastian, "they didn't know my mother was carrying me at the time."

Bastian tapped his hand on the table. "I have the proof." He waved his hand around, "which I'm still working on." He looked right at me, "Aldis Hayden, a Solrelm resident mysteriously went missing a little over one hundred and fifty years ago." He tapped the table a few more times, "I'm still narrowing down where he was taken, but," he glanced around the table, "the mere fact that Reagan has Alterealm and Solrelm DNA and the last name *Hayden* sounds all the right alarms for me."

There were several murmurs and conversations in the room. I wasn't able to focus on more than the fact that I had my father's last name. My mother hadn't made it up at all.

"I would like to be kept up-to-date on your progress with that." I told Bastian.

He nodded. "Not to worry, I have made it my new mission to find out what happened to your dear old dad." His look hardened, "and then have a very boisterous conversation with my own parents."

Victor cleared his throat loudly. "Were you able to find out if there are more of yours helping Willis Hubert?"

"Solrelm residents are helping Hubert?" A woman with white spiked hair asked.

"I'm afraid so, Elder Drusla." Arius informed her.

"That explains how they're finding humans with Alterealm DNA." Another of the female elders said.

"Yes, Elder Arian, that's how they've been doing it." Kara told her.

"Ten more." Bastian said abruptly. "That's how many more traitors from my realm are helping that insane lunatic."

He leaned forward on the table and clasped his hands. "Which is why I am requesting to join you in your hunt." He glanced at me, "so I can ferret out any among those you find."

"Should we get him to check the cells?" Leone turned to Arius. "Does that show up on the scan?"

Arius took a deep breath and then exhaled. "I don't recall when we've ever had one from Solrelm scanned until a few days ago." He frowned, "but there was very little difference in the scan results to know for sure." He glanced at Michael, "the scans are designed to detect humans, not others."

"I would like to take a look at all your prisoners." Bastian announced. "Especially any that were ill after being put there." He shrugged, "as you know we don't transport well to your realm." He frowned, "which is odd, we have no problems going to the human side or a few other realms…"

"We'll arrange it after this meeting." Victor interrupted.

Bastian gave him a nod.

"What do you mean you want to join the hunt?" Michael asked him. "I didn't think you were a warrior."

Bastian laughed, "not to the extent you are, but I can defend myself." He glanced to Troy, "my task would be to see if there are any among or nearby that are mine."

Elder Varus looked at me. "Can you see this as well?"

I looked from her to Bastian, "I don't think so. I see traces around others sometimes."

"Traces?" Bastian leaned forward, "traces of their DNA?" He looked at Crissy, "or auras like the little seer?"

I sat back and clasped my hands in my lap. "I don't think they're auras, but could be." I tried to think of a way to explain it. "The people that took the family in the garage, the trace around them was dark, near black." I glanced at Quinton, "when the prince was injured, his was bright red," I shrugged, "a trace."

"That's not their DNA, but it's useful in other ways I suppose." Bastian looked like he was disappointed. "Did you mother have that skill?"

I shook my head. "Not that I'm aware of." I looked at Victor, "we could ask her family."

Victor nodded but made no comment.

"It's not really an aura either." Crissy said. "What I see tells me what's in a person's heart." She nodded.

"We can't guarantee you can tag along to every incursion, Bastian, but anything planned in advance we'll be sure to include you." Michael looked to Troy who nodded. Turning back to him, he leaned back and crossed his arms. "How did you find out there are more of yours involved?"

Bastian grinned, "Have you met my brother, Trendan?" He motioned to himself, "I'm the nice one out of the three of us." He chuckled, "he sang like a songbird as soon as my brother walked in."

Arius chuckled. "Sounds like you have a lot in common, brother." He turned to Victor.

"You instill more fear than I do among the criminals, brother." Victor said in a monotone way.

"Speaking of fear." Bastian glanced around, "I have to be going. I'm on duty for the next few days." He stood up.

"It was nice to see you again, Prince Bastian." Elder Varus inclined her head to him.

"Might be seeing a whole lot more of me before we end this insane plot." He bowed his head to Troy, then nodded to Chase and walked out with Ira.

When the door closed, Elder Varus looked at Troy. "This has been very informative."

A few of the other elders nodded their agreement.

"There's more." Chase said with a serious look.

"More?" The Elder that was father to Nathas frowned and leaned forward.

"We found more symbols at the market and Romulus has just confirmed that a mage's magic was used." Chase turned to Quinton, "that's how they vanished in that shed."

"Was it a mage's portal or are they using porters?" Quinton leaned on the table.

"He's about eighty-nine percent certain it was a mage's portal." Chase shrugged. "Which I'm told is only something powerful mages can maintain, especially when large numbers go through it."

"Hopefully they landed in the snow." Kara looked unhappy.

"Arwan." Elder Varus said in a low tone. "It could be only Arwan doing something like that from a distance."

"That's what we thought too." Michael chimed in.

"I keep seeing something like fog." Crissy stood up and paced away from the table, "is there magic fog?" She spun around and looked at me, "and Reagan is connected to it."

All eyes were on me again. I shook my head to let them know I had no idea.

"Can we ask Clairee and Romulus about that?" Alona turned and looked at Bethany, "about the fog or something like it?"

Bethany nodded slowly, "yeah, I'll call her when we're done here."

"I thought the magic smoke was just for magicians on stage." Daxx said.

"Well, unfortunately, we're all learning new things here lately." Leone said in a serious tone.

"I'd like to be kept apprised of new developments." The Elder with the curly hair said.

"Of course, Elder Arian." Rafael said.

"I think we'll be having more of these update meetings in the future, or at least until Arwan and Willis Hubert are in one of our cells." An Elder with black hair and dark eyes said.

"I agree, Elder Marinus." Victor said, then stood up. "You will have to excuse us, we're to meet the woman Kara met at the asylum."

"The one with Alterealm blood?" Elder Varus asked.

"Yes." Victor motioned to Kara. "We had Kara set it up and want to get there with time to spare, so we can get a watch set up."

"We won't keep you any longer." Elder Varus stood up. She gave me a brief smile. "Welcome home, Miss Hayden."

I smiled back. "Thank you for allowing me here."

The elders exited the room without further delay.

Most around the table stood up.

Victor came over to me. "I contacted your family, there are many living relatives excited to meet you." He cleared his throat, "however we cannot permit a visit as of yet." He looked to Quinton where he stood beside me, "at least not until we speak with Gudrun."

I nodded. "Okay. Thank you." I watched Victor walk away and then just continued to sit there. I had my fathers last name and other relatives. My entire life, save thirty years, I'd felt like an orphan and suddenly I wasn't.

"Are you okay?" Quinton leaned down beside me.

"I'm—" I huffed out a short breath. "shell-shocked, I believe." I turned my head and looked at his deep brown eyes, "I have family, all of a sudden." I inhaled slowly and tried not to become emotional. "My mother was Keiragan Dalston and my father was, or could still be Aldis Hayden." I swallowed the lump in my throat and gave him a wide-eyed look. "Isn't that something I should have known before I was over a century old?"

Quinton gave me an understanding look. "Yes, it is." He picked up my gloved hand from my lap and squeezed it in his. "Many of our protocols are to blame for so many being stuck on that side, yet if you hadn't been, we wouldn't have answers we need now." He glanced at his phone, then straightened, still holding my hand. "Come on. I was going to check in on Gudrun before we went over for the meeting, you can come with me."

My look must have reflected my surprise.

"I don't know if he's well enough to speak, but you can still come if you want." He held my look.

I nodded. "I'd like that."

"We'll meet you over there." Quinton said gruffly. "I'm taking Reagan to see Gudrun."

Victor raised his eyebrows, but made no comment.

"Don't be late." Michael told him.

"We won't." He glanced at me, then winked.

The next moment we were standing in the medical building.

He released my hand and started walking, I almost had to jog to keep up with him. We entered a hallway with several doors. Quinton stopped. "I'll be right back, I just want to check on his status before we go in."

I nodded and stood on that spot. I watched him walk down the hall and go into a room. I breathed in deep and out slowly, to stay calm. I was meeting a member of my family. My mother's brother. She had never spoke of him. I frowned, as I did the math quickly. He would have already been missing before she went over to that side. I put my hand over my mouth and continued to stand there. In all the years I'd missed her and wished she were still here, none of them could compare with my wish right now. If she could have known her brother was found… Quinton came out and motioned for me to come with him.

I hurried down the hall to a door he stood by.

"He's in and out, but recovering." He paused with his hand on the door, "which the doctor says is nothing short of a miracle."

I grinned, "I understand, my mother hung on for years beyond when she should have." I blinked so no tears would form in my eyes.

I froze inside the doorway and looked at the man in the bed. He was thin, but still a large man. His hands were bound with little room for movement.

"Prince," his voice was hoarse, "forgive me if I don't bow."

Quinton shook his head. "It's not a problem, Gud."

The way Quinton said it sounded more like *good*, showing me that they had known each other well before my uncle had disappeared.

"Kerry?"

I jolted and looked back to the man looking at me.

"This is your sister's daughter, Reagan." Quinton explained.

I stepped to the end of the bed.

"Her daughter." He licked dry lips. "I have a niece." He looked at me with tired eyes. "You look just like her." He turned his head slowly and looked at Quinton. "My parents?"

Quinton put his hand on Gudrun's arm. "We lost your father during the influenza about a hundred years ago, but your mother, aunts and uncles are all fine."

Gudrun closed his eyes for a moment, then he looked back at me. "And Kerry?"

I shook my head. "I lost her over a century ago."

He didn't speak for more than a minute. Turning he gave Quinton an exasperated look. "The nurse told me how long I was gone."

"Too long." Quinton crossed his arms over his chest and looked down at him. "How did you end up over there?"

Gudrun closed his eyes. "I was on a routine patrol," he shook his head slowly, "next thing I know I'm in a room with no windows."

"Were you moved to that place then?" Quinton's expression was filled with anger, but his tone hid it well.

My uncle shook his head slowly. "No. I don't think I ever left the building again, until you found me." He smirked. "I thought I'd gone and died finally when I saw you." His eyes drooped shut a few times as he fought to keep looking at his prince.

"You rest." Quinton's tone was more commanding. "We'll talk to you soon."

"Yes." Gudrun cleared his throat, then looked at me. "Lovely to meet you, niece."

I smiled and gave him a nod, my throat too choked with emotion to speak.

Chapter Thirteen

"He believes that?" Michael leaned back against the counter. "He believes he was in that building all this time?"

"I find that hard to believe. That the building was a mental institution all these years." Leone scanned the windows as he spoke. "We need to know how he just suddenly landed there."

"Once he has recovered further, we will have to get more details." Victor spoke with authority as walked to stand where Troy sat on a stool.

I looked around to see the rest of the family scattered around the diner, waiting.

"This is a good location." Rafael nodded to Quinton. "Derian says he used it for meetings with ours living over here."

Quinton continued to stand with his arms crossed over his chest. "Helps that the owner is one of ours."

"I feel bad we're costing them business by closing the place for our meeting." Alona looked at Chase.

He gave her a smile. "They'll be compensated."

"At least we don't have to watch our backs." Daxx said as she sipped her coffee.

"She should be here soon." Kara looked at her phone.

"You keep your distance." Rafael gave Kara a steady look. "Listen, but stay at arm's length, please."

"You still think this might be a set up?" Paisley looked from Rafael to Arius.

Arius lifted one eyebrow. "We're not taking chances." He looked at the kitchen. "We have guards out back and down the street."

I hadn't known that. Although the entire royal family was here, minus Crissy. I looked in the corner booths, I didn't think she was here, but with her knack for blending and being unseen...

"Reagan, will you be able to see," Emil waved his hand around, "traces when she comes in?"

I nodded. "If she comes in with ill intent, I'll know."

Emil motioned to a table across from the door. "Have a seat there."

I got up and went to where he pointed. Before I was sitting, Quinton and Emil moved so they were between the door and I.

"Any trouble, you use your porter." Quinton told me in a quiet, but stern, tone.

I pulled the cuff of my jacket up so my porter was visible and nodded at him. I knew nothing about clandestine meetings and spies.

Derian walked in and nodded to Victor. All of the males in the room straighten up as he moved out of the way as a woman with short curly hair entered. Her look of surprise grew as she looked around.

She bowed her head. "Your majesties."

Kara glanced at Rafael and nodded.

"Please," Troy motioned to a table in the center of the diner, "take a seat."

She bowed her head again and quickly moved to sit down. "I didn't expect the whole royal family." She said quietly.

Daxx leaned on the table and looked across the room at her. "We're a tight-knit group."

The woman looked at her for a moment. "Yes—my queen."

"What's your name?" Autumn glared at Michael as he sat at the table with her.

"Oh, I'm sorry," She inclined her head in a respectful manner, "Lucina, but on this side, I am currently known as Sophia."

"You're from Alterealm?" Bethany asked as she moved closer.

"Yes." She clasped her hands together on the table. "I haven't been home in some time." She gave Michael a brief glance. "My pass expired, but I couldn't leave."

"Why are you working at that place?" Paisley stood up and sat on one of the stools closer to her. "You have to know how those from the realm have been treated."

"Yes, princess, I do. Its why I'm there." She turned back to Autumn. "A cousin of mine ended up there," she glanced at Troy, "he was a guard." Turning back to Autumn, she blew out breath, "he managed to get a message out to my uncle." She turned and looked at Quinton, "but no one was willing to do anything about it—to go look for him."

Quinton went over to the counter and picked up a waitress's pad and pen. He took it to her. "Write your cousin's name, your uncle's, and anyone that you know he spoke to."

She nodded but continued to look up at him. "Did you really just take them all out?"

Quinton nodded.

"Thank the gods." She closed her eyes for a second. "I couldn't figure out how to free them all, so I did nothing but monitor what was happening." She shook her head, "I helped some feed from time to time, but I have to *retire* and come back with a new identity every few years." She patted her head, "a new hair color, style, contacts…"

"How long have you been working there?" Quinton crossed his arms over his chest and studied her.

"Thirty years. Which is nothing considering how long it has been happening," she lifted her purse, then paused before opening, "may I?"

Quinton motioned to it.

Pulling out a thick handful of folded papers, she held them up to him. "There's something going on in the basement, a few of ours talked about it. I can't find a way down there. I did some research and tracked the address and renovations for the last two centuries," she looked at Victor, "I can't trace it back any further..."

Quinton flipped through the papers, his expression grim. With a grunt, he held them out to Michael.

"Did you find your cousin?" Bethany asked

She shook her head. "No. I don't know what happened to him, but I couldn't, in good conscience, leave the others from our realm there and just walk away."

Rafael looked at Emil. "Ask Derian to come in."

Emil stepped out the door.

I watched Michael hand the papers to Troy and walk to the other side of the room and stare out the window.

Troy glanced through them, looked at Chase and shook his head, before handing them to Victor.

Victor's expressions gave away nothing. He folded the papers and held them while Derian come in the door with Emil.

Alona got up and went over to Chase and said something quietly.

Chase gave her a look and nodded. "Lucina, would you like to go home and see your family?"

She stopped writing and looked up at him. "I..."

"A visit, we can bring you back if you wish." Chase added.

"Is it wise to..."

Chase held his hand up to cut off Victor's query. "She's been on the inside this long; we need her there for a short while more."

Victor's expression changed and he nodded. "I will see if we can secure schematics of the building."

Chase nodded and looked at Derian. "I need you to set up a fast method of contact for Lucina on this side."

Derian nodded. "We have many safe houses set up."

Crissy popped up behind the counter. She reached over and took the papers from Victor's hands and opened them. "We need Reagan to see in this basement," she nodded and looked at me, "I don't know why yet, but I know we do."

Everyone turned to look at me. I shook my head, not having a clue why.

"Kara isn't going back in there." Rafael said in a tone that didn't allow for argument.

Sophia paused and looked at Kara, "I thought you looked familiar." She smiled, "I don't know how you did it, but I'm thankful you did." Her expression became serious, "the voices were actually others' thoughts?"

Kara nodded.

Sophia sat back and then turned to Chase. "I have been checking files and there may be other patients that have our blood in their veins."

Chase looked at his twin, "we need someone else in there."

Troy nodded and looked at Arius, "you can make the *introductions* when we find someone suitable."

Arius crossed his arms over his chest and gave them both a quick glance before looking at Sophia, "We'll need you to list the routines, protocol, and every exit you know of."

She nodded. "I have a notebook hidden away, I make a record of everything." Heaving out a deep sigh, she put her hand over heart. "I'm so relieved this is almost over." She nodded, "I would like to see my family. I called each week from a different location, but to see them…" A single tear slid down her cheek, "thank you." She said without looking at anyone in particular.

"We're sorry it has gone unnoticed as long as it has." Troy said quietly.

"I will set up a secure location on our side for her to see her family." Victor said abruptly, "we'll need guards to watch over her kin until this is over." He looked at Rafael.

Rafael nodded, "I'll get Ira to select a few to rotate."

Sophia stood up. "My family will be in danger?"

"We can't take chances, there is much you don't know about." Troy told her.

Taking a deep breath, she nodded. "Then I don't wish to see them until it is over." She shook her head, "I won't put them in danger."

"As you wish." Victor said, a look of admiration was on his face.

"Derian, I want you to stay with Lucina until you have things set up over here." Rafael informed him.

"I can get the notebook for you." Sophia held out the notepad to Quinton.

Quinton took it and looked down at it for a moment, then put it in his pocket. He turned to Michael. "Get her a porter as well." He glanced at Troy, who inclined his head, "just in case."

Michael pulled out his phone. "We should get going, the whole family in one location too long over here is asking for trouble."

Arius held out his hand to Paisley. "I agree with that."

"Should we ask Bastian to take a wander through that place?" Daxx got up and walked over to Troy, "check the staff and see if any are his?"

Troy rubbed the bridge of his nose, "it can't hurt."

"The climax is so close." Crissy said loudly, "I feel it." She turned to Victor with an excited look, "my visions paused for a minute."

Victor raised one eyebrow, looked at me, then held his hand out to Crissy. "We'll discuss it further at home."

Chapter Fourteen

I lay there staring at the ceiling, hoping answers would pop into my head. I had no hints that led me to believe that Crissy was stating facts. I knew nothing of portals and the other things that had been happening because of a disgruntled madman and his crazy mage. Until the family sat me down and explained everything that had happened, I didn't even know magic, *real magic* existed.

Sure, my mother had told me of the various factions in Alterealm, but until now they were stories, like the palace on the mountain.

I sat up and looked around. The palace on the mountain. I giggled. Okay, so *some* of the stories were fact.

Sighing, I stood up. Best to go get this over with. When I'd agreed, it was more out of curiosity, but now that it was real, my nerves were getting the better of me. King Troy was going to look inside my head for clues. Clues that I apparently had but was unaware of.

I had to go through with it. If I, even unknowingly, had the answers to end this, there was no other option. At the time, I thought if we found the answer then I wouldn't have to go into a basement of a building where horrible things had happened. The modern facility was once housed inhumane and torturous procedures done in the name of curing mentally ill patients. More than one of us had tears in our eyes as the historian listed off procedures practiced in the name of cure. I didn't believe in ghosts or leftover bad spirits, but even I had to admit that a basement of torture had to harbor some sort of vibes. Vibes I really wanted to avoid.

Taking a deep breath, I nodded to myself and opened the door. Hopefully I wasn't late to meet Bethany. I was one step down the staircase when Autumn came rushing out of a room on the other side of the hall.

She stopped and pointed to me, a panicked look on her face. "I need help. Now." She ran back into the room.

I rushed to follow her. Had someone been hurt? When I stepped in, she stood there, a large book in her hand.

"If I can't even figure this out." She looked up at me, "how am I going to do the others?"

I went over and looked at the book. It was full of paint chips and fabric swatches.

"What color should a nursery be?" She blew out a breath, then looked at me. Not waiting for an answer, she hurried over and held the book against the wall. "What are you supposed to do, hold it against the wall and hope the right choices pop out?" She glanced over her shoulder.

"I-I'm not sure." I looked around the room. "Babies and homes are not something I'm familiar with." I watched as she came over to me. "My last home was an old utility shack on a roof."

She studied the book, before giving me a quick glance. "I lived in the back of a gym before here."

I nodded slowly. "Okay. So, uh, do we know if it's a boy or a girl?"

Autumn shook her head. "Not yet. I just want to have this started before Rena comes over, you know, so she sees I'm serious about raising the baby if she can't," she shrugged, "come to terms with how it happened."

I nodded slowly, then tried for an encouraging look. "Well," I motioned to window, "with the great light from that you could go neutral." I had no idea what I was talking about.

I looked back at the color choices and pointed to one, "like antique white." I nodded. "And use decorations," she frowned, "like pictures of teddy bears, or-or balloons for accents." I shrugged, "if it's a boy, you can change the pictures and curtains."

"Curtains." She nodded and pointed to one of the fabric swatches. "I was thinking something frilly."

I smiled. "The lace would look good."

"Okay." She heaved out a breath. "This is good." She nodded. "Do you think I should get a crib right away or one of those bassinet thingies?"

This was so far from anything we knew. "Maybe-maybe the bassinet and save the crib for when you know the gender, or the baby is bigger."

She nodded her head quickly. "That's a good idea." Eyes-wide, she pulled a piece of paper from the back of the book. "What about these safety things? For outlets and doors, should I get them now? Do you think I should do the whole palace?"

I looked at the printout she held. "Well, the baby doesn't come out running, so I think you could wait on those for now."

She considered it, then nodded.

"There you are." Michael came into the room and gave Autumn a look. "You didn't answer your phone." He said gently.

Autumn frowned and touched the pocket of her hoodie. "I think I left it in our room." She opened the book. "We need antique white paint." She gave him a serious look. "And curtains made from this," she tugged on the fabric swatch. "Where do I get a bassinet here?"

Michael looked down at the book briefly. "you do know you're a princess, right? You tell Mitz all of this and she will get the right people on it."

Autumn looked relieved. "I was worried I'd have to learn how to sew." She looked at the walls, "the painting would be good exercise though." Leaning into Michael's shoulder as he put his arm around her, she sighed loudly. "I want everything to be perfect when Rena comes over, you know, so she knows I'm serious about this."

Michael kissed the top of her head. "The number of times you go over to check on her, I'm sure she knows you're serious." He took the book from her hand. "Let's track Mitz down and get this started."

Autumn blew out a breath. "Yes." She turned to me. "Thanks for the assist, I was freaking out a bit."

"Can we take you anywhere?" Michael asked.

I shook my head. "I'm meeting Bethany to go see the king so he can look in my head." I raised my eyebrows, "I don't know how I feel about it." I frowned, "Doctors, tests, now a brain exam." I grinned, then sobered, "do you have an eye doctor here?"

Michael looked concerned. "Are you having eye problems?"

I shrugged. "No, not really, just sometimes lately I see like a green hue when I'm looking around. I just want to see if that's an issue." I shrugged, "might as well get those checked too, then I'll be good for another hundred years." I laughed, even though my nerves were getting the better of me.

His expression was serious. "Ask the doctor, he'll get you in touch with the other medical staff."

"Righto. Thanks." I left them standing looking at each other.

"Nothing that stands out." Troy announced to the others staring at us. He looked back at me, "you took a lot of chances during the wars."

I shrugged, "I don't like seeing innocents suffer." I tried not to look relieved, but I was. A few times I thought I felt something happening, but there was no pain. The king had to tell me to take a deep breath and relax a few dozen times, but other than my fears it had been harmless.

He inclined his head. "I agree." Sitting back in his chair, he glanced at Victor. "There are no faces I recognize." He rubbed the bridge of his nose, looking a little tired.

"Was there fog?" Crissy leaned forward on the table.

"None that I saw." Troy told her.

Crissy frowned, "there has to be a piece missing." She squeezed her eyes shut, "why can't I see it."

"It will come to you, heart, I have no doubt." Victor told her.

Opening her eyes, she looked at him. "Maybe my head is broken. I keep seeing a blank, nothingness…" she gave Daxx a wide-eyed looked, "how is that possible?"

Daxx shrugged, "I don't think your head is—broken, Criss, maybe you're not seeing it all yet." She glanced to Rafael, who also shrugged.

"You'll get it, little sis, you always do." Rafael assured her.

"If Crissy says Reagan and fog are somehow the solution we need, I believe her." Kara said. "She's always right, even when she can't explain it to us."

Crissy sighed, "if I'd told you to wear warm socks because you were going to end up in the middle of nowhere in the snow," she waved her hands around, "it would have changed everything you did up to that point." She nodded, "then you wouldn't have found Tawny."

Kara sighed. "You're right."

"Knowing before changes the during, then the after isn't right." Crissy nodded.

Everyone paused for a moment and looked at each other. I wasn't sure what she just said, but the others seemed to agree with her.

When I turned back, Troy was quietly watching me.

"I am sorry about your mother."

My breath got stuck in my throat. "You could see her?" He nodded, "I wish I could." I squeezed my eyes shut for a moment, trying to picture her, I opened them and looked at him again. "Her image fades more each year."

"I'm sure her family will have a painting or sketch of her." Alona said softly.

"She was a very strong woman." Troy's tone was low.

I nodded, "she held on for a long time."

"Unknowingly with your help."

I blew out another breath, "you saw that too?"

"Mmm, I did."

"You guys really need to set up a hotline or something." Paisley crossed her arms and looked at Troy, then Chase. "it wouldn't have worked then, but it will now."

"A hotline?" Arius looked amused.

She nodded. "Yes, anyone going over should have a number to contact in case they get stuck over there or something."

"An emergency contact number." Bethany nodded.

"There are safe houses for those that live over there, a number to call makes sense for those visiting." Alona gave Chase a steady look.

Chase held her gaze for a moment, then turned to his twin, "seems like a modern idea, brother king."

"While I agree, we need to focus on finding Arwan and Willis Hubert." Victor glanced at Crissy, "or there won't be realms for people to visit."

"If all we're doing is sitting here doing nothing, I have some thing else to do." Quinton stood up.

"What?" Leone asked him.

Quinton scowled at him. "More than sitting here."

"That helps." Rafael mumbled.

I studied the space around him, there was a faint trace around him that hadn't been there earlier. It wasn't red, but there was a faint enough trace for me to know he wasn't feeling well.

Giving Rafael a hard look, Quinton shook his head and walked out of the room.

I got up quickly, "I'll be right back." I hurried after him

When I caught up to him, he barely gave me a glance. "Are you all right?"

"I'm fine. I just hate sitting around and doing nothing."
With his brows drawn together he stared down at me.

"I was talking about your health. I can see..."

"I'm just tired. It's been months of broken sleep." He
started taking longer strides.

"Quinton." I had to struggle to keep up with him, without
jogging. "It's more than sleep deprivation."

He stopped so suddenly I almost went past him. "I said..."

"I heard you talking to the doctor." I admitted.

The expression in his eyes changed. "How much did you
hear?"

"Enough to know that you are not well."

With his hands on his hips, he stared at me, too many
emotions going through his eyes for me to define them. He
looked down the hall one way, then the other. "You can't tell
anyone."

"That something is wrong?"

"Yes. I caused my brothers enough heartache for a
century. I can't put them through that again."

I started to ask what he was talking about, but he
interrupted.

"Its complicated and everything else that's happening right
now is more important."

I couldn't argue with that, not when it involved more than
one realm. I held up my hand, "maybe I can help."

Quinton looked at my hand then took it in his own and
squeezed it. "This isn't something even your touch can
heal." There was a sad look in his eyes now, but he still
smiled. Touching my hair, he continued to smile as his gaze
moved over my face. "I always wondered." He said softly.
Releasing my hand, he stepped back. "Too bad it's too late."
He nodded at me, then vanished.

I stood there, my heart beating like an enamoured teen. I
had no idea why. I had no idea what he was talking about.
Biting my lip, I pulled out my phone. Smirking at the fact that
I had a phone. Opening up the contacts I touched the screen
and scrolled through them. I had no idea who to call in hopes

of an answer. One of his brothers probably had the information I needed, but family bonds and loyalty were strong. I considered each of the women but knew none had been here long.

"Are you lost, love?"

I jolted and turned to see Mitz standing behind me.

"No. Well not physically at least."

She smiled. "That's the easiest lost to be, physically."

I sighed, "very true."

She motioned down the corridor. "I was going to the kitchen for a cup of tea, you're welcome to join me."

No one did that anymore. Paused to enjoy a cup of tea. My mother insisted on a few quiet moments a day over a cup of tea. "I would love to."

She nodded, then paused. "Do you mind if we pop back to the chamber's kitchen? My favorite teapot is there."

I grinned. "Not at all. I love porting."

She laughed. "You were definitely meant to be here."

Chapter Fifteen

It seemed odd sitting in the large dining room with just Mitz, but it also gave me the quiet that had been lacking since I'd been here.

"Now," she topped off her cup, then gave me a knowing look, "we've covered all the small talk—why don't you tell me why you looked so lost in the hall."

"Quinton said some puzzling things."

"Oh," she looked surprised. "he's usually the straightforward one. What did he say?"

I took a sip, stalling long enough while I figured out what to say yet not tell her what had led to the conversation. "That he'd caused his brothers heartache for a century."

Her expression sobered. "Oh. I see." She looked into her cup, "that." She nodded. "Yes, that was a hard thing to witness." She glanced up at me. "He's a proud a man, so freely giving the details would be hard for him." She inhaled slowly. "To be honest, love, I don't know if it's my place to tell you—or if you'd understand the dynamics involved." Mitz smirked, "I'm probably making you more lost."

Titling my head sideways I gave her a playful grin, "just a little." I straightened up, "my mother educated me in all things Alterealm." I shrugged, then stared into the dark liquid in my cup. "It made her feel better, helped her hang on longer I think." When I looked back up, Mitz was giving me a sympathetic look.

"What color were her eyes when she fed?"

I knew what she was asking. "Green." Her expression was pained. "It was my fault." I nodded, "when we discovered my ability, she insisted we keep ourselves secluded." Her attention didn't waver, she just continued to sit there waiting patiently. "To keep me safe. We didn't know for years that wearing gloves would stop it." I shook my head, "that I needed contact with skin. For years we thought any contact would activate my—I turned my gloved hand over on the table and looked at it, "ability."

She made a soft sighing noise, "It must have been very hard for you." I looked back up at her, "to watch her fade."

I swallowed the lump in my throat. "I'd touch her, help her when she fell asleep." I leaned back from the table and met Mitz's steady look, "now I wonder if I prolonged her suffering needlessly."

"I'm sure she knew." She gave me a tender look, "Mothers just know things about their children."

I nodded slowly. "You're probably right." I took a shaky breath and exhaled it slowly, refusing to let the melancholy creep in again.

"Thank you." She nodded, "for sharing that with me." Her smile was genuine. "I'm sure she's watching over you, and dancing now that you're where you belong."

I gave her a wide-eyed look. "I still can't believe it." I motioned around the room, "I'm here. In Alterealm."

"Unless I'm mistaken, your arrival is very important. For more reasons than a prophecy." She took a deep breath, and nodded once. "Quinton is an essence feeder." She shrugged, "his eyes go red," she gave me a careful look, "he has fangs."

I knew about essence feeders, so none of this was a surprise to me.

Seeing what she'd said didn't move me, she continued. "Many find human essence to be more appealing, as are emotions I suppose."

"My mother didn't mention that."

She tilted her head, "I suppose it's different for each type of feeder." Clasping the cup in her palms, she stared at it. "Quinton was enamoured with a human from the city," she rolled her eyes, "before it was the filth it is now. I suppose it was just over a century ago." Her gaze shifted to a spot over my shoulder as she remembered. "It happens, passions override logic." I could see the pain of the memories on her face. "They got carried away and he took too much." She closed her eyes, "obviously that is forbidden, but no one knew what could happen as a result." Opening her eyes, she gave me a stern look, "it was like her soul and spirit wilted," she shook her head gently, "then her body followed." With a jerky movement, she put the cup on the tray with a clatter. "I cared for her until her spirit faded completely."

I didn't know what to say. I knew my mother was always afraid of going too far, but never knew it was possible with the other feeders.

"There are times I think it's more merciful for the victim." Her eyes were glazed with unfallen tears. "Quinton suffered as a result and it was far worse, he had to live through it for a century." She moved her hand in a circle in front of her face, "he was horribly disfigured," she paused, "but even worse, he was tarnished beyond recovery." She nodded slowly, "he was the enforcer when all this took place, and yet he broke one of our most important laws."

It made sense now, the tension I'd felt when I'd questioned why Leone was the enforcer in Alterealm. I frowned, "but he's," I felt my cheeks flush, "gorgeous. What happened? Was a cure found?"

"I suppose you could say that." She smirked, then sobered just as quickly. "He starved himself for a century, not feeling worthy of feeding." She inhaled a sharp breath, "I believe the only thing that kept him here with us was his love and loyalty to his brothers." She nodded slowly, "It was Daxx's essence that ended his suffering." She had a proud look on her face, "he was gravely injured," she paused for a moment, "even the healing blood from the royal family had no value, but the long-prophesized huntress was his cure." With a deep breath, she nodded abruptly and stood up. "Let's go into the kitchen, I feel like baking." She gave me a big smile and carried the tray out of the room.

I stood slowly, processing the information. It was like the last pieces of a puzzle finally fitting together. What would the ramifications of starving for a hundred years be, internally? I bit my lip and picked up my cup to follow Mitz, and how did I go about finding out?

I watched Mitz flit around the kitchen, gathering ingredients and telling me tidbits of some of the other girls' arrivals. I laughed at the last one, "Chase calling Kara cupid makes so much more sense now."

She nodded and took something out of the fridge. "Yes. Has he found a nickname for you?"

I shook my head, "no. Thankfully."

Mitz grinned, "yes after Emil's shocking moment, I'm sure it won't be complimentary for you."

I turned to watch her move across the room when something drew my attention back to where she'd been standing. There was green haze. I hadn't seen it since the market and was hoping I wouldn't again.

"Are you all right?"

I turned to see Mitz standing beside me. I rubbed my hand over my eyes, "yes, just—" I shrugged, "processing." I avoided looking around the room, keeping my focus on what she was doing.

Bethany, Paisley and Kara came into the kitchen.

"Mitz. We're taking stock before the big meeting to discuss positions and updating the archaic ones. We were wondering if you needed more help?" Bethany sat at the counter beside me.

"Help with what, dear?" Mitz paused in pulling out measuring spoons and cups.

"Everything you do." Kara leaned on the counter.

"Which is too much." Paisley tucked her hands in her pockets and nodded.

Mitz turned and looked at a large door, a pantry I thought. "I have the entire staff to help me, love."

"You always seem like you're running." Bethany said playing with the spoons.

Turning away from the cupboard, she came over and opened a drawer. Pulling out a rolling pin, she went over and set it on the table by the door and stood there. "Not at all. The staff does all the work, I just deliver the end result."

Quinton came in and looked at her, he studied everything she had sitting out. "Are you making those pastries?"

Mitz looked over her shoulder. "I was thinking about it."

Quinton grinned. Then turned to look at the rest of us, curiosity in his expression.

"We came to ask if she needed someone to help her with everything she does." Bethany explained.

He looked at Mitz. "Do you?"

Picking up the rolling pin, she smiled, "not at all, love." Taking a few steps, she moved past the pantry door, then grasped the handle as she raised the pin above her head. As she yanked the door open, she swung the rolling pin down. A man appeared out of nowhere and slumped to the floor. Pointing at him with the rolling pin, she looked at Quinton. "Find out if Romulus is missing *that*. If it's not his, then it's working with Willis." She crossed her arms over her chest and glared down at the man.

I jumped up from the chair. There was green haze hovering all around the room now.

Quinton jolted and went over and stood above the man. He pulled out his phone and tapped the screen. "Yeah, we need you in the kitchen," he nodded, "in the chambers. Bring your port box," he glanced to Mitz. "Mitz is not happy." He shook his head, "same as the time we had to paint *all* the hallways."

Michael appeared in the middle of the kitchen, his phone still to his ear, holding a little box in his hand. He looked at

Mitz, then noticed the man crumpled at Quinton's feet. "What—" he went over quickly, dropping his phone to the floor as he knelt down and lifted the man's face off the floor by his hair. Shaking his head, he held the box over him and the man vanished.

I would have expressed my shock and elation, but I was still looking at the green haze in the room. My heart was beating so fast I thought I might expire from it.

"A mage." Quinton said in a low tone, he looked at Mitz. "How did he get in here?"

Mitz crossed her arms, the rolling pin still in her hand. "I have no idea, but my skin was crawling." She scowled, "he was cloaked."

Michael nodded, as he picked up his phone, he tapped the screen. "Yeah. New one for you, he was cloaked and hiding in Mitz's kitchen." Michael shrugged and looked at the rolling pin she still held, "might want to check his head, pretty sure Mitz took him out with a rolling pin." He smirked, "me too, brother."

My breath was stuck in my throat. The haze was fading.

"Reagan?" Paisley was beside me, "it's all right, everything…"

I shook my head. "I saw it." I looked around the room, "*inside* this time." I turned back and looked at the pantry the man had been in, "it was there," I motioned my hand in the air, "I don't—don't think it's in my head." Someone touched my shoulder. I looked up to see a concerned Quinton watching me carefully. "A mage. They cast spells and such?"

He nodded, his brows drawn together.

"Could I see that?" His expression faltered, "could I see a trace when they do their magic?"

He opened his mouth and then looked at Michael.

Michael opened his in much the same manner.

"Oh for heaven's sake," Bethany came over and stood in front of me, "what do you see?" She moved her hands in the air around her, "as I do this." She motioned down her body and she slowly disappeared from my sight. While that was fabulous, I was more hyper focused on the white haze the hovered around where she had been. She reappeared.

"Did anything happen?"

My open hung open, my eyes bulging. "I saw—" I gaped at Quinton then looked back to her, "a white haze." Covering my mouth with my hand, I backed up, moving my hand I laughed. "Witch magic is white." I spun and looked at Paisley, "mage is green." My heart was racing, "OMG, I'm not seeing things, I'm seeing the haze left by magic…" With a screech, I dashed back to Quinton, reaching up, I grabbed his face and jerked it down to my level. Kissing him hard on the mouth, I released him, "get everyone here. Now." I covered my face and then laughed out loud. "She's right! Crissy is right."

Michael held his phone up to his ear and spoke quietly, looking at me like I was possessed. He nodded and then jammed the phone in his pocket. He looked at Quinton, who shook his head slowly.

"Do you need to sit down?" Quinton started walking toward me.

I waved him off, "no. I feel like I could run to the moon right now."

"Mitz, what did you guys drink?" Michael picked up my empty cup and sniffed it.

I laughed louder.

"What's going on?" Daxx came running into the room, a knife in her hand.

Troy appeared beside her, and gently pushed her hand down.

Autumn came charging in and if I didn't know her, I would have fainted with fear from the expression on her face. She turned in a circle and looked around. Michael shrugged.

"Crissy, where is Crissy?" I blurted out, "and a mage, we need a mage." I told Troy. "*Now.*" I added, "right now."

Mitz moved to sit at the counter, she was the only one not looking at me like I was a stark raving lunatic.

Rafael, Arius and Victor all ported into the room at once.

"Romulus at the cells?" Michael asked.

Arius nodded, then glanced at Paisley. "What have I missed?"

Paisley raised her eyebrows, "I think Reagan has had an epiphany."

Leone appeared, looking dusty and out of breath. He looked down his dirty clothes, "don't ask."

"We're here." Chase and Alona came in a different door, both looked half asleep.

Emil was the next to appear, he too looked like he'd been sleeping.

"Get Romulus here." Quinton told Rafael.

With a curious look, Rafael ported out.

Crissy came racing in, she skidded to a stop and looked around. "We're meeting in the kitchen now?"

I shrieked and went over and grabbed her and hugged her. "I saw it. It's real. Not in my head." I released her.

She giggled, "the fog? You saw the fog?" She jumped on the spot.

I nodded, then shook my head, "it's not fog." I enunciated each word slowly.

Her eyes widened, "what is it?"

"It's," I waved my hand around, "like a haze." I nodded, "similar to the traces I see, but not around a person and," I swung my hand around, "much wider spread." I closed my eyes, then opened them and smiled down at her, "I've seen it in the city, here at the market, all over the place for months and months." Putting my hands on my hips I took a deep breath and tried to settle down. "White haze is from witch's magic..."

Quinton was right there in front of me, grasping my shoulders, he looked down at me, his gaze steady, "you can see a where a mage's magic is at work?"

I nodded, "I think so."

"Let's test that." Troy said.

I turned to see a strange man, looking shocked, standing beside Rafael. I say strange because of the vibes coming off him, not his greasy pimp appearance.

"Romulus, do a simple cloaking—" Quinton lifted his hand and dropped it, "whatever."

Romulus inclined his head then started to wave his hand around.

I sucked in a breath, as he started a green haze began to swirl around him. I pointed. "That's it." I glanced to Bethany, "does anyone see the green haze swirling around him?"

Every head in the room gave me a negative response.

"That will be all, Romulus." Troy glanced to Mitz, then back to him. "The mage just sent to the cells, is he one of yours?"

Romulus brushed a hand back over his slicked back hair. "I haven't seen him for a few years."

Quinton crossed his arms over his chest, "how the hell did he get inside the chambers? I thought it was airtight?"

Romulus shook his head as he took a visible deep breath, "I don't know. We have the entire underground kingdom warded, just as the palace is." He looked at Quinton. "I'll double check *all* of it."

"Someone managed it." Chase kissed Alona, then turned to Troy. "Brother, let's go visit this mage."

Kara looked at them, "I'm coming." A worried look on her face, "it's a mess inside a mage's thoughts, but if I can hear something…"

Rafael nodded and held his hand out to her. "Let's go, get you set up before they walk in."

"Romulus, you need check the wards on the castle. Now." Autumn gave him a harsh look. "Rena is coming over soon and if she's not safe, I'm taking it out on *you*."

Romulus jolted like someone had smacked him. "I will begin testing it now." He inclined his head and then hurried from the room.

Crissy rushed over and jumped toward Victor. He caught her without hesitation. "It wasn't fog." She laughed and hugged him. Releasing him just as quickly, she jumped to the floor and dashed for the door. "I need to go to my tower, there are pieces."

I felt like a huge weight I'd been carrying for too long was lifted off my shoulders. I glanced around at the others, then paused to see Quinton looking at me oddly. I wasn't sure, but it looked like pride.

"I'm not one to jump up and down with excitement, but I might try it today." Daxx tucked her knife back in behind her. "You saw this green," she flicked her hand, "whatever in the city on our side?"

I nodded. "All over the place." I gave Autumn a quick look. "That's what led me to that shed at the market."

Autumn was grinning. "So, you find the green stuff, we find them." She turned to Michael, "she needs freedom." With a look to Daxx, she turned back to him, "we all do, so she can find this."

Michael gave Troy a hesitant look, "There are too…"

"Don't say it." Daxx warned. She pointed to me, "if she can lead us to traitors and any of Hubert's jerks, she needs to be out there looking." She put her hand on her hips and glared at Troy. "We all need to be."

Quinton shook his head. "It would be too risky…"

"We'll take our guards." Paisley looked up at Arius, "wander around the villages." She gave him a hopeful look, "say yes."

Bethany moved over and hugged her mate, despite his soiled condition. "We find the locations, you guys rush in and put a hurt on them."

Leone gave her a steady look, then glanced to Michael.

Michael closed his eyes and blew out a breath.

"Cristy saw it for this purpose." Victor's voice held great authority, "to end it." He nodded to me, "Reagan is here now, in this time to end it."

"So basically, we're to risk our mates well-being to bring this to a close?" Chase gave Troy a hard look. "I don't like it."

Alona leaned against him for a moment, "I don't like the idea of thousands being harmed in the realms if Hubert succeeds."

"The gods empower the royal blood to watch over the realms to vanquish evil from harming the innocent..." Mitz said quietly.

All of the men turned to look at her.

"Well." Chase sighed, "when you put it that way."

"Damn, Mitz, that's low." Leone mumbled.

"Perhaps," she smiled at him, "but still very true." She looked around, "your mates are of your blood now and the gods have brought them each here," she nodded, "at this time, each with a skill needed to help and to protect."

"Reagan's not a mate..."

"Don't try to think, Leone, you'll hurt your brain." Quinton blurted out. He turned to me, his brown eyes reflecting both pride and regret. "She is a mate." He turned to his twin brothers, "and to be respected as one." He nodded once, then looked at Arius. "Are we going to find out what the mage knows or just standing here with our gobs open?" He huffed out a loud breath, "I'll be at the cells." He vanished.

Rafael appeared and waved his phone in the air. "Why is no one answering..." he looked around with a jerky movement. "What have I missed?"

Troy grinned, then shook his head. "I'll fill you in later." His ported out of the room.

"Well then," Chase gave me a big grin, "today is proving to be very entertaining." He winked at me, then hugged Alona and they disappeared.

"Still processing that." Daxx tipped her head to where Quinton had been standing, "but later when we're not grilling a mage and hunting for green haze," she motioned between us, "we have to talk."

Paisley laughed, then bounded over to me and hugged. "Welcome, sister." She turned to Arius and tapped her finger on her chest, "this girl is done being a complacent princess."

She grinned at him, "better arrange the guard patrols or whatever because after we're done at the cells, I'm exploring Alterealm." Her eyes sparkled when she turned back to me and then ported out of the room.

One by one, they left until Emil was the only one left in the room with Mitz and I. He motioned to the door, "Come, sister, we'll walk to the cells and see what's happening."

I was still in a daze, I knew about mates and everything pertaining to it, I thought, but I hadn't realized I was so intrigued with Quinton because of it. I glanced at Mitz, she was smiling at me like she'd known it all along. I nodded. "Okay."

Chapter Sixteen

"You didn't know?" Daxx glanced over her shoulder.

"I knew." Crissy nodded and kept going.

"You knew Reagan was Quinton's mate?" Daxx paused and looked behind us.

Crissy nodded again, "who else could it be with the prophecy?" She shrugged and started walking again.

"Prophecy?" I stumbled over a lip in the walkway, "the nine sons?"

"It still irks me that you know all of this." Alona said quietly.

"Yes. That one." Crissy stopped and closed her eyes, "For our loyal brother filled with the deepest sadness, he will find the touch of his woman will renew his heart and she is the only one that will be able to heal him inside." She opened and eyes and looked at me, "I knew it was you."

"Wow, no pressure there." Bethany said with a smirk.

"Deepest sadness? He's the grumpiest." Paisley mused.

I shrugged and looked down the small street in the village. "I didn't know." I shrugged, "I always thought with mates there was uncontrollable…"

Autumn held up her hand, "don't go there." She titled her head and looked at me, "our stories with mates weren't all easy."

Bethany chortled, "that's putting it mildly."

"I'm drawn to him, intrigued if you like, but I didn't know that's why." I checked the other direction, then looked behind us to where our large entourage of guards followed. We weren't exactly moving through these towns and villages under the radar. I paused, trying to decide on a direction, everyone froze and watched me. I had to wonder if the prophecy was a metaphor or if I could really help with the illness he wanted to hide. I shrugged it off and turned to go down the one street. "he said something peculiar earlier."

"Quinton?" Bethany asked.

I nodded.

"They all say and do stupid things." Alona stated.

"Or rage." Crissy added.

"All the raging." Paisley laughed.

"What did he say?" Autumn stopped and looked back at the guards. "They're standing out."

Daxx looked behind us and nodded. "Yeah, I'm working on a plan for that." She turned to me, "so what did he say?"

"That he'd always wondered." I paused and looked to the outskirts of the village. "What's that way?"

"So, he knew you were his mate." Bethany glanced back at her guard and motioned for him to come.

"And then he said too bad it's too late." I continued to look out at the countryside at the end of the street.

"Too late?" Paisley shook her head, "for what?" She smirked, "as far as I know mates don't expire."

Alona laughed, "like spoiled milk."

I watched Bethany talk to Mac, who was shaking his head.

"Could it have something to do with how he suffered before Daxx," I pushed my hair back from my face, "cured him?"

A thoughtful look appeared on Daxx's face. "I don't see how."

"We'll find someone who knows, later." Autumn, motioned to Mac going back to the other guards, then looked at Beth.

"He said beyond this field is the wasteland." Bethany pulled her hair up into a ponytail.

"What are *the* wastelands exactly?" Paisley asked.

Dax snorted, "a burnt-out place. It felt soulless when I was dropped there."

"Nothingness." Crissy said excitedly.

"Yeah, a whole lot of nothingness, Criss." Daxx nodded.

"No. No, I mean it's the blank, the nothingness I've been seeing." She turned and looked across the field. "It has to be."

"Those people that ran from the market headed to the wasteland." Alona stated.

Daxx spun around and looked at me. "It can't be a coincidence." She looked at Alona for a moment, "the witch drops the prophesized huntress in the wasteland," she motioned to me, "then Reagan comes along and can *see* the magic or whatever," she turned to Bethany, "they don't even patrol the wasteland, other than the borders."

"You missed many steps in that summary, but yes," Alona nodded, "I agree." She motioned for her guard to come over. "Sith, you and the others need to get to the yard and get horses and send patrols to check the wasteland. *All* of the wastelands."

He hesitated, then looked at Daxx for a moment before back to Alona, "my queen…"

Alona shook her head, "there's something in the wasteland. We're sure of it."

One of the other guards came over, "we'll take you back…"

Crissy shook her head, "no, Bronx, Reagan has to be there to see it."

"We'll wait here, bring horses back." Autumn looked at her guard, "Woods, port back to the yard and tell Ira." She motioned to the field, "it's out there."

"In the wastelands?" He asked with a skeptical look on his face.

"Do you know a better place to hide, then the place no one willingly goes?" Bethany asked him.

"Why are they wastelands?" I asked, having no idea.

"I don't understand all the details, but I've nodded off a few times when Chase explains it's farming ground that has died off from overuse." Alona shrugged, "they rotate crops surrounding it and have three years rest or something, but it's still spreading."

"Yeah it's like the life has been sucked out of it." Autumn shrugged, "Michael was mumbling about it over the phone a few weeks ago."

Crissy darted toward the field, then stopped just as abruptly, she spun back and dashed over to Bronx. "I need a mage. Now." She tapped her head, "it was here all along and I didn't *see* it."

Bronx frowned, but pulled out his phone.

"See what, Crissy?" Bethany asked her.

"That mage." Crissy nodded, "Arwan, no one knew how he was living so long…" she shook her head, "it has to be." She pulled out her phone and waved it around, "I don't know who to call first," she stopped when Bronx held out his phone to her. "Oh." She took it and smiled as she spoke into it, "can a mage draw power from something else to do things?" She nodded enthusiastically, "so the larger the living thing the stronger the power?" She shrieked, "yes." Nodding, she handed the phone back to her guard. "Arwan is why the wastelands are nothingness." She smiled.

Daxx held up her hand, "you think this older than time," she made quotes in the air, "mage is sucking the life out of the ground to power up?"

Crissy nodded. "Yes." She sobered, "someone should tell the brothers." She turned to Bronx. "Go tell them." She gave him a wide-eyed look. "Now."

He hesitated, looked, then he nodded, then turned back to talk to the other guards.

Alona turned toward the field and held her hands over her cheeks. "Oh my god, I think she's right." Clapping her hands together she turned back to the other guards. "Sith, you and Bart get to the yards, and tell Rafael and Ira." She waved at him, then turned to Daxx's guard, "Tim, you and Woods go get us horses," she looked behind her at the field again, "and our weapons." She turned to Crissy's guard, "Bronx, take Felix and Mac with you, get the men back here, quickly."

"One of us should stay with you." Sith told her.

She turned and looked around. "We're perfectly fine, right here. Go. Hurry back."

"Don't make me use my ruler voice." Daxx said, a serious look on her face.

Tim blew out a breath, "*please*, stay here." He pleaded.

She nodded.

One by one the guards used their porters and vanished.

Daxx turned and looked back at the field. "We could walk across it and just take a peek."

Autumn nodded, "no harm in looking."

"I'm just happy to have company for the walk this time." Bethany said.

"Do you still see it?"

I glanced over my shoulder at Daxx. "Yes."

"Should we call the men?" Alona paused and looked at the dust on her boots. She made a hissing noise. "We're nowhere near where we said we would be."

"And tell them we're wandering across the wasteland without our guards?" Kara shook her head. "I don't think that's a good idea."

"Let's follow it a bit longer and see if it turns into anything." Paisley held her phone out in front of her. "I can't see the haze, even using the camera."

"Do we get reception out here?" Bethany glanced at Paisley, who nodded. "Okay. If they're concerned, they'd call." She looked behind us, "they'll be shouting orders and beating their chests."

Crissy laughed, then sobered and looked at me. "It must be part of her ability." Crissy looked completely animated.

"I'm so glad it was the strange fog I've been seeing." She looked at me, "it wasn't green."

"I'm glad it's real too, I thought something was wrong with my eyes."

"These boots are ruined." Alona sighed in a dramatic way.

Daxx growled softly, "I feel naked without my katanas." She looked back the way we'd come. "There's no landmarks out here, so I can't pop over to get them and find my way back."

"Aside from Autumn, the only one of us that is armed is Kara." Paisley looked behind us.

"I was just heading to practice." Kara shifted the case on her shoulder. "When you guys decided we should check more villages."

Autumn snorted, "if we find anyone, I have enough pent-up aggression I will manage."

Bethany grinned, "I hear that. Being under house arrest is starting to get on my nerves." She shook her head, "I'm almost tired of watching movies."

Daxx laughed, "that's bad."

Beth nodded.

I stopped and looked around. "It's getting thicker." I motioned even though they couldn't see it, "*now* it looks like actual fog, only it's green." I was still shocked that much of the wastelands had the haze over them, but some areas were thicker than others.

"Shh." Autumn crouched down.

Everyone reacted immediately and hunched closer to the dusty ground.

"Look."

I followed the direction she pointed. There was a stonework arch in the middle of this nothingness. Standing beside it were four men.

"Shit, don't move a muscle." Daxx whispered. "We have no cover here."

"Now do we call the guys?" Bethany whispered.

"Not yet." Paisley answered.

"Can you freeze all of them?" Alona leaned over closer to her.

Paisley shook her head. "They're too spread out."

"How is that here?" Crissy asked quietly, "in the middle of," her eyes went wide, "nothingness."

Everyone looked at her suddenly.

"The nothingness that is linked to the fog," Daxx looked at me, "that's linked to Reagan?"

Crissy nodded very enthusiastically. "The climax is close." She pointed to the arch, "it has to be the portal that we can't find. I bet it's not always visible."

"Even if it was, most would think it's just an old ruin." Daxx turned to Bethany. "Can you cloak us?"

Beth bit her lip. "Only if we don't move. I can't do movement yet."

Daxx nodded. "Good enough."

Beth got to her knees and took a deep breath; she closed her eyes and her lips began moving. As she moved her hand around us, she opened them. "That's the best I can do. We just have to stay in this small area we're in. Don't talk too loudly either."

Daxx knelt and looked back at the tree. "Is it green by them?"

"Yes. Very thick, bright green." I continued to watch it, waiting for it to disappear. Part of me wanted to giggle, just knowing that I wasn't seeing things and it was real. Well, at least to me it was. One of the men stepped into the densest green haze and then stepped under the arch and disappeared.

"Oh, fraggle, it *is* a portal." Kara whispered.

Another one of the men stepped into it and was gone.

"Okay," Daxx reached behind her and pulled out a curved knife, "Reagan, you keep your eyes on that portal, shout if your green haze fades." She glanced to Alona, "You and Crissy stay here, call the guys and then port them here." She stood up as the last man entered it. "We're going to see where it comes out." She started running toward it.

"Now we're talking." Autumn got up and followed her.

"We'll need you, Reagan." Bethany and Paisley got up at the same time.

"There better not be snow." Kara took off after them.

I started running after them. Later, much later I would have to seriously question my sanity. I was running into a magical portal without knowing what was on the other side.

Chapter Seventeen

I stumbled when I came out on the other side. I looked down at my feet. Pavement. Inhaling as I looked around, there was no mistaking that stench. We were in the city on the other side. We stood beside a building that looked like it was abandoned. It was an odd place to bring people out.

"Where'd they go?" Autumn was looking in all directions.

"There." Bethany pointed as her other hand clutched her stomach.

A car pulled up to where the four men stood. Three more males got out and stood beside it. One of them pointed to the car beside them.

Autumn quickly moved to hide behind an old beat up dumpster. "Seven." Autumn said quietly, then shrugged, "seems even to me."

The rest of us followed her.

"They're not heavily armed." Daxx mused, looking around the end of the bin.

One of the men went over to the other car and opened the door.

"Now or never, ladies." Daxx said and started walking toward them.

The rest of us followed. I reached to my side and then remembered I wasn't carrying my surujin.

"Here."

I turned to Bethany and she held out a knife.

"I don't need it."

"Hey, guys. Jump through any portals lately?" Daxx called out the men.

In a blur they all scrambled into the one car and took off.

Autumn ran toward them. "Damn." She stopped beside the car with one door still open.

The rest of us caught up.

"Anyone know how to drive?" Autumn leaned in. "The keys are in it."

No one spoke up.

"I saw someone being taught in a movie." Bethany said.

Paisley looked at Autumn and then got in the drivers' seat. Autumn ran around and climbed in the other front door. "Get in." She said to Bethany.

Daxx nodded and opened the back door. "They couldn't use a van?"

Not knowing what else to do I climbed in behind her and closed the door. It was crowded with the three of us in the back.

"Okay, turn the key and put your foot on the brake." Bethany instructed Paisley.

"Should I put my seatbelt on?" Kara asked.

"Someone keep an eye on them, in case they turn off." Autumn said.

"I am." Daxx was hanging over in the front seat.

"Now move the shifter until that little thing on the dash is on D." Bethany said. "Yeah. Now push the gas and go."

The car lurched forward, then jerked to left. I bounced off Daxx. We jerked forward again, then abruptly stopped.

"I got this." Paisley said in a tense tone.

"They're still on this street." Daxx said leaning further over the back of the front seat.

The car suddenly filled with all of our phones playing music. Sandwiched between the door and Daxx, I couldn't have gotten my phone out of my pocket if I'd tried.

"Trying to concentrate here." Paisley said loudly.

"I'll answer." Bethany said. "Hey."

She must have put it on speaker, because Leone's voice filled the small space.

"Where are you?"

"The portal came out in the city." Bethany explained.

"The portal is gone on this side." That was Troy.

"We had to bring Reagan so she could see if there were more." Bethany said, then bounced off the door as the car jerked again.

"Don't drive too fast." Autumn said. "In case they turn off."

Paisley nodded.

"Too fast?" That was Michael. "You're driving?"

Autumn snorted. "No."

"Thank the gods." Michael sounded relieved.

"Paisley is." Daxx called out.

"What?" There was no mistaking Arius' voice.

"Get out of my head, babe, I'm trying to focus here." Paisley said in a choppy voice.

The car jerked as she hit the brakes. I bounced my head off the back of the driver's seat. Bethany's phone landed on the dash.

"They didn't even look." Paisley growled, "just ran out on the street."

"They're turning." Autumn pointed.

The car lurched forward again. I was thrown back against the seat.

"Can you shoot the tires if we get close enough. Kara?" Daxx turned to her.

Kara shook her head. "Not unless I hang out the window."

"You are not hanging out a window." Rafael said very loudly through the phone.

"I guess you can't drive and stop their car at the same time, Paize." Daxx said with a sigh.

"Not if you want us to live." She answered.

The car slid as we went around the corner, all of us slumped over as it did.

"The gods hate us." Troy stated.

"Daxx," Alona was on the phone now, "give us a landmark."

"Yeah." Daxx started looking around.

"Guys, they're turning again." Autumn braced her hand on the dash, "slow down. It's fenced in."

The car jerked a few times as Paisley hit the brakes.

"Crissy." Daxx shuffled to the edge of the seat again.

"I'm here." Crissy answered.

"Pull it over here." Autumn pointed for Paisley.

Paisley nodded and the car jerked in that direction.

"The old wrecking yard that closed down." Daxx looked around. "Near the torn up old train station."

"I know it." Crissy told her.

"Bring the guys to the street here. And someone grab our gear." Daxx flew forward and hit the seat again as the car stopped.

"That wasn't too hard." Paisley said as she turned the car off.

"None of you move until we get there." Michael commanded.

"Just in stay in the car." Arius added.

The line went quiet.

Bethany turned in her seat and looked at Kara, "what do you think? Confined to the palace for ten years?"

Kara laughed, "much longer."

Paisley ran her hand through her hair. "That was pretty intense."

"We lived through it." Daxx grinned at her and then turned to Kara, "out. I'm not sitting in the car waiting for them."

Autumn nodded. "I want to see inside the fence and get a heads up on what to expect."

"You're sure?" Autumn whispered as she looked through the boards again.

Checking again, I nodded, "there's no haze at all."

"That's good for us, right? No mages." Daxx asked.

"We won't even discuss what's good for you." Troy's voice came from behind us.

We all froze and turned around in slow motion to see the men looming over us.

"This does not look like the car you're supposed to be in." Arius looked down at Paisley as she straightened up from the fence.

Paisley pointed, "it's ten feet away," she shrugged, "it was very cramped."

Arius blew out a breath, "you scared the hell out of us."

Autumn grinned at Michael, "we were fine." She jerked her head toward Paisley, "she drives better then some of the bus drivers around here."

"I had it until that jerk that ran out in front of us." Paisley hissed.

"Perhaps we can discuss your driving skills at a later date?" Victor suggested and went over to the fence and bent down and looked through the hole we were peering through.

"We haven't seen anyone." Autumn reported. "Rea says there's no green haze."

"No mages." Quinton nodded, not taking his eyes off me. "What about white from witches?"

I shook my head. "There's no haze of any color."

He nodded his head slowly, then turned to Rafael. "Arwan and Hubert aren't here."

Rafael shrugged, "but there are others that need our immediate attention."

Alona and Chase appeared with Crissy.

"We followed four through the portal and they met up with three others." Kara told him.

"Seven?" Chase looked at the fence, "doesn't seem fair."

"Since when do you care about fair?" Troy asked him.

"I don't." Chase grinned.

"There's a reason they came here, I suggest we go find out what that is." Victor stated.

Daxx nodded as she pulled out two katanas from a bag that Leone held open. Putting them in one hand, she pulled out a box like the one Michael had brought to the kitchen and secured it to her belt.

I looked around. "We're going to fight them?"

Quinton glanced in the bag and nodded. "We'd try asking them to give up, but that never works out." He turned and held a small leather pouch out to me.

Hesitantly I took it and opening it. It was a real surujin. My jaw dropped as I pulled it out.

"Be careful." Quinton came over and pulled the rest out. "Clip it to your side," he pulled the other end out and held it up, "the handle is also a blade," he put it in the slot of the case. "In case anyone gets too close." He gave me a steady look, "don't be afraid to use it."

I nodded and put the pouch through the belt loop of my jeans, "I've survived a few wars, I know when to fight and when to run." I felt giddy as I tucked the bladed handle into the case. "Is it wrong if I say I love it?" I looked up at him.

He grinned, "no, in this family loving a weapon is normal."

Autumn chuckled and tapped the baton type weapon she held; a curved blade popped out the end. Alona held up nunchucks.

Bethany wiggled her fingers, "built in weapons." She turned and looked at the fence. "How are we getting in?"

Kara opened the bag and pulled out a bow, in a few seconds she had it assembled and the case full of arrows on her back. She nodded at Rafael.

Quinton walked over and looked at the boards, he glanced over his shoulder at Arius. Arius shrugged and went over. They grabbed the one board and pulled together and it snapped in half.

Beth shrugged, "that works." She glanced at Paisley and motioned to it. "Tag team?"

Paisley nodded. "Tag team."

I watched the others go through the hole in the fence and hurried to follow, not even knowing what I was going to do. Quinton was waiting for me on the other side.

"Don't get separated," he motioned to the women, "they're scarier together than a whole army."

I nodded, trying to shake off the nerves.

"Aw, so sweet." Daxx said. She wiped an imaginary tear from her face. "There's a reason you're my favorite brother." She held up her phone, "connect to the group call."

Pulling the earpiece out of my pocket I put it in and then connected.

"Divide and conquer?" Chase said in the earpiece.

"The ladies can go down the middle we'll circle around from either side." Emil's voice came through it.

I startled and turned to see him coming through the hole in the fence with a man with long white hair.

"Works for me." Daxx said and started walking.

"One of these days, we need to work on your timing, my lovely mate." Troy said.

"You can talk all you like, my king, I like action." Daxx said.

"TMI." I said.

There were a few chuckles as the group split in three. Four of the men went to the left and four to the right, the women walked down the center like it was a normal stroll in the park. Autumn and Daxx were up front. I was at the back with Alona.

Crissy stopped abruptly. "Going high." She said through the call.

I turned to look at the large crane off to the right. It was covered in rust and had most likely been sitting there for a few decades.

"Have care." Victor's voice said in my ear.

"Give us a lay of the land, little sister." That was Rafael.

"Okay," Crissy answered without pausing.

I held my breath as she scaled the crane like it was a child's climbing gym. Turning to Alona, I expressed my concern with a look, she smirked and rolled her eyes. I took that to mean it was a normal thing with Crissy. We caught up to the other women.

"I see people." Crissy reported. "There's ten, I think. They're loading a van with wood boxes."

"Where are they, heart?" Victor said with a patient tone.

Kara paused and stood there looking around.

"Vic, you guys need to get to the middle fast." Crissy said, "I can't see the labels on the boxes, but it's taking two men to lift them."

"Straight ahead, Criss?" Daxx asked and glanced up at her. "Yes."

Kara looked left then started jogging left. "I'm finding a perch."

"Keep watch behind us, Crissy." Rafael said. "Kara, honey, save some for us."

Someone chuckled softly, "Better move faster then, Captain." Kara said.

Daxx and Autumn ducked down behind a long-abandoned car.

Alona moved to stand below the crane, I followed her. My heart was pounding in my chest. Deciding I was the only one that seemed unprepared for this, I pulled the surujin out and held the weighted end in my left hand and the handle of the bladed end in my right. Alona nodded to me and we began going forward.

"Almost there." Troy reported. "Wait for…"

Daxx and Autumn bolted in that direction.

"Need a hand, boys?" Daxx's mocking tone came through the earbud.

There was a sound of an annoyed growl through the call, I could only assume it was Troy.

When Alona and I caught up to the others it was mayhem. The unarmed men we had followed weren't without weapons now. Large swords, and even a sort of spear was in play.

"Spearman is mine." Autumn called out.

"Poor sap wielding it." One of the men said, but I couldn't tell who.

Alona seemed to be sticking to the outskirts of the action, but after watching her in action with the nun-chucks I realized she wasn't someone I would want to go against.

Daxx slid along the ground and used the vanishing box on a man that Bethany and Paisley had disarmed and knocked to the ground. I didn't quite understand how they did it, but it was amazing.

I nodded and decided what my task would be in this skirmish. I lunged to the left when Autumn and the man with the spear were going head to head. I didn't pause to admire her abilities, but with a glance I saw she had the man on the defensive as he was backing away from her onslaught.

I approached the man that Daxx was fighting with her twin blades, releasing the weight, I gave the chain a flick in his direction, it landed perfectly around one of his ankles, with a quick jerk he hit the ground. Daxx had a huge grin on her face as she bent down with the box and disappeared.

"You and me, Rea, lets clean house." She sounded so happy.

I nodded and picked up the weighted end again.

"I'll engage, you do your thing." She sounded out of breath as she bolted toward two men fighting with Quinton. "I'm borrowing the left one, Quint."

"All yours," Quinton grunted as he ducked the swing from the man on the left and turned his attention to the other one.

My heart was in my throat as I watched him advance on the man using a sword larger than the two the bad guy was wielding. The clash of metal beside me, brought me back to the task at hand. I turned and dropped the weight and did a wide sweep with my arm, sending it to unroot the man Daxx was fighting.

"Sisters with skills." Rafael's voice sung through the earpiece.

"Pay attention." That was Kara.

I turned to see a man lying at Rafael's feet, an arrow beside him.

"Giving you something to do, honey." Rafael grinned in the direction of the crane.

"Need back up." That was Bethany.

"This guy is a tank." Paisley said in a strained voice.

Daxx nodded when I sent her a questioning look.

I turned and went toward the very bulky man they were trying to knock down. "Call out when you're going hit him." I said as I ran toward them, spinning the surujin as I went. I would have more than enough momentum by the time I reached them.

"On three." Bethany growled.

"One," Paisley hissed.

I was almost there.

"Two," Bethany whispered.

I sent it flying, and jerked it around ankle, "three." The man tumbled to the ground. My surujin was still wrapped around his ankle, I jerked it again when he went to get up.

"Port box." Bethany said with an urgent tone.

The man was on his side again, starting to get up. I rushed over and kicked him in the face. Later when my sanity returned, I'd question such a move.

Leone was over him, grinning at me. He let me pull the chain free, then the man vanished. "Damn." He laughed and then spun, swords in hand again.

"One of them is getting in the van." Crissy reported.

"Not now he isn't." Kara said calmly.

The man with the white hair came rushing toward me, Emil beside him. Instinct told me to duck, so I did quickly. A man tumbled over top of me. My heart was no longer beating fast, it was now stuck in my throat.

The white-haired man put his foot on the back of his neck and held him down.

Emil stopped and held his hand down to me. "Head on a swivel." He said softly.

I nodded and got up. "or no head at all." I whispered. He winked and released me. Turning, he surveyed the area.

"Is that all of them?" Emil asked.

"I can't see any more." Crissy said.

"Keep watch of the gate." Victor said. "We're going to check in the building."

I followed Emil toward the van they'd been loading. Quinton paused and looked back at me, the expression on his face said he wasn't thrilled I had almost been decapitated. I blew out a breath and pulled the chain to put the surujin back in its case.

Daxx patted my shoulder as she went by and rolled her eyes.

Troy stood over one of the cases they'd been loading, shaking his head.

"Fuck me." Rafael whispered.

"Holy shit." Leone hissed. He turned to Bethany, "if you girls hadn't…"

"What is it?" Crissy asked over the call.

"A whole lot of bad." Autumn told her.

"If they'd gotten this wherever they were going…"

"Yeah." Rafael replied before Arius could finish.

"We need to know where they were taking it." Chase said in a harsh tone. "Arius get a hold of your cell guards and make sure they all are processed quickly."

Arius nodded and backed out of the group, as he took his phone out of the zipped-up pocket of this leather coat.

Curious, I weaved my way through the large bodies to take a peek. I physically jolted when I saw in it. "Is that explosives?"

Emil nodded.

I looked in the van, then back to him, "all of it?"

Leone climbed out of the van. "All of it."

"How could they get their hands on that much?" Quinton asked.

"We'll have to find out." Troy said as he rubbed a hand across his brow. "They most likely used magic to dupe someone."

"They weren't going to try to blow up the barrier, were they?" Daxx glanced around.

"I don't believe that is a possibility." Victor stated.

Quinton squatted down and leaned against the van. "We need to know what it was for."

I watched him for a moment, the trace around his was more visible. He looked up and saw me looking at him and his look hardened.

"What do we do with it?" Rafael asked. "I'm not porting explosives to Alterealm."

Troy turned to look at Chase for a moment, "we'll contact someone on this side to come and get it."

Rafael looked at the white-haired man. "Welsley you go with Quinton and bring ten guards over here until it's picked up."

The white-haired man nodded and turned to Quinton.

Taking a deep breath, Quinton got up. "Be back shortly." He stepped away from the others and put his hand on the other man's shoulder. They both vanished.

I couldn't help but think that whatever was wrong with him, he was almost to the point of being drained just now. I took a deep breath and exhaled slowly, it was time he and I had an honest chat.

"Ready to go back?" Bethany stood in front of me.

I startled, "yes."

"Thanks for the assist." Paisley inclined her head to me, "that guy was like trying to take down the hulk."

"Sisters with skills." Arius winked at me, then leaned down and kissed Paisley. "Go. Before I remember how my heart stopped when I learned you were in the middle of a high-speed car chase."

She gave him a timid look, then vanished.

Chapter Eighteen

I stood in front of the mirror and stared at my reflection. I felt like, for the first time in my life I had purpose. The problem was, I didn't know what to do with it. Turning away, I picked up the pouch with my new weapon and attached it to my hip. I was never going anywhere without it again.

Sighing, I sat down on the end of the bed and stared at the door. My initial purpose may have been to see the green haze and lead them to the clues they'd been searching for, but now—now I knew my purpose was to be the mate of a great man. All I had to do was find a way to get him to see that.

Nodding to my thoughts, I got up and walked out of my room. I stood at the stairs and looked up. In conversation I'd learned who resided in the palace and somewhere was Quinton's room. I didn't know if he was there, but with a big meeting having been called, I imagined everyone would be doing as I had done. Wash off the wasteland dust and wrecking yard grime to get ready before the meeting. I went up the stairs slowly, eyeing each room as they came into sight. I stopped at the top trying to decide, then froze when one of the doors opened.

Emil stood there for a second, then gave me a grin and pointed to the far end of the hall. Without comment he closed his door and went down the stairs.

There were no decorations on the walls on this floor, I wondered if Alona hadn't yet gotten to it, or the plain walls were the plan. Reaching the door, I took a deep breath and knocked on it before I could change my mind.

"Yeah." Quinton's gruff tone came through the door.

I opened it, "It's Reagan."

The door jerked open. "Is something wrong?"

I was momentarily speechless as he stood in front of me, naked from the waist up. His hair was wet and water droplets still glistened off his broad chest. "Uh, no, not with me."

He released the door and lifted the towel to his head and rubbed his hair with it. "Am I late? I thought we had an hour while they gathered everyone up." He walked away from me.

I stepped inside, noting the room was sparsely furnished. A bed, a dresser and single chair took up very little space in the large room. Glancing up, I stared at the ladder resting on the ceiling.

"Emergency escape. This was my parents' room."

I turned to look at him. "I suppose that makes sense."

He shrugged. "It's a great place to sit and think in the quiet too."

I smiled and stepped into the room further. "With all the family you have, I can see where that would be a great selling point."

Quinton smirked. "Yeah." He pulled a shirt over his head, then looked at me. "Why are you here, Reagan?" Crossing his arms over his chest he leaned back against the dresser.

He was straight forward, I appreciated that. "When did you know?"

He didn't even pause, he knew what I was talking about. "When you knelt over me in that garage."

I was surprised. "That long." I said quietly.

"Yeah." He shrugged. "I didn't plan on saying anything though."

"What changed your mind?" I mimicked his stance and crossed my arms over my chest and stood there.

His dark eyes assessed me briefly. "I didn't want anyone to question you."

"Being your mate gives me that allowance?"

He nodded. "It damn well better."

I smirked at his tone but left it there. I looked at him for a moment, the trace was faded again. "What does the doctor give you to help?"

There was no look of shock from him. "Some kind of elixir."

"It's not working as it did?"

Quinton shook his head. "No. It's becoming less effective each time I take it."

"Have other options been explored?" I tried to stand there and look as removed as he did, but I truly wasn't.

He nodded slowly and looked at the floor in front of him. "Yeah. I've been poked, prodded and scanned very thoroughly."

"And the prognosis is?"

"Not good." He straightened away and turned, opening the top drawer, he pulled out a folder and then tossed it on the bed. "That's the complete documentation. Take a look and see for yourself." He turned and went to the window and leaned a hand on the wall beside it.

I looked at his back as he stared out it, unmoving. Going over, I squatted down and opened the folder. There was a faded photo attached to the inside of the jacket. It was of him, I could tell by the eyes.

"That's what I looked like until Daxx got here." He said without turning.

"I've seen disfigurement before, so if you were plotting to shock me enough to run from the room, you're mistaken." I dragged my eyes away from his image and began to flip through the pages. Scanning for a quick summary of each. "So, starving yourself for a century did irreversible internal damage." It wasn't a question.

"My heart is still good." He said quietly, "other organs, not so much."

"Why haven't you told your family? Having support through…"

He spun around and looked down at me. "I spent a century standing on the sidelines," he scowled, "my *special* healing blood no longer heals me." He shrugged, "probably not others either."

My mother had told me stories about the royal family being blessed by the gods with their life blood being that special. "So, you're going to die quietly just so you can join the fight?" I closed the folder and stood up.

"Something like that." His brown eyes locked on my own. "I need you to not tell my family."

"And you will take my word for it if I agree?" I took a deep breath, trying to remain rational.

"Yes." His gaze searched my face for a moment, "you've lived through a lot and done it honestly, as far as I can tell, I don't think you'd be deceitful now."

It was a back handed compliment, but still a compliment. "You're right."

He nodded slowly and continued to stand there.

"So, what now? I'm supposed to nod and leave?" I crossed my arms over my chest again. "Just accept that I have a mate I'll never know and get back to it all?"

"Three hundred and fifty years." He said quietly, holding my eyes prisoner with his own. "That's how long I waited and wondered. I searched on this side and on the other side, not accepting that you were going to just appear in front of me." He made a soft noise of annoyance. "And then you did."

I kept silent.

"It's too late, Reagan." A pained looked crossed his face. "I wished to the gods it wasn't, but we can't be mated. I can't share my mark with you then give you the decay and pain that's inside me."

I swallowed the lump in my throat at the agony in his tone. His beautiful brown eyes were bleeding pain. "Maybe I'm the one that's meant to take the pieces and make you whole again." I whispered.

He shook his head. "It would kill you to heal everything inside me."

"A bit at a…"

With a quick move he was in front of me, gripping my shoulders and shaking his head. "No." He searched my face for a moment, then took a ragged breath and released me. With stiff movement he went back to his dresser and opened a box on top of it. Turning, he came back to me with something enclosed in his hand. "This," he held out his closed hand, "is an amulet made for my mate." A sad look appeared in his eyes, "it's obviously not the pendant of the enforcer, but it's still a royal title." He opened his hand.

I looked down at the silver chain pooled in his large palm.

"Its yours." His voice was rough. "Take it."

I took the pendant and lifted it out of his hand. The emblem on it was a sundial with crossed swords over it. "So that's it? I'm your mate, take this."

He gave me a hard look. "No one will question you if you have that."

"After your dead, you mean?" I closed my hand around it so I wouldn't throw it at him.

"Yeah." He clenched his jaw. "There is no happy ending here, Reagan."

I nodded slowly, "Ergo no happy for now either."

His brows creased as he looked down at me. "It's been hard enough watching my brothers find their mates, having that connection with them and knowing I'd never have it."

"That doesn't mean you have to be completely alone." I squeezed my eyes so the hovering tears wouldn't fall. "If you're hoping I'll say I understand and walk away, then you're in for a real shocker, sir."

"I can't pretend things are going to work out." He said with a gravely voice.

"I'm not asking you to pretend anything." I put the hand I held the pendant in against his chest. "Just don't ask me to watch you go through it alone."

With a shaking hand, he touched my cheek. "I missed you before I even met you."

"I'm here now." I whispered as unshed tears choked me.

He held my look for a moment, then leaned down and kissed my mouth softly. "Stubborn woman." He straightened. "Go. I have to eat often to keep my strength up." He stepped back, "the elixir burns through calories faster than I can put them in."

I nodded. "Don't think you're going to avoid me, my prince." I made the motion of an elaborate bow, then straightened and went out the door before I puddled on the floor in a heap of emotion.

I couldn't even explain how I'd ended up in a large gym, but here I was trying to burn off the frustration that was filling my every pore. I gathered up the surujin chain again and looked the padded post once more. I flung it, the weight caught in the wrong place and wouldn't release when I jerked on it. With a growl, I stomped over and untangled it. In a blur of anger, I stabbed the padding with the blade at the end of the handle. With a sound similar to a wounded animal I continued to stab it over and over and over again. Reality hit me and I stepped back, releasing the weapon and standing there looking at the carnage I had produced.

"Well, I don't think I've ever seen technique like that before."

I jumped and turned to see Michael and Autumn standing behind me. I looked back at the hacked-up post. "I am so sorry."

Michael shook his head. "I'm just glad you used a post and not my brother."

I snorted. "That obvious?"

He gave Autumn a quick look, "as the mating process goes it usually stirs up…"

"Stupid men moments." Autumn finished.

"Close enough." He rubbed his hand against the back of his neck. "We were sent to fetch you for the meeting."

I huffed out a breath and then looked back at my surujin. Feeling like a child, I went over and picked it up. I busied myself tucking it back into the case, so I wouldn't have to look at them. "I'm sorry you had to witness my outburst." I said quietly.

Autumn laughed, "we all have moments."

Michael hugged her to his side, "some of us more than others." He frowned, "Quinton is," he thought for a moment, "kind of a hardass, but I'm sure you'll work it out."

I offered my best fake smile. "Yes, we're in the process of doing that." I pulled the necklace and pendant out of my pocket, "am I to wear this all the time?"

Michael expression showed shock. "Ah, yeah—if he's given you it, then you should."

Autumn nodded, "guards won't harass you if you are."

I gave her a nod of my head to say thank you for the tip, and unclasped it. "Where is the meeting?" I secured it around my neck.

"Meeting room at the palace." Autumn told me.

I nodded and opened the porter, then paused and looked at Michael. "Could you get in touch with that Bastian man for me? I need to speak with him."

Michael's expression sobered. "He's going to be at the meeting." He gave me an understanding look. "I'll mention you need a private moment with him."

I nodded. "Thank you." I pushed the button to take me back to the palace.

Chapter Nineteen

I stood beside the thrones, trying to be unseen. The room was full of people, many more than other meetings I'd seen. Beth and Crissy sat on the stand the thrones were on, they were just as quiet.

Quinton came over and perched on the window ledge beside us. He watched servants bring in more chairs and set them at the other end of the room.

Bethany leaned around Crissy and looked at him. "Are more coming?" She looked around the room. "Good thing we picked this room for meetings."

He shook his head. "No, but we only planned for thirty seats around the tables."

Crissy said. "There's forty-five here," she shrugged "or will be when Victor gets here."

I watched Quinton for a moment. He'd avoided eye contact with me since our discussion. "All of the elders are here. Is that good?" I asked.

Quinton shrugged. "Saves us having a second meeting to tell them the same thing."

Bethany nodded. "Is that another royal family member with prince Bastian?" She glanced at me, "trying to learn who is who if I'm to pull off this princess thing."

"That's his guard, Tor." He crossed his arms over his chest, "the other realms are on full alert too."

"How many reported back with issues?" Bethany looked worried

"Two so far. The others are keeping an eye on things." He watched Michael go over and speak to Bastian. Bastian nodded and turned to look at me. Quinton turned to look at me.

"I don't see things for other realms." Crissy said quietly

"That's good." Quinton gave her an amused look, "I don't think you have enough head space for more visions and more realms."

With her eyes wide, Crissy gave him a quick nod, "I don't know if it's this realm or the one I was stuck in I see," she paused, "I think it's more the people that are important in them than the place."

Quinton looked at me after she said that, but didn't comment.

"Who is the woman with the gorgeous hair?" Beth asked him quietly.

I didn't have to look around to know who she was talking about, there was only one woman here I didn't know and she had long pale strawberry blonde hair, but that wasn't what made her stand out to me. Her skin almost glowed with flawless perfection.

"Princess Aireese of FaTerra." Quinton answered without looking.

Bethany looked back to him, but he didn't add any more.

Crissy leaned closer to Bethany. "She's a fae."

Beth's mouth dropped open. "Like a real fairy?"

Crissy nodded. "I read about them in the Alterealm library." She grinned. "Its fascinating."

I looked at the woman and the large man standing behind her. He was pretty for a man.

"Is that her guard?" Beth asked

Quinton nodded, "yeah. His name is Firo or something like that."

"Wow." Beth whispered, "a fairy princess." She turned and grinned at me.

"How many realms are there?" I looked at Quinton

"Six." He stated without any inflection whatsoever, like it was a totally normal thing.

I knew of three, but didn't ever stop to think that there might be more. I looked at him, "and you know all of them?"

He nodded. "I've only been to Solrelm and FaTerra," he shrugged, "the others are of no interest to me."

I shrugged and then gave Bethany a blank look.

She smirked. "I'm still trying to get used to here—I don't know if I'd want to go to yet another realm." She put her hand on her stomach, "especially if my body hates it as much as porting around here."

He tilted his head and looked at her. "It's worse."

"Uh, yeah, no thanks." She grimaced.

The sound of chairs scraping had us all turn. Victor was walking through the room speaking to the important guests.

"Let's hope they have ideas how to end this." Bethany got up and went toward Leone.

Crissy waited until Victor looked at her, then went toward him.

I got up and turned to Quinton. "Any protocol I need to know? Just so I don't commit any horrible offenses."

He looked at me for a moment, then leaned forward and pulled on the chain that had his pendant on it. "You're in Alterealm, so as long as you're entitled to wear this—" He released it and stood up, "it's them that should worry about offending you." Inclining his head to me, he motioned to the table. "We're to sit in rank order for this."

I nodded and went with him, having no idea about rank. Aside from kings and queens I didn't know what the order was, so I stood until the rest of the brothers and their mates sat down.

Emil gave me an understanding look as I sat down beside him.

"As most of you know," Troy began, "this was originally the time we'd allotted for a different meeting." He glanced at Bastian, "we've discovered some things that needed to be shared with the rest of you." Inclining his head to Princess Aireese, he glanced at Victor.

Victor didn't waste time with formal protocol. "Princess, have your guards been able to locate those working with Willis Hubert?"

The princess shook her head. "They haven't." She glanced to her guard sitting behind her for a moment before turning back to look at the twin kings. "However, we've confirmed the location where they intended to breach."

The elder with the curly white hair sat forward, "was it scientifically detected or was it more magic being used?"

The princess smirked, "I'm told it was a mix." She clasped her hands in front of her neatly. "I'm sure our experts would be glad for the collaboration, Elder Arian."

The elder looked pleased with this and nodded her head quickly and sat back again.

It occurred to me then, that I needed to start trying to commit names to memory. Beyond the royal family here in Alterealm, names were lost on me. I wondered if it was because I was solo for so many years and never had to remember people.

"And what of your realm, Prince Bastian?"

I snapped out of my internal dialogue.

Bastian leaned back in his seat and crossed his arms over his chest. "I'm told they haven't found a location, but we're still getting information from the traitors that were helping that lunatic." He glanced at Elder Arian, "perhaps we could combine skill sets to see if we can locate the barrier site they were targeting." The elder nodded.

"I'll set it up it up with your people to have mine come over and see what can be done." The Princess said with a quiet tone. "What else have you discovered?" She turned back to look at Troy.

Troy stood up and glanced around at his brothers briefly, "as you know Willis Hubert has been working with Arwan."

I watched the expressions in the room change to everything from fear to disgust.

"With the help of Reagan," he continued, "we've been able to find portals he's been using here and in the human realm."

Every eye in the room was now on me as he spoke. I had to fight to keep from sliding under the table to hide.

"I'm just waiting on the head of our magic factions to arrive to confirm our other suspicions," Victor looked at his phone and nodded at Troy, then got up and went over to a large board on the other side of the room. "Today we intercepted transportation of a tremendous amount of explosive…"

There were several audible gasps in the room.

"Are they thinking they can blow up the barriers?" Elder Arian sounded amused.

Troy opened his hands, "I don't think they're that naive," his expression was grim, "we're still working on discovering their plans."

"I think we can all agree they're not that naive." The elder with the long white braid stated. "Which leaves the question, what were they planning to demolish?"

"I agree, Elder Varus." Troy nodded slowly. "I've advised all realms to increase security." He nodded. "We've canceled all crossing, outside the teams working on this."

Bastian nodded. "We have done the same."

"As have we." Princess Aireese added.

The door opened and Romulus and Clairee came in. They inclined their head to Troy, then went over to Victor and spoke quietly.

Victor nodded and then looked at the map in front of him. His shoulders stiffened, then he turned back to the rest of the room. "It has been confirmed." He held up a marker. "A century ago, our wastelands were considerably smaller." He turned to the map and put a circle in the center of the orange area. "Each year it has grown," He glanced over his shoulder, "however growth has increased greatly for the past few decades." He circled the entire orange area and then put the marker down and turned to look at everyone. "Arwan has been drawing his energy and power from our lands."

"For centuries?" Elder Nodin looked concerned.

The mage, Romulus nodded. "Yes. Prior to that he could have used a simpler power source but," he looked right at me, "until Princess Reagan was here and able to see the traces of his magic, we had no way of knowing."

Again, all eyes were on me. Princess? I almost blurted that part out loud.

"The strength of his magic isn't his own." The fairy princess looked pleased with this.

"It doesn't make it any easier to find him." Bethany said.

The princess nodded slowly, "that's true, but if the source is cut off, he's weakened."

"I—" Clairee looked at Romulus, "we don't know how to do that." She gave the princess a quick glance, then looked to Troy, "we can on a smaller scale, but if he's drawing it from the land of this realm," her eyes widened, "that's a big source to try and contain."

Troy considered what she said for a moment, then turned to the princess, "perhaps your experts could collaborate with our magic factions and try to come up with a plan."

The princess nodded. "I'll set it up." She gave Clairee and sympathetic look, "I have no doubt it's going to be quite the task."

"If he can be tracked down, Kara can hear the spells as mages cast them." Rafael said looking at Kara, who looked like she wanted to crawl under the table.

"So, if you find him, you think you can stop Arwan?" The Princess asked.

"Oh, we'll stop him." Paisley nodded, "one way or another."

"If you can cut off his connection with the land, will his magic be weaker?" Daxx looked at the princess, then to Romulus.

"Considerably." Princess Aireese said with conviction.

Daxx nodded, then stood up. "I say that takes priority." She nodded, then pointed to Bastian, "as well as finding where they're trying to—" she glanced at Troy

"Take the barriers down." He finished.

Most in the room nodded. I just continued to sit there trying to grasp what all of it meant. Why would you want to break the barriers that kept one realm separate from another?

"We also have a location in the human realm that's been used for more than a century to port people over—" Chase didn't bother to stand up. "Many of our citizens were trapped in a mental asylum all this time." He glanced at Bastian, "we already brought out more than twenty of our own, but I'm wondering if you could look at the rest residing there and see if any from your realms are confined there."

Bastian nodded. "I can do that."

"Are you able to close that portal down?" The princess looked at Romulus.

He nodded slowly, "we should be able to disrupt it."

"We have to get to it first." Leone said. "So far," he glanced at Michael, "we can't find an access point from the outside to the basement."

Elder Varus looked right at me. "You'll be able to see any active portals?"

I nodded, "Yes. I've seen the magic trace in Alterealm and all over the city before I was brought here."

The Elder with the scariest demeanor stood up. He turned to address Victor. "Have patrols been set up with Princess Reagan to seek out all access points over here?"

Victor looked at Quinton for a moment before answering him. "We've only just confirmed that was what she was seeing, Elder Segos," he turned to look at Michael. "I am certain it is in the planning stages now."

Michael raised his eyebrows to his brother, then nodded and looked back to the elder. "Rafael and I will start selecting a team for this."

The elder looked pleased with this and sat down again.

"How soon do you need me to check the asylum?" Bastian looked from Troy to Chase.

The twins exchanged a glare before Chase sat forward in his seat again. "A few day's time." He motioned to the princess, "lets get the barrier locations found first, so we can get watches in place."

"Please let us know when you find out what they were planning to use the explosives for." The princess was looking at Victor as she spoke.

"Immediately." Victor told her.

"If that's everything, I should get back and arrange the team to work with Elder Arian." The princess stood up. "I'm also going to send more seekers out in my realm to ferret out any with the heart dark enough to be part of this." A sad look crossed her face, "there have been more rainbows lately. We knew something was happening."

"I'm sorry to hear that." Elder Varus said in a soft tone.

Rainbows were sad? I glanced down the table at Crissy, she looked like she was going to cry. Later I would have to ask why rainbows were sad.

"Keep us apprised of your discoveries, princess." Victor inclined his head to her for a moment.

"I will." She turned and looked from one brother to the next until she reached Emil. "Congratulations," she looked at the rest of us, "to all of you for your recent discovery of your life mates." She smiled at me, then looked at Alona. "The *extra* abilities many have in this room is electrifying, my wings have been vibrating with it." She inclined her head to Bastian. "Prince." With a nod to her guard, she went to the door.

Ira stood up and then left with them.

"Well," Bastian said after the door closed, "at least she didn't turn anyone into a tree this time." He smirked at the shocked looks from the Elders.

Elder Varus stood up. "If that is all," she motioned to a few of the other elders, "we have much to do."

Troy nodded, "that's all for now." He turned to Chase, before looking back to her, "and thank you for the lists of new job assignment suggestions." He waved his hand around, "that will be top of the tasks once we shut down Willis Hubert."

An elder with spiked white hair stood up. "Can we drop him in a bottomless pit this time?" She asked.

Arius got up. "It won't be a catch and release—I guarantee it."

Chapter Twenty

The royal family were talking to the elders that lingered, as Mitz brought in snacks. I smirked at how often she had food out for them. Then again since I'd been here there seemed to be no regular routine for the day or night. Prince Bastian got my attention and motioned to the hallway. I hurried to go speak with him.

"I was told you wanted to talk to me." He leaned back against the wall and looked at me.

His dark eyes still made all the alarms in my head go off. I guess some childhood warnings were life-long. "Yes." I bit my lip, "although now, I'm not sure how to ask you."

"Ask me?" He raised one eyebrow looking entirely too amused.

I nodded, "I wanted to know if I have—essence."

His looked changed to surprise. With a smirk, he eyed the pendant resting against my shirt. "I can only imagine why you're asking." He bowed with great dramatic moves. He straightened back up. "I don't see a tattoo, but the pendant screams 'soon to be princess'."

Crossing my arms, I frowned at him. "It's not what you think."

"I'm sure." His grin faded as he looked at me. "Why are you asking me? You are surrounded by essence feeders."

I took a deep breath as I dropped my arms back to my side. "I realize that." Actually, I hadn't thought of what sort of feeders I was surrounded by. "But you know more about me than they do," I motioned between us, "with my father being from—" I blew out a breath, "your realm."

Bastian ran his hand through his chaotic hair. "I know nothing about you or even what the mix of your two parents equates to." He glanced back into the room, "other than you can see traces of magic and a person's innermost personality flaws."

I tried to mask my anxiety with a polite smile.

His expression changed, making me understand I wasn't as good an actress as I hoped. "Anything living has some sort of essence." He shrugged, "or they wouldn't be living." He acknowledged his guard that signaled they were ready to go. "As to yours, it may be extraordinary," he shrugged, "or simply normal." He nodded to his guard. "Maybe you should ask one of the doctors here, I'm sure they'll be able to explain more than I can." He motioned to his guard, "for now, Tor and I need to get back and inform my parents that the proverbial shit is about to hit the fan."

I watched him leave with Ira, then turned around to see Quinton a few feet away. His arms were crossed over his chest and his expression wasn't very approachable. "He had news of your father?"

My mouth opened, I forgot to ask him. I snapped it shut and shook my head.

I watched his chest rise and fall with a deep breath. With a jerk of his head, he motioned back to the room. "Unofficial meeting, now that the VIP's are gone."

I bobbed my head quickly, and moved past him to go back into the room. I stopped a few feet from the door and turned to see he was right on my heels. "Quinton, I have an odd question."

He looked down at me, his expression somber. "About?"

I offered a polite, nervous grin, "do I have essence?"

His eyebrows went up. "everything has essence to a certain degree, or else it wouldn't be alive." His eyes darkened with what looked like anger. "Why?"

I shrugged, gave him another smile hoping to erase the dark mood from him, "I just—well, some of this is all new to me."

With a quick move, he lightly grasped my chin and tilted my head up. He leaned down close enough I could feel his breath on my face. "Don't even think about letting someone feed off you, Reagan." His brown eyes locked on mine, "It wouldn't end well for them." Releasing my chin, he stepped around me and went in the room.

"That," Bethany came up behind me, "seems to be a normal Whitham brother trait." She smiled at me, "growling." Motioning to the room, we started walking together. "You have more power over him than you think."

I made a sound of amusement. "Right."

She laughed, "you do. It's part of the mate deal, they will do anything to make sure their mates are happy."

I looked at her as we walked around the table. "I don't think we're there quite yet." I whispered.

She shrugged and sat down. "Doesn't hurt to test the limits."

Leone came over and gave her a curious look.

Bethany smiled up at him. "Girl talk."

Leone looked at me, "that never ends well for us."

I couldn't help laughing.

"There's just one more thing we need to discuss." Arius tapped his finger on a tablet. "I've been thinking."

"That never works out." Quinton smirked.

Arius gave him a bored look, then turned back to look around the table. "As I was saying, the probation farm is full—actually, it's beyond full. We need another building or somewhere those with lesser crimes can be sent." Arius scowled, "saving the cells for any involved in Hubert's cause."

Victor nodded. "Another facility would be wise."

"What about that old factory warehouse? I don't even know what that was for." Leone frowned.

Rafael nodded. "We could fence it in and renovate the building."

"Have them manufacture, something to work off their crime." Bethany suggested.

"I'll send some contractors there to take a look." Troy glanced to Chase, who nodded.

"I have an idea of who would be the warden of the new facility." Rafael turned to Arius. "You can't be everywhere all the time, brother. You need a few to run the farm and new facility and report to you."

Arius nodded slowly. "Who did you have in mind?"

"Ellis. I think he'd be good at it. He's very task oriented, good at organizing groups."

Arius glanced at Emil. "Do you think that would be of interest to your son?"

Emil grinned. "I think it would be. He's already decided he's never going back over." He looked at Troy. "Let me know when the contractors are going over and we'll tag along." Troy stood up, "we're going to coordinate with the men watching the asylum in an hour."

Victor got up, "that gives us time to work on some other details."

Kara got up. "I have my first archery class." She grinned at Rafael, "here's hoping we find a few good ones."

Rafael shrugged, "half the guard have all signed up to try it."

"Just make sure you keep a few to be *guards*, brother." Leone stood up and turned to Bethany.

She smiled, "I'm going to go see if I can do anything at the temple to help with all the preparations when portals are located."

Alona stood up and stretched. "I'm going to go see if the nurses need a hand, before I catch a nap."

Michael stood up and looked at Autumn. "I'd like to stay and be in on the plans." He turned to her guard, "take a few others and take her over for the lessons."

Her guard nodded, and pulled out his phone.

"I'm nervous. I've never been nervous when it comes to teaching self-defense." Autumn said. "These women we've found need to know how to defend themselves."

Paisley leaned against the table. "I think you're just aware of what some of these women went through." She gave her an understanding look. "I could go if you like."

"You wouldn't mind?" Autumn gave her a steady look.

Paisley shrugged, "that's what sisters are for."

Autumn grinned. "You got it twin, let's go."

They went out the door, their guards following them.

"I'm going to the library." Crissy jumped up, she paused long enough to smile at Victor then jogged out the door.

Emil turned to Troy, "I'll come help with planning if you don't mind." He shrugged, "Rena and her guard are going through things and packing." He rubbed his hand over his face, "Rena had everything she owned from our storage lockers delivered." He glanced at Michael, "says this will be her last move." He took a deep breath and let it out slowly, "I have to admit being able to go about your life without having to change your name and move every decade is a welcome thing." He glanced at me.

I nodded, knowing all too well how that went. "Sleeping in the same place is—new." I grinned at his exaggerated nod.

"I'm helping." Daxx looked at Troy, "with planning."

He smiled down at her. "Not that you ever stick to the plan."

She shrugged, "still good to know what the rest of you guys will be doing while I get things started."

Quinton started for the door, then paused and looked at me.

I glanced around as everyone was in motion. "I might just go rest."

He searched my face, then nodded. "We're going to the asylum in the morning, then looking for portals after that."

I made Derian and the other two guards stay outside the building and went in quickly. Having one shadow was bad enough, but now to even look out a window I needed three, or more.

I barely sat down before the doctor came through the door.

He stopped and gave me a concerned look. "Was I expecting you?"

I got up slowly, "No. I just had a few minutes while everyone is off doing their thing and thought I'd see if you had a moment"

He inclined his head. "I always have time for," he looked at the pendant resting against my shirt, "the royals."

I wanted to cover up the pendant but clasped my hands in front of me instead.

"What can I do for you?"

"I spoke to Quinton," I glanced at the floor for a second, "I know he's not well. I can see it." I rolled my eyes, "he would never have told me otherwise." The doctor stood there patiently. "He showed me the file." He still didn't move. I lifted my gloved hand up, "you know what I can do— do you think there's any way I could help him?"

"I'd be afraid of what that would do to you." He motioned to the chair.

I sat down again.

He perched on the edge of a chair. "Your ability doesn't harm you, but it does drain you." He paused with a loom of thought on his face. "I'd be worried your batteries," he made quotes in the air, "would drain completely."

I sighed quietly. "I was afraid of that." I felt strange about this but asked it anyways. "What about my essence? Do you think it would be super-charged because of my ability?"

The doctor looked at me for a moment, I couldn't make out what the expression meant. "There's no way of knowing that for certain." He motioned in the air, "nor am I going to suggest testing it." He pointed to the necklace. "It is the death penalty to even attempt such a thing from any bearing a royal amulet."

I opened my mouth then snapped it shut again. Nodding, I stood up. "Of course. Thank you."

The doctor got up. "I'm sorry I couldn't be more helpful, princess." He motioned to the desk. "We're trying a new serum for prince Quinton." He gave me one of those hopeful, fake doctor smiles. "We haven't given up yet."

I gave him back a fake smile and let myself out quickly.

I watched Daxx throw a second knife. "You're very good." I meant it, I doubted I could even hit the target at all.

She grinned. "Lucky shots," she pointed to Kara, "she's got mad skills."

Kara turned away from the map. "I had a lot of time to practice. Having no friends because I couldn't be near people."

"Until now." Bethany piped up. She leaned over the table and put a sticky note on the map. "You have more friends than you can handle now."

Kara laughed.

"Where are our guards?" Paisley stood in the doorway, looking out into the hallway.

"I sent them to the practice room. They were bored." Alona tossed the catalogue on the table.

Autumn was doing squats beside one of the desks. "Tell me again, why are we here doing nothing?"

Crissy looked up from her notebook. "Victor said they're checking the lay of the land around the asylum."

"Weren't we supposed to be going over today?"

Crissy got up and went to a corner and started bouncing a ball. I looked at Alona.

"It helps her sort through the visions." She said quietly.

"Today was postponed." Paisley said then went over and watched Kara and Beth at the map. "Something the person they have inside suggested."

Daxx paused. "Did they say why?"

Paisley shrugged.

Beth turned and looked at me. "Wouldn't it make more sense to take Reagan? She could look for portals and save us a lot of time."

Alona got up and went over to stand with Paisley. "What are you two doing?"

Kara leaned against the table. "We're marking areas where we found or caught people." She pointed to the map, "the market, the wasteland and where Autumn landed when they brought her over."

Bethany nodded, "the path those guys were on the day Kara arrived." She paused for a second. "That house. Where Leone and I were."

Autumn came over and looked. "Any pattern?"

Kara shook her head, "not yet."

I went over to get a closer look.

"Hold on." Daxx picked up the sticky notes. "There' the old mine—that's a mud pit now." She put one on the map, "and over here," she pointed, "is where I got sliced." She put another one on.

"Should we check all those areas?" I just wanted to do something.

"The guards have been patrolling the mine and that farm every day." Kara said while staring at the map. "What's in this direction?" Kara pointed to a spot. "The day they were going to blow up the palace tunnel—they came from that way."

"It's being patrolled too." Bethany said.

"But," Daxx looked at me, "they wouldn't see a portal."

"That's true." Alona nodded.

Daxx looked at her, "call our guards, we're going to check some of these out."

"It would take us all day to ride to them." Paisley studied the map.

"We can port to most of them." Daxx shrugged, "one or more of us have been to them."

I frowned. "Don't you need a porter?"

Autumn shook her head. "The blood-bond with royal brothers allows us to do it without," she made a face, "and not always on purpose."

I raised my eyebrows, not even knowing what to say.

Kara grinned. "When Quinton gets around to more than giving you a necklace, you'll be able to do it too."

I glanced down at the pendant. "I'm not going to hold my breath waiting for that." Part of me wished I could tell them why. I gave her a quick smile, even though I didn't feel it. "I'm happy to port along anywhere you go." I did grin to that.

"I actually haven't thrown up in a few days." Bethany nodded her head quickly. "Maybe I'm finally adjusting to it."

Alona rolled her eyes. "I do not miss that."

"You called?"

We turned to see Sith in the doorway.

Alona smiled. "Yes. You'll need full gear," she glanced at Daxx, "and we'll meet you in the armory."

"Are we going over with the kings?"

Alona shook her head. "No, we're going to check a few locations over here."

He gave her a skeptical look.

"Just checking for portals." I told him.

He nodded but didn't look convinced. Taking a deep breath, he exhaled slowly. "We'll meet you at the armory." He inclined his head and left.

"Okay, ladies, go get changed and meet at the armory." Daxx said then vanished.

Autumn looked happy. She grabbed my shoulder. "I'll take you to your room. It's faster."

Chapter Twenty-One

I looked around to see where we were this time.

"Is it weird I feel disappointed that we found nothing at the last four locations?" Paisley asked while looking around.

"No." Bethany pulled her hair up into a pony. "You're just thinking like I am—"

"That the guys can't be as mad if we find a portal?" Kara asked.

"Yeah." Paisley looked behind us. "We brought our guards this time, so they can't be as mad."

"Is anyone else looking forward to this ending?" Daxx looked all around us. "When we can do what we want again?"

Alona nodded. "What are we going to do all day-or night then?"

Crissy tucked a ball into her pocket. "I want a job." She nodded, "I've never had a job."

"Yeah, they're going to have to find us jobs." Bethany went over to the edge of the overgrown road and looked both ways. "I don't think princess is a job." She turned and looked at Autumn. "This is where you fought them?"

Autumn nodded, then pointed down the hill. "We had to port down there and run up because the ward thing was messed up."

Paisley put her hands on her hips. "Let's see where this goes."

As soon as we started walking, we were flanked by our guards.

Bethany turned to look at Mac, "where does this lead?"

Mac shook his head. "I don't know. Guarding the palace is before my time."

"Is there a lake at the bottom?" Crissy asked.

Daxx stopped walking. "A lake?"

Crissy nodded. "I keep seeing water." She made a face, "not in a good way."

"Oh jeeze." Bethany whispered.

"I have had enough of swimming to last a few lifetimes." Paisley said her eyes huge.

Autumn nodded. "I don't know how to swim."

Crissy looked at her for a moment. "I think we all need to learn how to swim."

Kara sighed, "is that one of those hints, but not a warning because it would change things?"

Nodding, Crissy started walking again. "I just have to figure out how rocks float."

Alona looked at Daxx, then started after her. "Floating rocks?"

"Yes." Crissy didn't look back, "I asked Victor and he said maybe it was a metaphor." She glanced back at Alona, "I don't see metaphors."

Paisley groaned, "bad water and floating rocks."

"Do we tell the men this?" I asked.

Daxx shook her head. "They have enough going on right now, better to let them stay on task."

Crissy stopped again, then her shoulders dropped, "maybe it's not here." She stared at the ground. "There's a woman and a bus."

"A bus?" Autumn looked around. "I don't think we have buses over here, do we?"

Alona shrugged, "I have no idea. First thing I'm doing when we have our freedom back is going on a tour of this realm we rule over."

Daxx nodded, "That. I had to approve a report, or finding," she shook her head, "I don't know what it was. Troy was busy at the cells and someone showed up at his office with a clipboard full of papers." She blew out a breath, "Troy said I did the right thing, but it would be helpful if I understood things."

"Another reason I can't wait for Rena to take over all the *reports* that flood Chase's desk." Alona glanced to Daxx, "most of them are trivial and not need to know." Groaning, she pulled her phone out of her pocket and answered it. "Hey." She gave Alona a wide-eyed look, then shrugged, "we're just out for a walk." She nodded, "yes, all of us—guards included." She turned and looked up the hill at the palace, "just outside the palace." She looked at the ground and all around our feet, "how would I know that? Are there markers or something telling us where the ward starts?" She glanced at Bethany, who shrugged in reply. "I am." She rolled her eyes. "How's it going over there?" She listened for a moment, then nodded. "There has to be a door or something." She stiffened, "okay I'll see you when you get back." She tucked the phone back in her pocket. "They can't find anything over there, no visible entrance."

"Maybe they should have taken us, or at least Reagan so the most likely invisible entrance can be found." Kara said with a scoff.

Daxx nodded, "Yeah, but they'll have to figure that out on their own." She started walking again.

I couldn't help looking over the countryside as we went. It was a thing of beauty. I decided right then I was staying in Alterealm. Not that I had a choice really, with a dying mate I had to figure out how to help—without letting the rest of the family know. I was here to stay. I stopped so quickly Bethany walked into me.

"What is it?" She hissed.

I stood looking at a group of trees to our left, white haze floated above the ground. "Is there actual mist up here?"

Autumn came over and stood beside me and looked at the trees. "I don't see any fog or mist." She flipped her hood back and pushed up her sleeves.

"What color?" Daxx came up quietly.

"White." I whispered.

"Oh good, not a mage." Bethany moved past us, Paisley at her side, both of their hands were raised. "Maybe it's just a cloaking." She whispered.

"Can you do something with that?" Paisley asked quietly.

Bethany nodded and moved closer, then started to wave her hands around.

The white mist intensified as she did, but when she stopped there was a woman hunched down beside the tree.

The guards went past us quickly, swords drawn.

The woman looked up, her eyes were a pale purple.

"Wait." Daxx pushed past Tim and Sith, "Wanda?"

"Oh my goodness, my huntress queen." The woman dropped to the ground in a dramatic display of what I think was meant to be a curtsy. "I am so glad it's you."

Daxx waved her hand so the guards would back up. Slumping her shoulders briefly, she went over and put her hand on Wanda's head. "Get up and tell me what you're doing here."

Wanda stood up. Her eyes were no longer purple, but one was blue and the other green. She put her hands over her mouth, then dropped them. "I went into hiding—as you know." She nodded, "and Clairee said it's safe now that..." Her eyes filled with the look of fear.

"He's locked up for eternity in the cells."

Wanda whooshed out a breath. "Oh good. I went into hiding but if Marcus is apprehended, he can't harm me now." She looked relieved, then smiled at Paisley, bowing her head. "Princess, I was at the ball. I still hum that song often."

Paisley chuckled, "good to hear." She looked around us. "So, why are you hiding in the trees?"

Her mouth gaped open, "right." She looked out the ground for a second, then sighed. "I've been disguising myself, since," she nodded and motioned to Daxx, "that happened." She looked at Paisley for a moment, then back to Daxx, "they tried to recruit me." She whispered. "I was going to tell Clairee, then thought—" she bit her lip briefly, "what if I find out more information." She motioned into the trees, "so I followed them, cloaked." She nodded. "I panicked and came back, that's when you found me."

Daxx studied her for a moment, then pointed in the direction she did. "What's in there?"

Wanda turned and looked at it, "some kind of cave in the hillside. They went in, no one came back out."

"Should we call the guys?" Alona asked.

Daxx glanced at her, then looked back through the trees. "Let's take a look first." She nodded, "I don't want to drag them here for nothing." Tim gave her a hard look. "I'll call them after we look, Tim, relax."

"I just don't want another scene like after that apartment." He grimaced, "our kings are quite fierce when it comes to you ladies."

Alona made a sound of annoyance. "We'll protect you from the backlash."

Sith turned and looked at Tim, then to Alona, "I just don't want to be on the wrong side of a cell wall."

Alona grinned, "it will be fine."

Daxx motioned to one of the other guards. "Keep Wanda with you."

"Oh," Wanda piped up, "I could help." She gave Daxx a sheepish look, "now that I'm not alone."

Daxx considered it, then looked at the guard again, "anything happens, Felix, you get Wanda out of here."

"My queen." He inclined his head.

"Okay," Bethany raised her hands, bright orange arced off her hands, "let's go look."

"Oh, that's marvelous." Wanda exclaimed quietly, "Clairee told me you were a natural witch, but to see it."

181

"Focus." Daxx looked at her.

"Right." Wanda bobbed her head, "of course."

We moved quietly through the trees until there were only a few scattered about. Daxx squatted down, then looked over her shoulder at me. "Reagan, do you see anything?"

Keeping low, I moved up to crouch beside her and then looked where she pointed. It was a small cave entrance mostly covered by overgrowth of plants. Almost covering the entrance was thick swirling green haze. "Green." I whispered, "a lot of green."

All of us crowded around Daxx, staying low to the ground and silent.

Daxx looked over her shoulder, then sighed, "okay, I'm calling." She turned the other way, "Sith go stand out on the road, then the men can find you."

Sith nodded, then darted back into the trees.

Daxx sighed again and pulled out her phone. She looked at Alona and rolled her eyes. "Hey. So, we found something." She dropped her head down, then sighed again, "just listen. On our walk we found Wanda," she nodded, "yes that Wanda." She shook her head, "she found a cave and Reagan sees a lot of green..." She glared at Alona, "outside the palace, where Kara shot the arrows that time." She nodded, "Sith is standing on the road waiting for you." She held out the phone and looked at it. "I better get bonus points for calling them." She mumbled and put the phone in her pocket again.

Not much time passed before we could hear the men moving through the trees. Autumn turned and looked at them when they came into sight. "You guys need to practice stealth."

"Just out for a walk—in full gear?" Rafael looked at Kara's bow, then at her.

Kara shrugged and offered him no explanation.

Michael gave Autumn a look, then went over and squatted down next to her. He turned to look at me. "You still seeing green?"

I looked at the cave. "Very thick green."

Quinton was right beside me. "That means there's some mage crap going on right now."

Emil was on my other side suddenly. "Let's go see what they're up to."

Quinton nodded, then reached behind him and pulled out his swords. "Better than wandering around some building looking for a door that's not there." He mumbled.

Bethany moved back in the group until she was beside Wanda. "Can you keep watch on the entrance? Do something showy if any of them come out?"

Wanda hesitated, then nodded.

"Good, okay." She turned to one of the guards, "Mac, you stay with her, dial into the group and shout if anyone but us come back out or someone is trying to come in."

Mac nodded and pulled out his phone.

I watched a few of the others pull out their phones, then did the same as Quinton watched me. Before I put the earpiece in I gave him a look that I hoped told him to be careful. Reaching over, I put my hand on his chest near his heart. His brown eyes searched my face for a moment, then he nodded. Putting the earpiece in, I tapped the screen on my phone to connect. Opening the pouch at my side, I pulled out the surujin, then glanced around to see everyone was ready.

"Stealth." Autumn hissed into the mic.

I took that to mean for the men to move silently.

Even Daxx nodded and hunched down as she started moving toward the cave entrance.

Bethany held up her hand when we got there. With a quick look at Leone, she stood up and moved her hand down over herself. She disappeared from our sight.

"Just look." Leone's voice came through the earbud.

Someone made a gasping noise through it, I glanced around to see it was none of us on the outside.

Bethany reappeared. "There's about twenty men in there." She whispered, then looked at Leone, "heavily armed." She gave Michael a hard look, "there's boxes and crates all along the one wall."

"Any water?" Crissy asked.

Bethany shook her head. "No water."

"Oh good." Paisley whispered.

I looked at the entrance again, it wasn't that big. The hillside it was in wasn't large either.

Kara nodded and looked at me, like she understood what I was thinking.

"Reagan," I turned to see Michael looking at me, "stay to the back and tell us if you see any portals."

I nodded.

"And any mages or witches inside." Quinton said quietly. "Paisley and Beth will deal with them until we can send them to the cells."

"Are we going through any portals if they're there?" Daxx turned to look up at Troy.

Troy paused for a moment, "only after we deal with those inside." He said

Daxx nodded, "got it." She turned to Alona, "you and Criss get to the portal to make sure none of them escape through it."

Alona nodded. Crissy bent down and pulled the long blade from the strap on her leg.

Arius came back to the group. "Intake cells are ready." He tapped his screen and then put the phone in his pocket and zipped it up.

"Fight well, brother." Chase said.

"Same, brother, no injuries today." Troy replied.

"Let's party." Daxx whispered and started moving toward the entrance.

I went in after everyone else, two guards, Alona and Crissy were with me. The others must have moved with lightning speed because they were all over the large cavern, weapons swinging and the sound of metal on metal rang out all around me. I quickly sought out Quinton and watched as he took on a man his size. They were both wielding only one sword, I glanced around his feet to see his second sword on the ground. I frowned wondering if he'd voluntarily relinquished it or if he wasn't as fully charged as he led his siblings to believe. I looked around him, checking if his health was bad and felt a small measure of relief when I didn't see the tell-tale signs. Someone touched my arm, I turned to see Alona motioning in front of us. I'd momentarily forgotten my mission. Nodding, I moved further into the cave and looked all around. It wasn't hard to locate the source of a high concentration of magic, as the green haze became almost a solid object between two men standing with large axes on either side of it. I pointed.

Alona's shoulder dropped. "Problem with Criss and I watching the portal. Battle axes." She said calmly into the mic.

There were a few sounds of annoyance as replies.

"Arius and I will dispatch them." Victor stated. I watched him weave through the bodies trying to cause injury to each other.

"At least they're not giants." Arius said in a breathless way.

"Any mages or witches?" That was Paisley.

I dragged my eyes away from the men fighting against the portal guards to look around the cave. "I don't see white or any other green."

"Good." Quinton grunted into the mic.

"Paize," that was Daxx, "behind me," she growled in annoyance, "there's some man huddled in the corner like a scared cat." I watched her duck under the swing of some man, then she came up behind him.

"Detain him." Michael said quickly.

"On it." Paisley ran over to the darkened area behind Daxx. "Hey, it's okay. Just stay there."

"I've got her back." Bethany said.

I tried to see in the corner. "Going to check if he's— magic." I said, not knowing how else to say it.

"I've got you covered." That was Kara.

I glanced to see her standing near the entrance with her bow drawn, aiming it in Daxx's direction.

I ran over, sticking to the outer edge of the cave until I was close enough to make out the man hidden in the shadows. I looked right at him, then around him. "He's not magic."

"He's wearing a stabilizer, Arius." Paisley squatted down beside the man and was holding his wrist.

"Ours?" Arius grunted.

"No." Paisley looked at me, then back to the man. He was saying something, but wasn't loud enough we could hear it.

A motion beside me had me turn, a larger man was heading toward us, I swung the surujin out and wrapped it around his leg. He went down.

"Michael." Paisley said.

I turned to see her standing in front of the man with her hand out.

"I've got him." Michael came running out, with the box in his hand.

Paisley lowered her hand and squatted back down.

The man disappeared.

"He says they're holding his wife hostage…"

"Someone's coming." It was Mac's voice. "A man with a woman, her hands are bound."

"Mac, you engage him." That was Victor.

"Mac, get Wanda to get the woman and cloak them in the trees." Bethany hissed out a breath.

"Will do." Mac replied.

I gathered up my surujin and turned to see Bethany send a man flying back with the fire balls from her hand. Leone grinned at his mate, then used one of the boxes. There was a sound of a grunt, then the cave was silent. Sounds of panting and a sudden quiet were all I could hear through the earpiece.

Troy and Chase both came toward Paisley and I. Paisley nodded to the man and he stood up slowly.

"They have my wife." He stated, his voice shaking. "If I don't let them use my place, they're going to hurt her."

Troy nodded and glanced at Chase. "Mac?"

"I'm holding him on the ground." Mac reported.

"I'll go." Michael darted for the door.

"Have Wanda, bring the woman in here." Daxx glanced toward the cave entrance.

"Okay, they're coming." Mac said breathlessly.

When they came in the man darted toward them, "Chelsea." He called as he ran. She jolted and ran toward him, then they collided in a hug.

"His wife." Paisley said, glancing at Arius.

"You guys need to look in these." Quinton said.

Everyone turned to see him and Rafael opening boxes. "Enough supplies for an army."

"Is anyone else annoyed that they've been this close to the palace and we never caught on?" Daxx asked as she went over to look.

"I guess they still intended to reside in it someday." Leone said.

Michael came back, Mac wasn't with him so I assumed he was standing guard outside. "Sir," Michael went over to the man with his wife.

"Dean." The man told him.

Michael inclined his head, "where is your place?"

Dean kept his arm around his wife. "I don't know where this is." He looked all around the cave, "but whatever that is," he pointed to the portal that Victor still stood by, "it takes you out to my warehouse." He looked at his wife for a moment. "I refinish boats, so I have a large warehouse I work at near the harbor."

"Water." Crissy said.

Michael looked at her for a moment. "You've seen this?"

Crissy bit her lip, then shook her head. "No, not that kind of water." She glanced over at Victor, "I don't think this was a harbor in my head, or the floating rocks."

"Floating rocks?" Rafael hissed out a breath.

"Focus people." Daxx went over to the man. "How many are in your warehouse?"

Rubbing his hand across his brow, he closed his eyes for a moment. "A lot. They come and go constantly."

Troy turned to Michael, "get him pictures of all the top players and see if he recognizes any of them."

Michael nodded, and pulled out his phone.

Chase turned around and looked at Alona. "Duchess, go back with Sith and get Romulus and Clairee here." He glanced at Victor, "we don't want that closed yet, but we need someone to check it out."

Alona nodded and went over to Sith.

"Are there men or women in your warehouse with different colored eyes?" Bethany asked Dean.

He nodded. "There's one man," he looked at his wife, "we thought him to be a bit strange, or wearing colored contacts."

"A mage." Quinton said coming back over to the group.

I studied him and saw the faint reddish hue surrounding him. I gave him a look that I'm sure he interpreted the right way, when he scowled down at me, then turned to look at Dean.

"How long have they been using your warehouse?"

"For many months." Chelsea answered for him.

The twin kings exchange a look.

"Is there any other family they can use against you?" Alona asked with a calm patient tone.

Dean shook his head. "No, it's just us."

Chase nodded, then turned to one of the guards. "Bronx, you and Bart take them to one of the safe houses until this is over," he glanced at Derian, who nodded, "and make sure there's a guard there."

"We need people on the other end of this." Daxx motioned to the portal. "Surround them before the rest of us go through." She turned back to Dean. "Is the portal always open or is there someone on the other end opening it?"

Dean shook his head quickly, "I don't see them do anything when they're in my shop, just walk *through* the wall then come out here."

Daxx turned to Victor, "we need guards stationed here, lots of them until we go over," she turned to Troy, "we'll need to plan this out."

Troy raised both his brows and looked at her. "I agree," he gave her a curious look, "never thought I'd hear those words from your lips, but yes we need to get others in place on the other end." He pointed to the portal.

Daxx shrugged, "I don't like going in blind and having no idea what I'm charging into."

Chase chuckled. "You might be wearing off on her, brother king."

"Har-har." Daxx looked from one king to the other. "Less talk. We need the address of this warehouse and to round up the teams." She nodded her head slowly and turned to Autumn, "then we can kick some butt."

Autumn nodded, then lifted her hands and waved them around, "what are we doing lollygagging around here? Let's get moving people."

Bethany held her hand out, "good use of the word. High five."

Autumn tapped her palm against Bethany's, "who would have thought I'd win in a word game."

Paisley shrugged, "I need to up my game."

Chapter Twenty-Two

I paused outside his door with my hand in the air. I knew how this was going to go. After the very informative discussion with the Alterealm princesses, I needed to try. I knocked firmly against the ornate wood.

"Yeah." Quinton called from inside.

I opened the door and went in, pushing the door slowly closed behind me. Quinton stood in the middle of the large room putting his leather vest on.

"Rea, is something wrong?" He shrugged into it, then stood there looking at me.

I shook my head, "not what you think." I took a deep breath, then let it whoosh out, "I think it might be a good idea if you stayed out of the fray today—if possible."

Gone was his concerned expression. It was replaced with a hard stare as he put his hands on his hips. "That, right there, is why my brothers don't know."

"I have kept my word and not told anyone." I said with resolve. "I just saw how quickly you become drained and today we don't know what we're taking on."

"We have people watching the warehouse right now, getting us numbers." He did up the vest while eyeing me.

I didn't know how to broach the subject of a blood bond. It was hard enough talking to the other women, without explaining why. The moment I'd heard that Chase had been able to connect with Alona and help her, and give Daxx a boost of strength through it, I knew it was what I needed with Quinton. I didn't know if I could actually figure out the mechanics, but I had to try.

"What's on your mind?" He came toward me. "I can see the wheels turning up there." He tapped the side of his head.

"That transparent, am I?"

He shrugged, "or I've just had a few hundred years of observing people."

"A few." I smile briefly. I decided to just say it. "The women were talking about the benefits of a blood bond…" his brows drew together turning his expression into a scowl, "I wondered if that was something that would benefit us—" I motioned to him, "you."

I watched his chest as he inhaled slowly. "You think you can work the blood bond and send me what—" he motioned in the air, "healing energy through it."

I nodded, then shrugged, "I don't know, but I think it's worth a try." I lifted my hands, "you won't let me try this," I lowered them and gave him a stern look, "I've never been sick a day in my life, so clearly my ability is more than just my touch." I moved to close the space between us.

Quinton stood there, a mere foot separating us. The emotions going through his eyes were flashes as he thought it through. I wasn't about to speak and disrupt his process. I honestly pictured him shooting me down before I uttered a complete sentence. "I don't know, Rea."

Him using my given name in a such a soft tone meant more to me than I had ever imagine it could. "Surely a small amount of your blood can't cause harm to someone with healing running in hers."

"I don't like the idea of you being distracted because of me." He huffed out a breath.

"I'm distracted watching you as it is." I gave him an earnest look, "your skill at combat is both remarkable and terrifying." I bit my lip, "I was sidetracked wondering if you'd elected to use one sword or didn't have the strength to wield two in that cave."

He shrugged one shoulder, "it was a matter of space to move." He rubbed his hand over his jaw, "I didn't want to hit one of my own brothers or their mates with two swinging."

I opened my mouth, then closed it quickly. "I hadn't considered that." I inhaled through my nose and then blew it out, "but perhaps a bond would help so I don't pause to deliberate your motives." He was still not sold. "Don't think I'm doubting your ability as a warrior or stamina, in any way—I would just like to know if you run into trouble or are injured." I moved to close the space between us and placed my hand over his heart. "If you were injured, your brothers would insist I heal you," I tilted my head to the side and continued to look up at him, "we both know that's not as simple as they believe."

"It could kill you to try." He said with a gravelly voice.

"I know. I understand that now. Your fear of what will happen to me." I said softly.

"I'm not willing to take that chance." He said in a low tone.

"I understand." I had no more words to try to convince him. "So, how does this work?" I gave him a curious look, "the blood bond. Do we drip it into cups like vampires or—"

He grinned. "No." He huffed out a breath, "but it does involve fangs and to be honest with you, I don't know if I'm strong enough to just take a taste of your blood."

I raised my eyebrows, "says the man that's been powering through a gradual death unnoticed by others."

He snorted softly, "I didn't say it's been easy."

"And yet you continue to do it."

His eyes were locked on mine. "I have no choice."

I couldn't look away from him if it had been dire that I needed to. "Do this for me, for my sanity." I tried to smile and failed, "I haven't the time you've had to adjust to this."

The serious expression in his eyes lightened to something close to humor. "That's a pretty lame line."

I grinned. "Social interaction is a new thing for me, I'm faking it completely."

He chuckled softly, "I've noticed." He nodded slowly, "I spent a hundred years wandering alone, so I get it." Taking a deep breath, he blew it out and undid his vest.

I dropped my hand away and tried not to stare at his muscled chest, failing once again. "On the outside you are the image of the perfect male."

His mouth quirked, then he sobered again. "You will have to take blood from my chest." He watched me for a reaction, "I'll have to bite you to get yours."

I raised my eyebrows, "is it odd I don't find that frightening?"

He inhaled slowly, then breathed it out, "no, it just means you're definitely of Alterealm blood and my mate."

I watched the battle taking place inside his head through the reflection in his eyes. "Let's do it then. The others are gathering for food before we go over."

He was all business at the mention of that. With an abrupt nod, he reached behind him and pulled out a blade, then paused. "It's been three hundred years since I did this." He stated quietly.

I patted his chest, hiding my own anxiousness, "you look pretty good for an old guy." I joked.

He smirked and shook his head, "we really need to work on your social interaction, Rea, it's rusty."

I rolled my eyes, then sobered immediately as he dragged the blade across his chest.

He touched the back of my head, "I don't heal as fast as my brothers anymore, but let's not let me bleed out."

I jolted and leaned closer, touching the tip of my tongue against the blood running down his skin. The taste wasn't metallic at all, which I noted to think about later. Closing my mouth over the wound on his chest, I sucked gently. Quinton made a soft noise, but held me close, so I continued.

Lifting my head, I watched his chest as it closed slowly. It was a marvel to see. "Was that enough?" I looked up to see him standing there with his eyes closed. He opened them slowly and I felt a rush of heat as he stared down at me with red eyes. "Red is definitely your color." I whispered.

He smiled and I got my first sight of fangs. They didn't frighten me at all.

"You're not afraid of them at all." He stated.

I shook my head, still looking at them. "Quite the opposite." I said with barely any voice at all.

He made a soft growling noise. "This is killing me, in new ways." He stated, then reached and tilted my head to the side. I was like a boneless doll in his hands, willing to let him bend me to his will. He leaned down in slow motion and my heart kicked up to beat faster than ever before. When his breath brushed over my neck, I found myself clutching the arm holding my head. I closed my eyes when he bit into me and felt the tingle of excitement course through my whole body. He lifted his mouth away then sucked on my neck gently. I wanted him to bite me again but knew he wouldn't comply.

When he licked over my neck, and lifted his head, he hugged me against his body. "See," I cleared my throat to find my voice, "you are strong enough."

His chest was rising and falling rapidly. "Barely." He said in a hoarse voice. Squeezing me briefly, he then stepped back and began to button his vest with shaking hands. "We better get down there before they start harassing me." He glanced at me and I was almost disappointed his eyes were brown again. "I'll send you emotions through the bond while we eat so you can see how it works."

I flipped my hair back from my face. "Hopefully I'll be able to figure it out."

Reaching over, he flipped my amulet around, so it was lying flat. "It's all based on emotion and feeling, the stronger the emotion, the easier it is to relay."

I nodded, even though I had no idea what he meant.

Chapter Twenty-Three

"No heroics." Arius' voice came through the earpiece.

"Follow your own advice, babe." Paisley said.

"Someone tell me again why we got left over here in the empty cave?" Daxx turned to glance around at the other women.

"You're coming through the portal." Troy said.

Daxx nodded. "I know, but I wanted to be on the team to breech the warehouse."

"They're just sore because we found the cave and they couldn't even find a door at the asylum." Autumn moved over and stood in front of the portal. Tim and Bronx stood guarding it. "Just shout when we jump in this portal." She said impatiently.

"To clarify," Alona glanced around, "I'm to stay in this empty cave with Sith?"

"We need someone there in case the cowards try to escape." Chase said quietly.

"Wait for our go, ladies," Rafael said in a hushed voice, "we're just going to go in and take a peek in case the numbers are insane."

"I haven't seen any enter since I got up here." Crissy reported. "I think I want to try sailing, Vic."

"Mm, we'll discuss it at a later date, heart." Victor replied quietly.

"Okay." Crissy said quickly.

"Fight well, brothers—and warrior women." Chase said.

"Better than you, brother, now get the damn party started." Daxx growled.

"What she said." Paisley moved to stand in front of the portal with the rest of the women.

I followed her and stood ready, my surujin in hand. My task was one main thing, find magic. Of course, no one else knew I had a secondary to-do—keeping my mate from injury or worse.

"The gang's all here." Leone whispered.

"All, all?" Daxx asked looking more excited.

"Don't see Willis, but there are a lot of big names here from the guest list we've been accumulating." Michael reported.

Daxx and Alona exchanged a look. I was guessing they weren't aware of this list.

"Office is heavily guarded." Quinton said softly.

"Maybe Hubert's in it?" Bethany asked.

"Rest of the team is outside." Arius told us.

"Then we're ready." Chase said.

"Daxx, give us sixty seconds to be well inside, the portal is a busy place, let us draw their attention away so you can get through." Troy said quietly.

Daxx nodded, "We'll give you seventy seconds, chief, 'cuz some of you are slower than the rest." She said with a smirk. "Starting," She pulled her phone out of her pocket and tapped the screen, "now."

"I've never gone into battle with a time limit before." Chase blurted out.

Autumn stared at the phone Daxx held in front of her.

The sounds of fighting came through the earbuds. Autumn nodded her head and faced the portal again.

Daxx put her phone in her pocket and pulled one of the blades off her back.

"Ready or not, here they come." Alona sang out.

Autumn and Daxx went through together, Paisley and Bethany were next. Kara and I went through, followed by the guards. There were men all over the place fighting. Ours were easiest to spot as they were all in black. I doubted that was why they chose to dress that way. Not that I really cared, they all looked like gods of war.

Bethany stopped and pulled out her phone, as she did Paisley held her hand up and looked all around them. When Beth was finished, they reversed roles.

"Connect. I'll cover you." Kara said with her bow up and arrow drawn.

I took out my phone and tapped to rejoin the group call. Tucking it away, I stepped in front of Kara so she could connect. By the time she was done, Bethany and Paisley were nowhere to be found.

The guards behind us were flanking us now. Kara turned and looked at one, "get out there and help them."

I turned and motioned to the ones near me, "go." With reluctant looks, they moved out into the commotion.

"If I'm to be left guarding dismal caves, I want body cams so I can see what's happening." Alona said.

"It's chaos." Crissy said. "I can't even see what is happening."

"Watch," Victor grunted, "the entrances, heart."

"Yes. Okay, Vic." Crissy said quickly.

"Is Daxx on the call?" Troy sounded out of breath.

"I don't think she or Autumn paused when they came through." Bethany said.

"Need a port box." Paisley said.

"Any magic in the building?" Quinton's voice brought me back to the reason I was here.

"Checking." I told him and moved away from Kara.

"I've got your back, Reagan." Kara's soft voice came through the earpiece. "Rafael, watch yours." She said with a note of urgency.

I glanced over to see Rafael standing over a man lying on the floor.

"Thanks, honey." He grinned at her as Leone slid in with a box and the man vanished.

I ducked when Derian and another man fighting got too close. That made me realize I didn't have time to gawk around at my leisure. It also brought back memories of being too close to battles during the wars. I looked to the end of the building near big doors, then tried to not get distracted by Quinton going one on one against a large man. He was using two swords and quite vigorously, I noted and then looked away to check for magic. There was a door at the far end and green haze surrounding it. "Door at the far end from the portal. There's green haze outside it."

"Mage." Quinton growled.

I was suddenly knocked into some stacked crates. The man Derian was fighting stumbled into me.

"Rea?" Quinton said.

I scowled. "I'm fine." Getting up, I swung the surujin and flung it toward the man my guard was fighting. I jerked it and he landed on his face. Rushing over, I kicked him in the face when he tried to get up. "Port box." I growled into the mic.

"Rea has bite." Chase sounded amused.

"Paize, babe, hold the office door shut." Arius went running by me.

"On it." Paisley left Bethany and rushed to the other end.

"Let him be in there." Chase ground out through his teeth.

"Kara, honey, can you go listen by," Rafael made a fierce sound, "that door." he finished in a huff.

"Read my mind." She said quietly and started moving that way. As she went, she released an arrow and a man in her way dropped to the ground. "present for someone with a port box."

"I like cleaning up after you." Michael said and appeared by the man to dispatch him with the box.

Later, I had to ask her what sort of arrows she used that rendered her targets unconscious.

A noise had me turning to see a man rushing toward the portal. I lurched in his direction, the surujin swinging. Releasing it, I tugged when it connected and pulled his leg out from under him. Victor stepped into my sight and used his box on the man. He rushed back into the fray before I could blink.

"Daxx is down." Bethany said.

I looked, then spotted her across the room. She was on her knees hunched over holding her arm against her stomach. "I've got her." I told any listening. Bethany stood over her, with her hands out and large bright arcs of orange and red coming off them. I'd seen her knock a man down with small balls, so I could only believe anyone getting too close would be knocked to Timbuktu, or further.

By the time I weaved through the crowd of bodies, Troy was taking on any man that got too close. I nodded to Bethany as I knelt down. She gave me a worried look and moved further away. Pulling off one of my gloves I tried to assess what was wrong. There was no blood.

"A damn pipe." Daxx growled, "he whacked my shoulder with a damn pipe."

Troy glanced over his shoulder at us, his eyes were red as he checked over his mate.

I struggled to get the jacket undone and expose the flesh, Daxx hissed out a breath trying to help me.

"Get me back in the game, Reagan." She said breathlessly.

"I'm going to try." I placed my hands around her shoulder and exhaled slowly. "It's not broken." I could tell by the draw against my hands.

"Troy. Find that jerk with the pipe and hold him for me." Daxx barked.

"Sorry, sister," Rafael said, "I think Leone just sent him to the cells."

Daxx hissed in annoyance. "I'm still smacking him with a pipe."

"I can't keep up with whatever this mage is doing." Kara said in a panicked tone.

"My love, has Romulus arrived at the cave?" Chase asked.

"He has." Alona replied.

"Shove him through the portal, a guard will be there to greet him." Chase said quickly, then ran past where we knelt.

"Reagan." Quinton's hard tone vibrated in my ear.

I lifted my hands away and blew out a breath. Daxx lifted her arm and nodded.

"I'm good to go." She started to get up.

"Better connect to the call." I told her as Troy hovered over her.

She rolled her eyes and quickly did so.

I picked up my surujin and then a hand appeared in front of me. Pulling one glove on, I took Quintons hand, stood up, then quickly put the other one on.

His gaze moved over my hair, then face. "You good?"

I nodded. "It was just bruising mostly." I looked above his head, then connected with his eyes again. "You good?"

He smirked. "Of course." He motioned with his head, "go cover Kara while she listens in on that mage."

I nodded and went that way.

"Getting tired of staring at the door." Paisley said in an annoyed tone.

"Romulus is here." Rafael said, "Kara, mute your mic so you can relay to Romulus the words you catch."

"Okay." Kara replied.

I went over and stood beside Paisley, my back to the door and watched that no one came close to either one.

"Truck pulling up by the big doors." Crissy said with concern.

"They're not here for the boat refinishing." Leone said in with a shortness of breath.

"Quinton, Arius, cover the doors." Victor said in a flat tone. I glanced over to see if he was even fighting as he didn't sound out of breath. He was with calculating control and I felt sorry for anyone going against him.

"On it." Arius said.

Kara's voice came back over the earpiece, "the casting thoughts have stopped." she was quiet for a second, "I think there's someone in there that interrupted him."

"Oh, let it be Willis." Michael said in a lethal tone. "Bethany, Rafael, get on that door." Michael grunted a few times, "wait for Victor and I to get there, Paisley, then release it."

"Romulus is ready. Said there was some spell on the door, he took it down." Kara reported.

I glanced back to see she had her bow ready again and raised toward the door.

"Reagan and I will watch your backs." Daxx came running over and stood by me.

"Sparky, when I say, blast that door with all you have." Chase said.

"My king, keep your ass away from that door." Alona said.

"What she said, Troy. You and Chase need to be clear of it." Daxx said.

"What?" Chase didn't sound happy.

"They're right, my brother kings." Victor sounded commanding. "You cannot be anywhere near Arwan."

"Come help us." Arius said. "Fresh bodies have arrived."

There was a growl of annoyance, but no verbal rebuke.

I watched the kings go toward the door where Arius and Quinton were fighting five men. I was silently relieved they went to help. Taking a deep breath, I searched to see if I could feel if Quinton was fatigued. I felt something but couldn't be sure. I saw a slight hue around him, but not enough to warrant any intervention.

"Okay, Paisley, on three." Michael said.

I wanted to turn around and watch but didn't want to leave Paisley's back open to anyone attacking her.

"One." Michael's tone was hushed, "two."

"I'll freeze anyone inside." Paisley said and moved behind me.

"Three." Michael growled into the mic.

I stepped back so I could watch both the people on this side of the door and anyone nearby. I caught Bethany flinging her hands toward the door and the sound of shattering wood echoed in my ear with the earpiece and the one without. There was a rush of bodies at the door, I wasn't able to see what was in the room.

A shout beside me had me turn in time to see one of our guards rushing at a man running for the portal. With fast steps, I headed toward him and released the chain my hand. Jerking on it, the man only stumbled for a second, but I'd bought the guard enough time to get himself between the portal and him.

"He just vanished." Daxx's voice had me glance back to the office.

"Had to be a porter." That was Kara, "mages can't just vanish right?"

I looked at the mage beside her. Romulus was nodding.

"Brothers," Victor voice was loud, "I just dispatched Willis Hubert to our cells."

"Yeah." Arius cheered, "just the celebrity I've been wanting to entertain."

"Arwan?" Quinton asked.

"He ported out." Daxx stated.

"Shit." Quinton again. "We could use a hand cleaning up the last few." He didn't sound amused.

I turned to see four men left and most of those looking in the direction of the door Bethany had blown off its hinges. The trace around Quinton was getting brighter. Ignoring my own light-headedness, I rushed in his direction with the chain spinning. When I was close enough, I sent it flying at the ankle of the man trying to chop him to bits. I jerked on it and the man went down, meeting Quinton's knee as he raised it in anticipation of what he knew I would do. The man bounced off it and slumped to the floor.

"Port box." Quinton said breathlessly.

I looked him over, he even looked exhausted now. I nodded to him, and hoped he'd step back and let his brothers finish up. A slight dizziness had me put my hand to my head.

Quinton scowled and came over immediately. "You all right?"

I nodded. "Too much excitement after helping, Daxx."

He made a sound of annoyance. "I'm taking Reagan back over, she hit those crates pretty hard."

"We'll see you at the dining room shortly." Troy said.

"Quick snack then to the cells." Arius stated.

Daxx came over to me. "Thanks for getting me back up." she looked at my hair. "You'll be okay?"

I pulled a section of my hair to where I could see it. It was barely streaked. I nodded. "Yes. It's nothing a hot tea and biscuit won't fix."

"Duchess, we've decided to leave the portal open for the time being. If Arwan doesn't close it we may catch a few strays wandering through to the cave." Chase said.

"Leave Sith here until a watch arrives?" Alona asked.

"Yes. Derian is coming to keep him company." Rafael said.

"Cristy. I'll see you at home." Victor said.

"Okay, Vic. Porting home now." Crissy told him.

Quinton paused to watch Michael look in the boxes stacked up along the wall. "Send a team to bring that home, Michael."

Michael turned around and nodded. "My thoughts exactly, there's food here and other items we can distribute."

"I'd like some of it to go to shelters on this side." Paisley said.

"As you wish, babe." Arius nodded to me as he went over toward her.

"Ready?"

I looked up at Quinton and nodded as I stepped closer to him and put my hands on his arm.

Chapter Twenty-Four

"I can't believe you don't even have a bruise." Daxx said over her shoulder.

I caught up to Daxx as she went around the corner of the cell. She stopped suddenly as Troy walked by us going the other direction.

"Troy?"

He kept going. She watched him for a moment, then hurried in the direction we'd been going.

When we stepped into the area outside the cell Nathas had been in, the others were all there. Kara stood in the center shaking her head.

"What happened?" Daxx asked.

I looked at the wall to the cell, but no one was visible.

Chase stared at it. "It's not him." He said quietly without looking away from the wall.

"That's not Willis Hubert?" Daxx demanded loudly.

"Oh, its him." Rafael answered.

"Then..." she looked at a few others, "what do you mean it's not him?"

Quinton crossed his arms over his chest. "It's not him running the show, Daxx." He looked at her, "Arwan's plan, Willis was only brought in to recruit."

I felt anger, almost rage. I knew it wasn't my own and looked at him. His brown eyes were already watching me. He'd intended to share that.

"He," Daxx's mouth dropped open, she turned to Kara, "you're sure?" She looked at Arius, "Troy saw it?"

Arius nodded.

"I didn't see it." Crissy said with disappointment in her voice

"Even you, my heart could not have seen this coming." Victor told her as he put his arm around her.

Daxx shook her head and went over to a panel and did something on it. The wall revealed an older rounded man. She hadn't made it so we could hear him, but sound wasn't required as he was in the center of the cell, doubled over laughing hysterically.

"Damn." Daxx whispered, then changed the wall again. "Two hours." She said bluntly. "Two hours and we go to the asylum." She nodded and started walking quickly from the room, "I've had enough fail for today."

Everyone had left to go about whatever they needed to do until it was time to go over to the asylum. I had nothing to do. It took ten minutes to realize I wasn't able to rest in my room. My mind was going at top speed and with the flurry of thoughts came energy I couldn't contain. I tried the stairs at the palace, running up and down them. Anyone who saw me gave me the kind of look you'd give a lunatic.

I ported to the girl's office in the chambers, then decided the only thing I could do was run off the thoughts threatening to consume me.

"Reagan?" Quinton called after me.

I stopped and wiped the sweat off my forehead.

"What's wrong?" He closed the difference between us.

I swallowed, trying to catch my breath. "Running off some," I flipped my hand in the air, "energies."

"Energies?" He gave me an odd look.

"Yes. Anger, frustration, annoyance..."

"Those are feelings." He put his hands on his hips.

I nodded. "Yes, they are giving me all the wrong kind of energies."

His look changed to concern. "What's happened?"

I debated on hitting him. Actually, raising my hand and hitting him as hard as I could. "What's happened?" I scowled at him. "You're irreparable, I'm in Alterealm trying to help find a madman's pet mage before they take over the world," I paused, "worlds. I can't go outside and breathe fresh air without a guard and people are calling me princess and practically bowing to me."

He rubbed the back of his neck and glanced down the hallway, "they're calling you that because you're wearing a royal family amulet." He lowered his voice even though the hall was empty, "you are a princess."

Putting my hands on my hips, I stared at him, "I am not." I lifted the pendant and then let it drop again, "we are not married, or mated or anything, Quinton. I may be your intended mate, but I'm fairly certain a single kiss doesn't seal the deal."

He looked like he wanted to smirk, but then sobered quickly. "We can't." A haunted expression came over his face, "I can't." Shaking his head, he stepped closer and leaned down so there was barely air between us. "To bind you to me as my mate would cause you too much pain." Lifting his head, a look of resolve filled his eyes, "I'm dying, leaving a mate behind is condemning them to madness and grief." His gaze moved over my face. "I won't do that to you."

"And that's it. End of discussion? I'm supposed to bow my head and accept it?" I was charged again and would need to run longer I decided.

"I can't change it. I'm sorry." He started to reach toward my face, then dropped his hand and shoved it in his pocket. "We're going over to the asylum in an hour. You should save some energy."

I nodded. "I'm aware of the plan. I'll be ready." I backed up a few steps, watching him, waiting for him to say more. It was obvious he wouldn't, I turned around and started jogging again.

"Anyone see anything?" Leone sounded anxious.

"There are no doors or entrances that are for a basement." Paisley said.

"And you ladies thought we were just slacking." Rafael chuffed.

"Not slacking," Kara said, "you should have brought Reagan though."

"Then we wouldn't have gotten bored enough to port all over Alterealm and find the cave." Bethany said.

"I see nothing from up here." Crissy said.

"Where are you?" That was Daxx.

"I climbed a tree." Crissy stated, "I wanted to see if I could see something from up here."

"Cristy, come down." Victor said quietly.

"Oh hi, Vic." Crissy said, "I'll be right down."

"Reagan, have you checked the whole exterior?" Arius asked.

I stood back and looked at the back of the building. "Quinton and I have walked all around it, there's no haze that I can see."

"Let's expand the search area." Victor said.

"I agree." Chase said quickly.

"Maybe it's inside the building." Bethany motioned to Leone for them to start walking to the left.

Quinton and I watched them walk away. He started going in the other direction, I followed. We were walking into a forested area.

"It would be too complicated for them to come and go." Troy stated, "We already discussed that possibility with Lucina and Alodia confirmed it."

"Alodia?" Daxx asked.

"The nurse, other nurse we have on the inside." Chase answered.

"Maybe there's a marker or something." Paisley mused, "like the stone arch in the wasteland."

"Anything could be a marker." Alona said softly.

Quinton and I looked at each other for a second, then to the trees. "There's a lot of trees here, it could be one in hundreds." He told them.

"Just shout if you see something you think I should look at." I told everyone. We were about three feet into the treed area when I glanced down at the ground. I had an idea. It had been several decades since I'd had to track anything, but even in a modern age, the basics would still be the same. I glanced up at Quinton, who frowned down at me for a moment. I motioned to the footprint in the damp soil.

He nodded and we continued walking. "Look for worn paths too." He said into the mic.

The path we were following was worn enough that the grass was trampled. I glanced around, still not seeing any haze. We kept going. We stepped out of a thick area of growth to a small clearing. There was a faint green haze. I nodded to Quinton.

His expression changed to serious. "We may have found something." He whispered.

"What's your location?" Troy asked.

"Back of the building, walk into the trees," I whispered as I paused and looked around to see if the haze was in the whole clearing, "you'll see a path where the grass is trampled."

"You a tracker too?" Leone asked breathlessly.

I smirked. "There weren't always fast food restaurants."

Quinton chuckled softly.

"You used to hunt?" Bethany asked

"I did. Kept my mother and I fed for a few decades." The haze was getting thicker.

"I couldn't hunt." Crissy said.

"Only hunting I'll ever do again is *in* a supermarket." Alona said, "oh wait, no I won't I'm a queen."

"Found the path." Daxx said sounded pleased.

I turned to ask Quinton if we should wait and he wasn't beside me. I turned in a complete circle. "Quinton?"

"What did he do now?" Rafael asked

"He's gone." I turned slowly, trying to see if the haze was thicker in this area. I spotted a stone. There was green haze over it. "The stone." I said and went over to it. I looked to my left then right, nothing. I pulled the surujin out, not feeling comfortable with the situation

"Reagan stay where you are." Emil said, sounding like he was running.

I nodded, as I lifted my foot to lightly tap the stone, thinking it could open or trigger something.

I struggled to sit up. My head was pounding. My phone ringing helped me to snap out of it. I pushed the earpiece and hoped it answered, because I wasn't sure if I could function to get my phone out. "Hello."

"Reagan. Where are you?" It was Paisley.

I looked around in the dim light. "I don't know."

"Is Quinton there?" That was Rafael.

"Quinton?" I rolled onto my hands and knees and tried to focus.

"Where are you?" Daxx told me.

I heard grunting and sounds of a struggle. Pushing to my feet, I took a deep breath and then regretted it. The taste of mildew filled my mouth. "I think we're in the basement." The grunts and sounds of struggle continued, followed by the sound of metal banging together. "Quinton?" I said as loud as I could. "Oh, it better be you." I mumbled. Finally standing, I focused to walk toward the sound, feeling for the pouch on my side at the same time. Stopping, I opened it and felt inside it, then I remembered I had just pulled it out when I ended up here. My foot connected with something, I leaned down and felt around. It was a pipe. "It's so dark in here."

"Use the flashlight on your phone. Access it the same way as when you check your battery." Paisley told me.

Nodding, to myself in the dark, I got the phone out of my pocket and turned on the light. Parts of the walls and other items were scattered all over and it looked worse than it smelled. "I think I liked it better dark." With one hand on my forehead, I held the phone up. "What happened?" The sounds I'd heard had stopped.

"Rea, I'm going to call Quinton's phone, listen for it." Leone said.

"Okay." I stopped where I was and closed my eyes, listening. The faint sound of music echoed. "I hear it." I listened as I started walking. Reaching a door, I looked in. "Keep it ringing. There are halls and doors down here." The music continued. I went in the direction it was coming from and then it stopped.

"Hang on." Leone said.

The ringing started again, I moved faster this time navigating through the rubble and other debris lying on the floor. It was louder when I stuck my head in a door. I shone the light ahead of me and saw him on the floor. "I've got him." I announced to all and hurried to him. Dropping down on the floor, I held the flashlight over his face. He opened his eyes.

"Get him on the call." Troy said in a harsh tone.

The phone rang again, I patted his pocket and found it and pulled it out, then answered the call.

"Brother?" Troy said in a quiet tone.

"Is everyone else okay?" Quinton panted as he spoke.

"We're fine." Arius answered.

I was moving the light up and down his body, when I spotted the blood on the floor. Dropping the phone, I struggled to get the jacket undone, when I opened it, I grabbed the phone again and saw blood covering his abdomen. I jerked my glove off, then switched the phone to the other hand and took off that one.

Quinton grabbed my hand and shook his head. "Where the hell are we?" He squeezed his eyes shut. "Someone come and get Reagan."

"Is he injured?" Victor asked.

"Yes. There's a lot of blood." I answered while glaring at Quinton to release my hand.

"Reagan, use your porter." Michael said in a steady tone.

Quinton shook his head. "I can't...port." He grunted a sound of pain.

"Shit." Michael sounded like he was running. "We're checking in the damned trees for a way in."

"Let me stop the bleeding." I pleaded with him.

He shook his head and held my gaze. We both knew I could end up passed out trying to heal his injury and the damage inside him.

"Just the bleeding." I leaned down closer, so our faces were inches apart and mouthed, *please.*

"Brother, let her slow the bleeding until we find a way in." Chase sounded out of breath.

"Can't." Quinton said with too much conviction.

"Can you port to him Troy, through the connection?" That was Daxx.

"Quinton's mind is on lockdown all the time." Arius said, "he's harder to connect with then Victor."

I stared into the brown eyes locked on mine. He was wordlessly asking me to let it end here. A tear rolled down my cheek. "You stupid, stupid man." I whispered. "What about feeding?" I said louder.

"That could help enough until we find him." Michael said.

"We haven't tried blood since Daxx fixed him." Rafael added.

I looked back to Quinton, he shook his head. "You have a choice, sir, my essence or let me heal it enough to slow the bleeding."

"You tell him, sister." Paisley voice quaked with emotion.

Quinton's brows drew together.

I held his glare, not giving in. "Pick one."

"Quinton. You heard the lady, pick one. That's not a request." Troy said in a very kingly voice.

"Punk." Quinton mumbled, then took out the earpiece and flicked it away from us. With a shaking hand, he reached up and put it behind my head and pulled me down closer.

When he stopped with our faces a few inches apart, I blinked the tears out of my eyes. "Just say yes." I told him and tried to contain the emotional overload that was just under the surface.

"Yes." He whispered breathlessly.

I nodded and dropped the phone and leaned down closer to him, so my neck was near his mouth. When his lips brushed over my throat, I reached down with my other hand with the intention to slow the bleeding while he was occupied.

Quinton grasped my hand in his and held it just as he bit into my neck.

I closed my eyes and tried not to cry. Being close to someone, to him after so long brought too many emotions to the surface—even though he was bleeding to death beneath me. I wanted to cry at the loss I knew was coming because he was stubborn man.

"There has to be a door somewhere." Emil growled out. "Look for cellar entries, they could be overgrown by now."

Quinton licked my neck, then shifted enough that our foreheads were resting against each other.

I felt a tear fall and knew it would bathe his cheek in my sadness. He suddenly squeezed my hand harder and started groaning low. That turned into the male version of a screech of pain. I sat up, "Quinton," I surveyed his body as he withered in pain and tried to see what was wrong.

"What's happening?" Arius asked.

"I don't know. He fed, shouldn't that have helped?" He was almost crushing my hand now. I tried to pull it free, but he wouldn't release it. "Quinton," I leaned down and got right in his face, "what's happening?"

He grit his teeth and opened his eyes briefly. "I don't know. I'm on fire inside." He hissed out.

"Reagan. Use the damn porter, now." That was Michael. "Take him to the courtyard, we'll meet you there with the doctor."

I nodded. "Yes." I grabbed his phone and set it on his chest. Leaning down I kissed his forehead, "I'm porting us to the courtyard." I told him. He moved his head, but he wouldn't release my hand, I took that as acknowledgment and opened the device on my wrist. "Porting now." I told the others. I leaned on top of him as, I pushed the button.

There were people shouting and coming at us from all directions when I opened my eyes.

"Brother let her go, so the doctor can look." That was Arius.

I felt hands on my shoulders, pulling me back. Quinton still wouldn't let go of my hand, so I shuffled to kneel by his head and held his hand between my own. "Let them help you." I said looking down at his face that was filled with so much pain it hurt me.

"Brother, drink." That was Troy.

I looked to see him holding his wrist over his brother's mouth. Quinton's mouth was squeezed together in pain.

"Hurry doc." Autumn said.

The doctor knelt down and pulled his shirt apart, with a cloth, he dabbed at the blood covering his skin. "It's healing." He said with amazement.

"He fed from me." I paused until the doctor looked at me. "Then started screaming. Is my essence harming him? The Solrelm part?" I wiped a hand over my eyes to clear the tears so I could see clearly.

"It shouldn't have any bearing on it." He turned to Rafael, "hand me that case."

Rafael hurried over and grabbed a fair-sized black case and brought it over.

"Portable ultrasound." The doctor said as he opened it up. "The charge is only good for about three minutes, but it was help me see where the issue is."

Quinton was absolutely still now, his face was more relaxed. I hoped that meant the pain was subsiding.

The doctor put gel on Quinton's abdomen, then gave Rafael a nod. Rafael switched the machine on. I looked at the small screen, had no idea what I was seeing, so I watched the doctors face instead.

"That can't be." He said quietly, then moved the wand over to the other side of Quinton's stomach. He stopped and looked at the machine, then reached over and smacked his hand on top of it. "This can't be right."

"How bad is it?" Daxx asked.

"What do you see?" Autumn was staring at the monitor.

"I don't see any damage, aside from the laceration that seems to be slowly closing." The doctor said with a strange look on his face.

"That's good then." Leone said, nodding.

The doctor leaned back and switched off the machine, then looked up at Troy. "You don't understand." He glanced to Quinton, a hesitant look on his face. Despite the glare Quinton was giving him, he continued. "Your brothers internal—state has slowly been decaying over the past," he gave Quinton an apologetic look, "hundred years. Nothing I've tried has been successful." He motioned to Quinton's exposed upper body. "I don't see any decay now."

Quinton's head snapped to look at him. "What?"

"My prince, I don't see the damage that was there on last weeks scans." The doctor shook his head, his face filled with awe.

"How?" Quinton whispered.

"Damn, Reagan, what kind of essence do you have?" Rafael asked loudly.

I opened my mouth, then closed it. "I don't know."

"It could have the healing properties as her touch does." The doctor said quietly.

Quinton finally released my hand but rested his hand on my knee instead. I started to brush back his sweat-soaked hair, then froze. There were markings on my hand, I turned it over and looked at it, then shoved up my sleeve. "I don't want to be dramatic, but I've grown a tattoo." I said in shock.

Quinton lifted his hand in the air and looked at it.

"You marked her." Leone sounded amused.

"I did not." Quinton turned his head and looked up at me. "You marked me." He said with a blank look on his face.

"I—" I looked around at the others than back to him, "have no idea how to go about that." I finished quickly.

"I've heard of accidental markings, but there's usually less clothes and no blood involved." Chase said with a smirk.

Quinton pushed up onto his elbows and looked at the doctor. "Marking healed Bethany and Autumn, is that what happened here?"

The doctor stared at him for a moment. "I can't be sure, but," he pointed to Quinton's stomach, "that is not like what we saw last week. I'd like to run some tests…"

Quinton lifted his hand so the doctor would stop talking. "I'm not dying now?"

The doctor nodded slowly, "from the glimpse we just saw, I would have to say no. I want tests to confirm it's permanent."

Quinton sat up completely.

Daxx came over and smacked him in the back of the head. "You were dying and you didn't tell us?"

Quinton rubbed the back of his head. "Ow! It wasn't anything new." He said in a gruff tone.

"I don't care if it was new or not, you should have told us." She put her hands on her hips, then turned and glared at Troy. "Talk to your brother."

Troy raised one eyebrow and looked at her, then turned his head slowly and looked down at Quinton.

Quinton nodded. "Yeah I get it." He shifted and got to his knees, then stood up. Reaching down he held out his hand to me and pulled me to my feet.

I paused and looked at our hands together with the intricate designs wrapping around our wrists. I looked up at him. "What now?" I was completely shaken, I couldn't process. "I understand mates, but," I looked at my arm again.

"Its not complete." Crissy blurted out, "there has to be the blood bond." She nodded at me, then turned and gave Quinton a hard look. "I can't be mad at you when you're covered in blood, but after you wash it off," she poked in him the chest, "we're having a talk." She bobbed her head once, then stomped away.

"We still have an active blood bond." He said quietly, "from when we went to the warehouse." He gave Crissy a sad look and took a deep breath and exhaled slowly. "I get it." He looked around at the others slowly, "and you can yell all you want later." He looked down at his torn shirt and blood-stained skin. "If you don't mind, I'd like to go wash off." He lifted our still joined hands, "and explain to Reagan what this means in the long run."

"I hope she doesn't talk to you for weeks." Leone said in a serious tone.

Bethany shook her head. "He didn't deceive her, Leone." She motioned to our hands, "for all we know she did it." She shrugged, "we may never know."

Leone looked at our hands, then scowled at Quinton. "We'll see you for breakfast." He held out his hand to Bethany, "I need some sleep before we go back to that basement."

I didn't see everyone else as they wandered away or ported, I was too busy looking up at the man as he looked down at me.

He leaned down and kissed my mouth softly. "Thank you. For saving me."

I gave him a small smile. "I don't know that I did." I lifted our hands and looked at them, "but someone saved someone in that dingy place."

He blew out a breath. "We still have to figure out how the hell we got there." He cringed. "I don't know who attacked me, but there's a dead body down there waiting for us when we go back.

"There's a rock, stepping on it activates the portal." I released his hand. "I am not going back there." I gave him a stern look. "Ever."

He smirked. "Go shower. I'll get Mitz the bring some food to my room and we'll talk."

"Are we sitting on the floor to eat it? You only have one chair."

He frowned. "We'll sit on the roof and look out over the countryside as we eat."

I looked up at the sky. "Dinner on the roof at sunset." I shrugged, "that could work."

Chapter Twenty-Five

I was still dazed by the recent events. I don't think I picked up the soap in the shower, I spent the entire time studying the design on my arm. I was mated. To a prince. In Alterealm.

I picked up the amulet and looked at it. If there was ever a moment in a daughter's life she needed her mother's council, it was now. I grinned at my reflection, of course she would have been jumping up and down and screaming in excitement over this. I was just looking very lost. Securing the chain around my neck, I looked at the woman in the mirror again. I was a princess in Alterealm. Sighing, I turned and picked up my jacket and went to the door. I pulled it open to see Quinton standing on the other side.

He gave me a sheepish grin. "I can feel what you are." Quinton grinned. "It's shed a whole new light on what my brothers have been going through."

I raised an eyebrow and looked up at him. "I can't feel anything, myself."

He sobered, "well, part of your churning emotions and thoughts are probably mine." He blew out a breath and looked down the hallway, "Controlling this link is nothing like controlling the one my brothers and I have."

I shrugged, "that makes me feel a little bit better." I shook my head, "I don't regret that you're alive and—" I motioned up and down his body, "well. I'm just…" I lifted both hands and then dropped them, not knowing how to explain it.

"Yeah." He nodded. "I get it." He motioned down the hall, "lets go eat and talk."

I stepped out and closed the door.

Quinton walked beside me as we climbed the stairs, "The doctor wants to run all the tests again."

I nodded, "I think that's wise."

"If this turns out to be permanent…"

I stopped at the top of the stairs, "If? You don't think it is?"

His chest rose with a deep breath, then fell as he exhaled slowly, "I don't know what to think." He started toward his room, "I spent the last century hoping the doctor could find a way to fix it." He opened his door and went in, "but every day I was convinced I deserved it."

I put my hand on his arm as he reached the ladder going up to the roof. "It was a mistake." He looked down at me, "there was no malice intended when it happened."

A sadness went through his eyes, "no, but it doesn't change the outcome." He looked at my hand on his arm, "I took an innocent's life." He began to go up the ladder.

I waited until he'd reached the top before following him. He extended his hand and pulled me up the last step until I was standing on the roof. Of the palace. I paused for a moment, turning and looking around. "It's breathtaking." I whispered.

He motioned to some cushions and blanket on the roof. A small lantern lit the area. "It is." He made a sound of exasperation, "now." Sitting down, he looked around, "Arwan had control of the palace," he paused while I sat down, "we don't know for how long. No royals or anyone with magic in their blood could come near it." He looked around the roof, "Autumn climbed up here to get to the trap door while some magic-wielder tried to electrocute her." He looked at the roof surface, "but she did it to get inside and break the magic so we could enter it."

"That's—" I gave him a wide-eyed look, "horrifying." I smirked, "and yet, fantastic at the same time."

Quinton nodded slowly, "The past—" he waved his hand around, "I don't even know how long since Daxx appeared," He shrugged, "but it's been one crazy thing after another." He opened the basket and looked inside.

I watched as he took the food out. "I'd like to hear about it." I nodded when he looked at me, "everything that's taken place since Daxx."

He pulled out two wine glasses and then looked at them. "I guess I can drink again." His gaze flicked to me briefly, "I couldn't before while taking the elixir."

I grinned. "Please don't get tipsy and fall of the roof." I sobered, "one miraculous healing is enough for today."

Quinton laughed. "Yeah, we've made history today, I'm sure." He took out the bottle of wine and looked at it. "You like peach?"

I gave him a surprised look, "I do, actually."

He nodded, "Yeah, Mitz definitely packed this." He opened it and poured a glass, then handed it to me. He was quiet as he poured his and put the bottle back in the basket. "I don't even know where to start." He sipped the wine, then nodded slowly. "It's been one moment of insanity to another since I found Daxx in the wasteland." He frowned, "my appearance didn't scare the hell out of her." He said softly, "I knew there was something about her," he glanced at me, "like when you recognize someone you haven't seen in a long time."

I nodded, "I guess on some level you knew she was the huntress."

He grinned, "I began to suspect it when she was in Troy's office, surrounded by most of my brothers, and threatened to slice Welsley a whole new lifestyle."

I snorted, "Yes, she is quite blunt."

He nodded as he opened a container and looked inside it. "I'm hungry, but not starving like I have been for decade after decade."

"That's good I suppose." I picked up another container and opened it.

He nodded, "you have no idea. I could stuff my face, then be hungry ten minutes later."

"I've been hungry before, so I do understand." I said softly and picked up a plate.

Quinton studied me for a moment, "you lived through a lot of changes." He stated.

I nodded and held up my tattoo armed, "apparently I still am."

He held out his arm and turned it from side to side. "Yeah it's—surreal. I never thought I'd see this on my skin."

"Ditto." I picked up a sandwich and put it on the plate. "So Daxx arriving was a bit unexpected?"

He chuckled, "that's putting it mildly." He pulled out another container and opened it. "It was chaos, all my brothers tripping over each other trying to be around her," he shrugged, "except Victor, he said the prophecy was," he frowned, "hog spittle, I think."

"Yes, Crissy mentioned the prophecy in passing, the wording. I guess it's not hog spittle." I grinned at him.

"Nope. It could have been less cryptic though." Picking up a plate he debated what he wanted to put on it. "Mine makes total sense—now."

I chewed slowly, processing that for a moment. "So, which mate arrived next?"

He paused in taking a bite, "Crissy." He shook his head, "that was," he continued to shake his head, "terrifying at times. I've never been afraid of Victor in my entire life, but he was hell bent on," he took a bite and didn't speak until he'd swallowed it, "I don't even know what."

"They're an odd mix."

With his eyes-wide he nodded. "I know, but apparently she was who he needed." He shrugged, "they work." He took another bite.

We ate in silence for a moment. "Was Alona next?" I picked up my glass, "I feel like she's been here longer."

Quinton nodded, "yeah she was." He grinned, "I never thought anyone would be able to take on Chase and last."

"They seem to be good together."

"It helps that she's an empath and that he feeds on emotion." He took another bite.

"Oh," I grinned, "I suppose that makes them a perfect match."

He studied me silently for a long awkward moment. "They all are."

I knew he was thinking about our match as his gaze moved over my face. I wasn't ready for deep emotional talk just yet. "Who came next?"

He took a sip of the wine. "Bethany." He grinned, "she highjacked Leone's mind and led him into a trap set up by Willis' people. They were going to use him to trade for this one mage," he shrugged, "and her best friend, a witch."

I opened my mouth, then snapped it shut.

"It's worse than that." He took a deep breath, "Leone was, is, a human essence addict and when he realized his mate was…"

"A human." I covered my mouth.

"Yeah, it wasn't good." He closed his eyes, "then she fell off a fire escape and broke most of her body, so it was a really rough time."

"OMG." I whispered.

"We all thought we were going to lose him." He stared off into the night, "after just getting him back from being kidnapped."

"That's incredible. Someone should write a book about these," I waved my hand around in the air, "events."

Quinton studied his plate, "it would have to be a comedy."

I grinned, "there are entertaining aspects, I'm sure."

"You have no idea." He mumbled.

"Okay, so Leone obviously has his addiction under control now."

He nodded, "all it took was his mate." He frowned, "stupid punk scared the hell out of us so many times."

I smirked, "being a big brother to so many must be hard."

He gave me a bored look, "it's been a long three and half centuries." He blew out a breath, "sometimes I almost wish it was still Victor, Michael and I." He sighed, "but then I realize I'd miss out on those other idiots and life wouldn't have been the same."

"I wished for a sibling for many years." I twirled the liquid in my glass, "my mother never looked at another man after me."

"Your father was probably her mate." He tilted his head, "I don't know how that would work between the two races though."

I blew out a breath, "a discussion for Prince Bastian, once we get other—things resolved."

Quinton nodded, "yeah those *things* need to end soon."

I cleared my throat, "which woman disrupted your world next?"

"Paisley." He blew out a breath, "that was a rough ride." He set the glass down and picked up his plate again, "that's also when we found Emil's daughter on an island where they housed women for their breeding campaigns."

"Holy." I hissed out quietly.

He nodded, "Paize was one of those women, she got away and dove off a cliff into the lake." He set the plate back down, "Crissy saw her in a vision and it was a mad scramble to try to find her before she drowned." Shaking his head, he leaned back on an elbow and looked up at the stars, "Arius almost drowned when we breached that island."

I completely lost any interest in eating and set the plate aside. "So, Rena's child is…" I didn't know how to say it.

Quinton's gaze met mine, "yeah, it's from the island."

"Autumn is going to raise the child?"

Quinton nodded, "she and Michael." He paused, "none of us know a thing about babies."

I smirked, "I'd imagine all your brothers are going to find out at some point."

He frowned, "do you know how many nieces and nephews I could end up with?"

I chuckled, "a lot."

He bobbed his head. "Uncle Quinton." He said softly.

"Most likely uncle Quint or Q." I shrugged.

He nodded, then was silent for several seconds. "Anyway, Arius has always been the scariest bastard among us, but Paize tamed him like a fuzzy puppy."

I grinned. "I'm sure he'd be thrilled to hear your thoughts on it."

He snorted. "I have no problem voicing my thoughts around them."

"Just didn't tell them you were dying for the last century." I blurted it out without thought.

He sat up, "it would have changed *everything*." He took a deep breath, "I always intended to tell them, I just kept…"

"Hoping the doctor would fix it so you didn't have to." I finished for him.

"Yeah, something like that." He picked up a container and held it out. "These are the best pastries in *all* the realms, possibly the entire universe."

I raised my eyebrows and took one, "I guess it would be a crime to not eat them."

He nodded and took a bite of one, then closed his eyes like he was savoring.

I took a small bite and smiled while I chewed it. "They are divine." I told him.

"Right." He took another one, then handed me the container. "So, Autumn was next." He shook his head, "damn she can fight."

I swallowed the bite. "I've seen some of it." I nodded, "she's very good."

"She should have kicked Michael's ass." He gave me a serious look, "she almost died," he shrugged, "I don't know how many times, before he had to mark her to save her life." He winced, "Mitz was even furious with him."

"He didn't want a mate?"

He looked back at me, "it's not a matter of a want," I lifted his hand then dropped it, "I can't explain it, *but* in Michael's case he was hung up on the ghost of a girlfriend he'd lost hundreds of years before Autumn was born."

"I'm sure it's more complicated then you know."

He shrugged, "maybe, but he let her suffer and put herself in harm's way instead of manning up."

"I don't know about that, but I'm pretty sure if Autumn decides she's doing something, no one can stop her."

Quinton huffed out a breath, "that's true." He smirked, "I'll never stand in her way."

I smiled, "I don't think I would either. A surujin wouldn't stop her."

He sobered, "we'll work on teaching you some more fighting techniques." He looked out into the night, "although I'm hoping after we find Arwan, we can take a break from fighting."

"Daxx will be heartbroken."

He chuckled, "yes she will." He shrugged, "we'll find her someone to beat down occasionally."

"Kara was next?"

He grinned wide, "she shot Rafael..." he waved his hand quickly, "Raf has always been our little playboy brother." He laughed softly, "Kara shot him in the ass with an arrow." He leaned back and laughed loudly, "most poetic thing I've ever seen in my long life."

"That reminds me, how does she render her targets unconscious?"

"Oh, she doesn't want to hurt people, so the elders and science people made her arrows that shock people enough to knock them out." He shrugged, "I didn't ask for the specifics on how it works."

"Ah, I wondered if she had more special abilities than hearing a person's thoughts." I paused, "which in itself is amazing." I frowned, "although I'm sure she hasn't always thought it was."

He shook his head. "No. Her own family had her locked up in that asylum."

I gave him a wide-eyed look. "I hadn't realized…"

"Yeah. Raf found the family, but she won't let him go straighten them out." His tone was quiet.

"I suppose she's decided to leave it in her past." I studied him for a moment. "Your brothers can't right every wrong ever done to their women."

He snorted, "we sure as hell can try." He huffed out a breath, "some things are *not* acceptable or okay."

I smiled at him.

"What?" He gave me a confused look.

"My mother was right." I motioned to him, "she always told me the royal brothers were incorruptible, with morals harder than the hardest metal known to man."

He looked at me, "I don't know if—" he shrugged, "we're all that, but there are just some things that are not acceptable."

I smirked. "I suppose I'm next in the story of the princes' mates?"

His look changed several times before he spoke. "You are *and* you're the key to ending this with Arwen."

I nodded and looked down at my gloved hands, I pulled off one slowly, then the other, "I have to wonder if that's because I can see the traces of magic or if it was to heal you." I looked up at him, he was staring at my hands, "losing one brother would render this family helpless."

His gaze flicked back to my face, "I don't…"

I shook my head, "it would. You're each a part of the other, you may be nine separate bodies, but you function as one," I nodded, "and now with your mates it's like watching an intricate puzzle be completed." I rubbed my hands together, needing to feel my skin and not leather. "Even in battle you're a huge unit working as one."

Quinton sat there in the low light looking at me. "You make us sound like much more than we are."

"Maybe because I can step back and look without bias." I clasped my hands in my lap. "Or I could before." I looked at the intricate design on his arm. "Since our markings appeared, aside from the immediate confusion, I feel connected." I blew out a breath, "I haven't felt a connection to another since my mother passed."

"Give it a few hundred years and you'll be wishing you didn't have all those people connected to you and trying to get inside your head." He grimaced.

"Big tough brother, wanting his baby brothers to think he's a rock and unmoveable." I said in a low tone.

He shrugged.

I smirked. "How am I measuring against the other women when this," I held up my arm, "appeared?"

He laughed then, deeply. "gracefully in comparison." He shook his head, still chuckling, "Daxx and," he closed his eyes for a second, "Bethany," he shook his head again, "let's just say they didn't take it very well."

I smiled, more for seeing him laughing, "Mitz told me some of it." I gave him a brief wide-eyed look, "your brothers didn't do a very good job explaining," I motioned to the air, "Alterealm to them."

He sobered. "No. They did not." With a gentle look, he studied me silently for a few moments. "You're taking all of this very well."

I gave him a half shrug, "I grew up knowing of Alterealm, so that helps." I smiled, "that's not saying I still may not freak out, but fate knew what she was doing."

"How so?"

I stared at my palm while I spoke, "I don't usually rush into the middle of a fight with a group of unknowns and heal someone." I glanced at him through my lashes, "yet for reasons unknown to me, I *had* to help you."

He considered this. "While I'm grateful, now, that you did," his eyes connected with my own, "I will lock you in a room if you ever put yourself at risk like that again."

I laughed. "You can try." Inhaling slowly, I breathed it out. I hadn't been joking, at some point all of this was going to sink in and I may very well freak right the f out. I tilted my head and gave him a serious look. "What if I'm not the final key in this."

Quinton frowned, "what do you mean? You can see where Arwan's magic has been used." He nodded, "we've found out more since you came than all we learned before."

"The prophecy, there's one more brother."

His brows drew together, "you think the nine brother's prophecy is linked to all of this?"

I shrugged, "seems possible. Each mate has had some key to figuring it out and reaching the end."

He stared at the roof beside him for a long moment. "Emil," he shook his head, "he was born on the other side, spent three hundred years over there."

"I gathered that from our conversations."

"He's had five wives, many children—three are still alive." He shrugged, "I'm sure he's has a long list of descendants he keeps an eye on, watching for the longevity of the Alterealm blood…" He looked over at me, "you'd think if he had a mate one of his wives would have been it."

I lifted my shoulders slowly, then let them drop. "Is he part of the prophecy? The one about mates?"

Quinton opened his mouth, then closed it and tilted his head. "yeah." He said slowly. "I don't remember what it says though." He exhaled loudly, "so you think we won't be able to end this until he's found his mate?"

"Could he have already met her and not known?"

He snorted, "no." He gave me a hard look, "trust me if we get without fifty feet of our mate, we know it." He closed his eyes for a second then gave me a gentler look, "I thought I was hallucinating from blood loss when you appeared over me in that garage."

"You looked afraid, or angry, I'm not sure which."

"Yeah, well, I was mad that if you were my mate it was way too late… then your hair started to lighten like I was sucking…"

"Oh. I understand now."

He nodded, "yeah, I thought I was killing you—too." He said softly.

The air between us was tense again. I held up my hands, "a picture of health." I smiled, "but that explains your reaction to me."

Rubbing a hand over his face, "I could have probably handled it a bit better."

I smirked, "maybe." He continued to sit there and look at me, his expression was unreadable. I cleared my throat, "so, what are we doing?" I lifted my marked arm and then lowered it, "about this."

"I want to see what the doctor…"

"Quinton," I interrupted, "I know you've spent the last century hanging on doctor's results, but this." I held up my arm again, "is already done now." I looked at my arm, "if the results are bad news, it's too late."

"Fuck." He whispered, "you're right." He looked at his arm, then ran his other hand over it. "I guess my brain hasn't caught up yet to the…"

"Quinton," I whispered, he looked up at me. "I think you should kiss me."

He looked at my mouth, then back to my eyes.

I shrugged, "unless you plan on this being a platonic union for all eternity."

His eyes widened.

"Hadn't thought about that either?"

He scowled at me.

I grinned, "or you have." I got up on my knees and moved closer to him, "I don't know about you, but I'm tired of living every moment of my life alone, in my thoughts, physically, emotionally…"

He grasped the back of my neck and pulled me to him in one smooth move. I found myself in his lap, my mouth crushed beneath his in a matter of the single beat of a heart. I wasn't some shy schoolgirl, hadn't been for over a century, but this felt—new, unfamiliar.

I wrapped my arms around his neck and matched his heated kiss with my own pent-up passions.

He growled in the back of his throat and tore his mouth from mine. He rested our foreheads together, "I wanted to take the time so you could get to know me."

I lifted my head away, "we have several hundred years to get to know all the annoying quirks we have."

He grinned and lightly grasped my face between his large hands, "after we find Arwen, I want us to go away for a month."

"Go where?"

"Anywhere, everywhere—wherever you want." He whispered.

I nodded as best I could with him holding my face. "If that's your way of proposing, or courting," I tried to nod again, "yes. Yes."

He made a noise in the back of his throat and then crushed my mouth with his again. He shifted and I found myself under him without breaking our kiss. My whole being was revealing in his nearness.

With a sudden move, he lifted his head and cursed. He pulled out his phone and glared at it. He answered it, "this better be life and fucking death, brother." He growled into it. The hard look faded and he sat up, "what? Hang on." He tapped the screen, "it's on speaker, she's here."

"Thank the gods." It was Chase. "We tried calling, Reagan, then found your phone in your room."

I sat up and tried to shake the lust from my head. "I must have forgotten it."

"Quinton, where are you?" Chase sounded out of breath, "hold on." We heard muffled voices.

"We're on the roof." Quinton said.

"Of *course* you are." Chase sounded out of breath.

"What's going on?" Quinton demanded.

"Bastian is looking for Reagan, says it's important." Chase said. "He's already here."

"Is it about her father?" Quinton stood up and waited while I grabbed my gloves.

"He wouldn't say, said Reagan deserved to be the first to know."

He pulled me to my feet, I went over and looked down the hole to see Chase looking up at me. With a nervous quake I went down the ladder.

Chase gave me a quick appraisal. "I wouldn't have disturbed you if it weren't important." He gave me an apologetic look.

"Yeah, you would." Quinton stepped off the ladder and hugged me to his side.

Chase grinned, "yeah, I would."

Chapter Twenty-Six

"Bastian had to speak with Elder Arian for a moment," Arius said, "he'll be here shortly."

I nodded, then looked to Quinton. He stood by the door, his arms crossed over his chest, watching me.

"You two giving each other looks is cute." Michael said with a smirk.

Leone nodded, "yeah, despite wanting to pound you into the ground for not telling us about what was happening with you all these years," he glanced at Rafael, "it's entertaining to see you mooning over Reagan."

Quinton looked at him, then to Rafael, "I'll pound you all into the ground if you don't shut up." He turned to Michael. "You too. Did you look into my idea?"

"What idea?" Troy got up from where he'd been perched on the table.

Michael cleared his throat and gave Quinton a wide berth as he came further into the room. "Uh, comparing locations of where Detrick, Gudrun and the others we got out of that place were when they landed there."

"And the conclusion is?" Victor straightened away from the papers he'd been looking over.

Michael went over to the map. "It's not that easy. Detrick and Gudrun were both on patrol when it happened to them,

232

but it was two hundred and fifty years apart, so trying to pinpoint it on a map is hard." He tapped the map Victor had shown them when we had the meeting. "The wasteland was barely there when Gudrun was still in Alterealm…"

"Was it a wasteland for Detrick?" Bethany asked.

Quinton nodded and went over to the map. "Yeah it was out to here," he tapped the map, "when he disappeared."

"Okay, so," Chase came over and looked at the same map, "the three of you that remember no wasteland need to sit down with the historians and cartographer and figure it out." He looked at Alona, "are any of the others that we brought back coherent?"

Alona didn't look hopeful. "Not too many, but a few are."

Chase nodded, then turned to Victor, "if three or four can confirm a location, that's all we need."

Arius looked at Quinton, "what are you thinking?"

Quinton glanced at me, then to his brother, "I doubt everyone ended up in that basement after wandering through the trees and stepping on a rock." He turned to Victor, "Det landed in the basement right from the wasteland…"

"Then there's another portal in the wasteland." Daxx sat down, then looked at the map, "that's a lot of space to search." Her head snapped around to give me a look, "and there's only one that can *see* the damn portals."

"Simple, we narrow down areas and start there." Paisley turned and looked at the door.

Bastian stood in it.

"I'll get on it." Michael said nodding.

"Leone, Raf, you help." Chase told them in a tone that was not strictly brotherly.

Both men nodded.

"Prince Bastian." Emil said in a groggy way, "we're here and awake, what is so urgent?"

Bastian looked around at everyone, then zeroed in on me, he smirked and glanced at Quinton. "I ask for one and get the whole family."

"Why did you need to see Reagan?" Quinton's tone wasn't jovial.

Bastian sighed loudly, then came toward me, "it's pertaining to your father," he glanced at the others, "would you prefer to talk in private?"

I hugged my waist and shook my head. "No."

He nodded slowly, then motioned to a chair, "please sit—" he looked at my arm, "princess."

I sat down slowly. I heard chairs scrape the floor as the others did, but didn't look away from the dark eyed man giving me a sympathetic look.

"I found your father." He said softly.

I inhaled sharply, but then realized he wasn't finished speaking.

"They," he huffed out a breath, "reset him, his mind," he glanced to Quinton who stood beside me, "it's the only way I can explain it."

"What does that mean?" I asked.

"He's alive, but has no memory of your mother," he sat back, "or ever being over in that realm."

"His memory has been wiped?" Arius asked.

Bastian nodded.

I just sat there, not sure what I was feeling. "So, I'll never know the man that was my father." I said quietly. "He'll never know he has a daughter."

Bastian didn't nod or make any sign of a movement for several moments. "I'm still looking into who is responsible. I talked to one of my brothers—he's just as livid as I in discovering you are even possible."

"Is there any way to undo what's been done to him?" Alona's expression showed as much pain as I was feeling.

"I don't know." He turned to Troy, "I don't know who I can talk to, or trust, right now." He leaned on the table, "between looking for those helping with the barrier fiasco, and who is responsible for hiding the fact that a realm that few females are born into can indeed mate with those from other realms…"

"It's not the time." I stood up and shook my head. "We'll deal with the barriers and finding this Arwan lunatic, then," I nodded, "then we'll figure it out."

Bastian cocked his head to the side. "You're certain."

I sucked in a sharp breath, "Yes. I've had no father for one hundred and fifty years, longer won't matter."

Quinton came over and put his arm around me, sending me comfort I couldn't have possibly felt on my own in the moment.

Bastian stood up slowly. "I won't give up until I have answers." He said with great conviction.

"I appreciate that." I nodded and leaned closer to Quinton.

Bastian looked around. "Any closer?"

Troy rubbed his hand over the back of his neck. "We apprehended Willis Hubert—only to discover he's not running the show."

Bastian looked from Troy to Chase, then back to Troy again. "The ancient mage is?"

Troy nodded, a somber expression on his face.

"I checked the asylum. There are no patients from other realms but there are two with Alterealm DNA. I gave the room numbers to your red-eyed nurse." Bastian rubbed his hand over his messy hair. "Let me know if I can do anything, but right now I'm chasing my tail trying to find our own traitors."

Troy nodded. "We'll keep you up-to-date."

Bastian nodded, then looked to me and inclined his head for several seconds. "Princess, I will find those responsible for the injustice done to you."

I couldn't speak, so I nodded at him briefly.

"I must go." He bowed his head to no one in particular. "Until next time, royal family."

Everyone watched him leave, then turned to look at me.

"I'd like to go rest." I nodded and moved away from Quinton.

"Call if you need someone to talk to." Alona said. "I've got my own horrible father story."

"Same for us." Paisley said while looking at Autumn.

"Thanks, I just need to—process." I told them, but wasn't able to offer even a polite smile.

Michael moved over to Quinton and patted him on the back, then gave him a little shove.

Quinton scowled at him. "I'll come with you." He said, still glaring at his sibling. "I was going to anyway, you moron. I'm not one of you idiots." Shaking his head, he came toward me and put out his hand.

I took it and felt better, knowing I wouldn't be alone.

We reached my room, I looked at the door. "Come in with me." I tugged on his hand as I opened the door.

Quinton stopped right inside the door. "I'm sorry." He said in a rough voice.

I released his hand. "For what?"

"About your dad." He said quietly.

I gave him a grimace, "I thought him long dead." I sat on the bed. "Then thought maybe there was a chance he was alive," I looked at the floor, "but to find out he had his mind scrubbed because he'd been with my mother," I shook my head, "I can't even process it right now."

He came over and sat beside me, "we haven't slept in close to twenty-four hours, that could be part of it."

I looked at him, "how do you do it?" I motioned in the air, "just keep going day and night."

He smirked, "oh, there are decades of nothing to do, so we rest then."

I brushed my hair back from my face, "I don't know how you did it, all those years, keeping your health a secret and still functioning."

He shrugged, "I did it because I had to."

I touched his cheek with my gloved hand, "you are an incredible man, Quinton." I tilted my head, "and the most stubborn being in any realm."

He chuckled, then stood up. "Rest. We're back at it in a few hours."

I jumped up and grabbed his hand. "Stay here. I may still have an emotional eruption and don't want to call anyone else."

He gave me a skeptical look. "I need to go feed."

I raised one eyebrow and lifted my chin, baring my neck. "I can do that." I lowered my chin, "I want to, for you."

His chest rose and then lowered slowly, "I'm a bit afraid I might fly like superman with your essence this time."

I laughed, "brave enough to chance it?"

His eyes were shining with amusement. "Guess we're going to find out."

Chapter Twenty-Seven

"We all have flashlights?" Bethany asked.

"Yes, for the tenth time, all of us have two lights with us." Leone said, sounding annoyed.

I glanced over my shoulder to see he didn't look as annoyed as he was trying to sound.

"I think we should go in pairs." Michael said, "a few seconds apart."

"So we won't land on top of each other?" Leone asked.

Michael nodded. "Just don't use your box and try to send anyone to the cells." He told him.

Leone looked at the box clipped at his waist, "yeah I know. I get the dead or injured."

Quinton and stopped when we stepped into the clearing.

"I don't know why I'm getting to guard the rock. Again." Alona said, coming out of the trees.

"Someone needs to have Romulus' back." Chase told her with a steady look.

"Fine, but don't think you're leaving me in the safe zone forever, my king." She hissed out a breath.

"Cristy is on overwatch again," Victor stated, "we'll connect as a group once we're in the basement."

"Yes." Troy nodded looked at Daxx, "as soon as we're in the basement."

"Yeah, yeah." She looked around at everyone. "None of the guards are coming?"

Rafael shook his head, "no, they're spread out around the building and down the road to keep an eye out, should we trigger anything to bring company to us."

Paisley rubbed her hands together, "I'm totally juiced." She looked at me, "if you see anyone with any kind of magic that isn't Bethany, you shout, I will immobilize them."

I nodded. "It was too dark to see anything last time."

"Everyone ready?" Quinton waited for nods, then walked slowly forward. "That rock?" He looked over his shoulder at me.

I nodded, "Yes."

Victor moved by them. "Our kings go in last." He stated.

"What?" Chase shook his head.

"I agree." Quinton looked at his twin brothers. "If it's a trap, we can't let them get you."

Chase looked at his twin. Both of their looks changed to reveal they were both annoyed. "Fine." Chase said under his breath.

"Trap?" Kara asked. "You think it's a trap?"

"One can't be too careful." Victor told him. He turned to Michael and nodded. "We wait for everyone and then explore together." He nodded again.

Michael gave Autumn a quick look, then moved over to stand on the other side of the flat rock. When they vanished, Autumn and Daxx stepped quickly to where they were standing despite an annoyed looking Rafael and Leone. Daxx held a flashlight in one hand and katana in the other. Autumn nodded to her and pushed her hood back off her head.

"Let's do this." Daxx said.

Rafael and Leone went next. Right after them Arius and Emil stepped up and vanished without comment.

"Okay." Bethany nodded and rubbed her hands together, then lifted them and bright arcs came off them. "No flashlight needed." She whispered as she stepped over to the rock.

Paisley stood beside her and then nodded.

Chase looked at Quinton. "Get on with it." He pulled a sword off his back.

Quinton glanced at Kara, she had her bow ready.

"I'll go over with our kings." She told him.

"Our own royal archer." Chase said with a grin.

Quinton and I moved over to the rock. "Ready?"

I clicked on the flashlight and nodded.

As soon as we came out the other side, I knew it was the same place as before.

"You could have warned us about the stench." Leone said.

I pulled out my phone and connected to the group call.

"Yeah, well I was too busy trying to live to sniff the air." Quinton said beside me and in my earpiece at the same time.

"I feel better being here." Alona stated. "Kings inbound."

The twins and Kara arrived at the same time. They wasted no time. "Which way did you go from here?"

Quinton looked at me, I shrugged and shone the light around the small space. "I think that way." I motioned to the far side.

"Should we split into two groups?" Daxx motioned to the door on the other side.

Michael shook his head. "Reagan has to be present to see if there's any more portals."

"No pressure there." Autumn looked at me. "Let's go the way they didn't first."

With that decided, everyone started to move toward the other end.

"It smells worse than the tunnels Crissy ran us through." Leone said.

"That's good." Crissy's voice came over the earpiece. "No witches have been there to cleanse it."

Leone looked at Rafael and shrugged. "I'm good with that." He replied.

"Less noise." Victor said in a hushed tone.

"Anything?" Quinton was beside me now.

I shook my head, and tried to focus on looking around me and not what I might step in. "The only haze is where we just landed."

Quinton nudged my shoulder so I would look up at him. The look on face was asking if I was all right. I nodded and then looked around some more.

"I'm glad I didn't know this basement was down here when I was stuck living here." Kara whispered.

"Yeah, nightmares would have been your own then." Paisley agreed.

We moved through the hallway in silence. There were two doors in the short hall. Michael stepped in front of us all and turned, he motioned to one door and then the other. Leone and Quinton nodded and they moved to stand on the other side of the doors. Michael backed up and made room so that Arius, Emil and Rafael could stand in the hall facing the doors.

Quinton snapped his fingers. I looked at him, he pointed to the one door, then the other, I realized he was asking if there was magic. I jolted and hurried to get a closer look. Paisley was right on my hip when I stopped a foot from the men and looked at one door. I shook my head and then turned to the other. There was no haze around either.

Michael nodded and put a hand on Emil and Arius' shoulders as they faced the doors. The other men stood weapons ready. Bethany was now on my other side. Michael lifted his hands and two brothers kicked open the doors. Leone and Quinton rushed in with swords drawn. A second later they came back out.

"Just storage." Quinton reported.

"Same here." Leone motioned to the room, "we should have Reagan take a look though."

I quickly moved to stand in the one door. Old steel bed frames and outdated IV poles were shoved to the one side, decades of dust coated them. I shook my head, then turned to look in the other door. More long forgotten equipment. "No haze." I said quietly.

"That clears this way." Daxx said.

For so many, they moved silently back the way we'd come and began going down the other hall. The hair on the back of my neck stood on end, this place was plain eerie.

"Anyone else wishing we weren't here?" Beth whispered.

"I'm with you." Kara answered.

"Brother, I'm not seeing a body." Victor stated.

"Could be further down. I stumbled around after trying to find a way out." Quinton said.

"Nothing here." Rafael said looking in the next door.

"Or here." Michael stood outside the one I'd found Quinton in.

"Someone's been here, cleaned up after you." Leone looked at Quinton.

"Be on the alert." Victor said softly.

"If I get any more alert, I'll freak out." Paisley told him.

I moved to look in the one room, then the other. I shook my head while watching Quinton stare at the floor where he'd been laying. "No haze."

"Steel door down here." Autumn said in a hushed tone.

"Steel?" Michael moved past Victor to go look around the corner. "Much newer than anything else in this forgotten place." He said quietly.

"Reagan, come take a look before we touch it." Quinton looked at me from the corner.

I nodded and moved past the twin kings. When I could see the door around the large bodies, I was able to see a faint haze. "It's not really a bright haze, but there's a faint one along the floor."

"Trap?" Michael squatted down and looked at the floor, then the doorframe. "There's some space under the door, maybe it's coming from inside the door?"

"Touch it and see." Arius said.

Emil shook his head. "I've learned not to touch doors to places people may want to keep others from entering." He looked at me.

"I'll do it." Leone moved by Emil and went up to the door. He held his hand out from it, then touched it quick. Nothing happened. Opening his palm, he placed it against the door. He shook his head.

"Stand back further and try the handle." Chase suggested.

Leone found it locked.

"Now what?" Daxx asked.

"We don't want to break it down," Troy looked around, "if possible, I want to set a trap here for others."

"Our locksmith is in a tree outside." Rafael looked at Victor, who shook his head.

"What kind of lock it is?" Crissy's voice rang through the earpiece.

"Looks like a normal doorknob, Criss." Daxx told her.

"You can do that kind, Bethany." Crissy said.

Leone looked at Beth and raised an eyebrow.

Bethany smiled, "she's been showing me." She shrugged, "you never know when we might need to get in somewhere." She pulled something out of her pocket and went over to the door. Rafael looked over her shoulder.

"You have lock picks?" He grinned.

Bethany sighed, "I couldn't do it with paperclips like Crissy can." She bent over and started working on the doorknob.

"Stand behind us, my kings." Victor said looking at Troy, then Chase.

Troy looked unhappy, but moved so there were four brothers between them and the door.

"This protect the king's thing is getting old." Chase mumbled.

"You've never had to go up against the most powerful mage that's ever lived before." Alona's tone was not as light as usual.

Chase exchanged a look with Victor and then moved to stand beside Troy. "I'm out of harm's way."

"Good." Alona answered.

"It's unlocked." Bethany said as she back up. Tucking the pouch back in her pocket, she raised her hands again.

"Ready?" Arius put his hand on the door handle and opened the door when Leone raised his sword.

They both rushed in the room, then stopped.

The rest of us went in one after the other. The room was clean and only contained a cot, a camp stove and few boxes.

"This seems like a good place to lay low." Rafael went over and opened one of the boxes. "We're going to want to take these home with us." He stated in a dry tone.

Quinton gave him a curious look and went over to see why. "Illegal porters and stabilizers." He turned and looked at Victor.

Victor nodded and did something with the port-box he used to vanish people. He went over to the cardboard box and held it over it. It disappeared. He looked at Michael. "Send someone to the landing room in the chambers to retrieve that."

Michael nodded and pulled out his phone.

Emil stood looking at the door on the other side of the room. He shook his head, "still not touching it."

"There's a haze around it." I told him.

Quinton looked around the room, "could that be what you were seeing before we opened the other door?"

I glanced around the room again, "there's no other hazy areas but that door."

Leone walked past Emil to the door. He grabbed the handle and sparks flew from it. Jerking his hand back, he cursed quietly.

"And that's why." Emil stated.

"Warded." Quinton went over to it and stood looking at it. "Alona. Shove Romulus into the portal."

Rafael moved out the door we'd come in. "I'll get him." He pulled out a flashlight and shone it down the hall.

Kara went out the door behind him. "I've got your back."

"I'm going to guess this is an outer door." Paisley looked over at Arius, "inner one wasn't warded, so it makes sense."

"I'd like to know where it comes out." Daxx said. "We looked everywhere outside this building."

Rafael came back into the room with the mage.

"Take down the ward." Troy told him.

"My king." Romulus inclined his head and went over to the door. As he waved his hands around more haze appeared. When he lowered his hands, Victor motioned to where the kings stood. "You're coming with us in case we encounter more."

As we stepped out the door, there were several explicit words. It didn't lead outside, it led to a tunnel.

"I didn't think to look for tunnels here." Michael stated.

I studied the construction of the walls. "There would be no map with these on them." I told him. "This is a tunnel used during the war to get out of the building without being seen." I looked at Quinton, who watched me. "This one is very old, it could have been used in a few wars."

"Let's see where it goes." Rafael moved down the narrow space.

"Cristy, has breaking the ward caused any notice?" Victor asked.

"Nothing has changed." She answered.

He nodded to no one in particular. "You and Alona can go home. We'll deal with the portal in the trees after we're finished here."

"Okay, Vic." Crissy answered.

"I'll see everyone at the meeting room." Alona said.

The tunnel was long, the rough ground causing more than one to trip as we filed through it. When we reached the other end, there was no ward on the outer door. Stepping out into the light I squinted.

"Where are we?" Daxx turned in a circle.

"That is well hidden." Paisley stated while looking at the door.

It was in the side of a shallow ravine, nothing else was visible but trees and fields.

"Someone needs to take Romulus back through to put the ward back on that door and close off the rock portal." Rafael said as he looked around.

"I will take him." Victor said, looking back at the door. "Cover this back up as it was."

"I'll go with you." Emil went back to the door.

"Set a warning spell on this door." Bethany looked at Romulus, "so we know when someone uses it."

Romulus looked at the wooden door. "I doubt it would reach us at home."

Paisley snorted. "This will." She pulled a small camera out of her pocket. She grinned at Arius' surprised look. "Never know when we need to keep watch somewhere."

"Good work." Alona's voice was back on the earpiece again. "I'll get the laptop booted up here, Paisley."

Chase shook his head, grinning, but made no comment.

"We're going to look around the immediate area and see if there's anyone nearby." Quinton said.

Victor paused at the door. "I don't think you'll find any, brother." He looked around. "I believe this is only known to one."

"Arwan." Troy nodded, "we have all the others, and someone moved that body."

Daxx heaved a loud breath. "So now what?"

"We go find the portal that sent Gudrun and Det here." Quinton told her.

Daxx nodded and looked at me. "You up for some wandering around?"

I looked around at the others, "I am."

Leone held up his hand. "We need to go get the two with Alterealm DNA out of there."

Troy motioned to Chase, "we'll come. We can port in and out if needed."

Chase looked at Kara, "message Lucina and tell her we'll be at the back door."

Kara pulled out her phone. "Okay."

"Hurry." Daxx told Troy. "I want to go portal hunting."

Chapter Twenty-Eight

"I'm tired of riding." Kara turned and looked at Paisley.

Paisley nodded. "I'd be happy if the view would change."

I looked at the orange dust kicking up around the horse's hooves. "Did they figure out how to cut off his drawing power from the land?"

Chase rode up beside me, Alona was sitting sideways in his lap. "They did just a few hours ago." He grinned. "It took eight mages, five witches and three powerful residents of FaTerra."

Daxx made her horse stop and turn before she looked back at us. "So, each time he does his mage stuff, he'll weaken now?"

Chase nodded. "That is what I've been told."

"Will he know it's happening?" Bethany and Leone came up beside us.

"Not right away." Chase said, "not until he does something big and tries to recharge."

"I'm looking forward to this all being green and alive again." Michael turned in the saddle and looked back to us. Autumn continued to sit across his lap, looking straight ahead.

Rafael turned and rode back toward the rest of us. "GPS on my phone says we're almost to the area we suspect." He looked at me. "Want to ride up front, Reagan?" He turned to Kara briefly, "we don't need anyone, or horses accidently go through portals."

Kara stopped her horse. "I'm good with following."

"How big is the area we need to check?" Crissy bounced in the saddle as she rode but looked thrilled to be doing so.

"It's pretty big, sis." Rafael motioned to me, "we're hoping Reagan can see the haze from a distance."

I glanced at the dust being stirred up again. "Then we're going to have to go slow. Riding as a pack is causing a lot of dust."

"Alright everyone, back off and let Quinton, Rafael and Reagan go ahead of us." Troy smirked as Daxx was awkwardly steering her horse in a circle. He went over and grabbed the bridle and guided her horse to face in the right direction.

Kara pulled an arrow off her back and put it in the hand with her bow as she nodded to Rafael.

"I'm getting it." Daxx said with a serious look of concentration.

"You're doing great." Troy smiled at her.

"My ass isn't." she mumbled and began to follow Chase's horse.

We walked the horses slowly, trying not to kick up any dust.

"It's in this area that Gudrun hit a portal." Rafael said quietly.

Quinton nodded, "Det wasn't far from here either."

I looked around, "I know it wasn't always like this, but why would someone be out in the middle of nowhere?"

Rafael shrugged, "could have been going this way on their way to somewhere else."

"Before this was wasteland it was green and a good place for quiet..."

"I understand that part. Sitting in the quiet of nature." I saw a single stone on the ground and steered the horse around it. There was no haze, but I wasn't taking a chance.

Less than a minute later there was another stone. I stopped the horse and turned to look at the last rock.

"What is it?" Quinton was beside me.

I looked ahead of us and saw another rock. "Rocks." I finally said.

Rafael was beside me now too. "That's not uncommon out here." He looked at me, "I guess Arwan can't suck the life out of a rock, so that's all that's left."

I nodded and started moving again. "It's just odd they're in line with each other." I pointed to the next rock.

"She's right." Quinton went past me to the next rock. He looked back, "there's another up ahead."

Rafael gave me a blank look then jerked the reins so his horse would go to the left of us. "There's a row of them over here."

"I feel like he'd use rocks again, after the one that sent us to the basement." I focused harder, looking for haze around the stones.

"What is it?" Daxx called out.

I lifted my hand, one finger up, telling them one moment. I went in the opposite direction from Rafael. When my horse was in line with Rafael's and Quinton's horses. I saw more rocks, much closer together. "I bet they form a circle." I said loud enough for Quinton to hear.

He nodded and nudged his horse to ride past Rafael. He rode in a large circle until he was back to me. "It's a circle."

I turned to see the others galloping toward us. "A few rocks," I shrugged, "okay, but a circle of rocks after a trail of them?" I shook my head, "they have to be markers." I got down out off the horse.

The dust was stirring with the motion of the other horses, so I walked past a few of the rocks marking the circle.

"Don't touch them." Quinton warned.

"I don't plan on it." I told him. I paused and looked at the center. It seemed blurry. "There's something..." The dust stirred as Quinton came toward me. I looked over my shoulder. "Everyone needs to stop moving." I told him.

249

Frowning, he held up his hand and made a fist. Everyone stopped all movement.

I stared at the center, then glanced around to some of the rocks. Those closest to me had a faint white haze hovering over them. "These rocks are protected by some sort of witch magic." I said loud enough for all to hear. "I can't see the rocks on the other side of the circle, it's blurry in the middle."

"Blurry?" Daxx moved with slow careful steps, taking care not to stir up any dust at all. She stopped beside me. "I don't see the rocks on the other side at all, and the center is just empty to me."

Bethany came over and waved her hand over the rock. Straightening, she nodded, "it's a witches spell." She glanced at Leone, "maybe a warning alarm." She turned to Troy, "we need Clairee and maybe some other witches."

I continued to stare at the middle of the circle. "I think its so no one can see inside it." I nodded, "I'm willing to bet if I could it would be filled with green haze."

"Get some mages too." Daxx said.

"I'll get the witches." Rafael came over and looked at the rock, then turned to look at the next ones. With an abrupt nod, he vanished.

"I'll go get the mages." Leone came over and looked at the rocks too before he disappeared.

"Why did they do that?" I asked Quinton.

"Committing it to memory so they can get back here." He gave me brief look, "we need a landmark or something specific."

"That's how you guys do that? A picture in your memory?"

"Pretty much." He nodded.

"That's—fabulous." I smiled.

"Be careful what you wish for." Autumn nodded and crossed her arms over her chest. "accidentally porting isn't all that fun."

"This circle is big." Paisley said softly.

"I don't like that Reagan or Daxx can't see anything in the middle of it." Alona turned to look at it.

A few of the men drew their weapons and glanced at each other.

I stared at the middle, trying to focus past what the magic on the stones was doing. There had to be a way in. How else did people end up accidentally porting? Was that a green hue in the blurriness? I squinted and looked at it with complete focus.

I was suddenly standing looking at the whole group I'd come with. They were panicking and looking all around them. I turned slowly. I was *in* the center of the circle now. I winced and quickly pulled out my phone and connected to the group. "I think I just ported."

"Reagan. Where are you?" Quinton didn't sound pleased.

I looked around again. "I'm in the center of the circle and there's a lot of green haze in here."

"What?" Daxx was loud. I watched her step closer to the surrounding rocks.

"Don't move." Bethany said slowly, "you didn't port anywhere once you were inside, and Romulus said he closed the portal on the other end but that may not be where this goes."

I nodded. "Okay. Not moving." I turned and thought I saw someone walking toward me in the green haze. I squatted down, "Beth, cloak everyone. *Now.*" I looked down and saw my amulet hanging from my neck. I quickly tucked it in. "I'm not alone in here and I can see you."

"Got it." Bethany whispered and motioned to the witch Clairee.

I watched and exhaled when I couldn't see them. "Don't move." I told them.

A tall man with black hair came up to me. "Are you all right, miss?" He couldn't' have been much older than twenty-five, but he spoke with a stiffness that told me he was older than he looked.

"Don't let them see your tattoo or amulet." Paisley said.

"I—yes, just a little disoriented." I stood up slowly, making sure to not move my feet. As I did, I pulled my sleeve to make certain my arm wasn't visible above my glove.

"Tell them your porter malfunctioned." Quinton whispered.

I pulled up my other sleeve to reveal my porter. "I think this is broken."

He moved closer. The hair on the back of my neck stood on end. I tried to look around him without making it obvious.

"Perhaps there was an error in programming it."

I looked around. "In—for the middle of nowhere?"

His cool hand touched my arm, "that's quite an expensive porter."

Panic hit me. I turned so he wasn't touching me, "its—it's my mate's—I wanted to know what it was like—to-to port."

"I see. Your mate much have an important position to have a model such as that."

I nodded slowly, not sure what to say.

"Historian." Paisley's voice hissed through the earpiece.

"He's a historian." I said quickly.

"Ah," he smiled, or it was something similar to a smile, "a fairly important position." He nodded, "recording history for the future to see."

I nodded again.

"Get out of there." Quinton said in a tense voice.

"Do you think I should try it again?" I glanced at him and saw the darkness surrounding him this time.

"I think you should get it back home, before it's discovered missing." Another forced smile, "wouldn't want your mate distracted from his important job."

"Yes." I gave him an awkward grin, "I think you're right." I looked around us again, making sure no one on the outside was visible. "Enjoy your stroll—out here."

"Oh, I shall." He inclined his head to me.

I pushed the first button my fingers touched.

I was in the courtyard. With my hand shaking, I got my phone and dialled back into the group. "I'm safe at the courtyard."

"Any idea who he was?" Daxx asked.

"No." I sat down on the stone bench before my legs gave out. "He just appeared in the middle of the protected circle—and he's not a good person. Can you stay cloaked and get away from there?"

"We're on our way now." Kara reported. "Raf ported all the other witches and mages out, we have Clairee riding with us keeping us cloaked."

Quinton appeared in the courtyard.

"Except Quinton." Leone said.

"I see that." I smiled at him.

"We'll port as soon as we're far enough away and Clairee and Emil will bring the horses back." Rafael stated.

"Wait." That was Michael. "Tell Quinton to get to Ellis. Someone just entered the tunnel at the asylum."

I nodded and stood up, "someone just entered the tunnel from the asylum."

Quinton held out his hand.

"I'll talk to you in a few minutes." I informed everyone and took his had so we could port.

"That's who was in the circle with you?" Michael turned and looked at me.

I nodded. "Yes."

"Is that Arwan?" Daxx asked, "he doesn't look ancient."

Troy crossed his arms over his chest and glanced to Chase. "Is there anyone that would know what he looked like in his youth?"

Chase looked skeptical, "I don't think anyone is that old."

"I contacted our historians." Victor stated, "they are looking for any sketches of him, or artwork of any sort."

Bethany leaned closer and looked at the screen. "If it is him, that explains why the wasteland is so big now." She straightened up, "he's using it to look younger and for magic."

"That's been cut off though." Kara said quietly.

Bethany nodded, "he's not going to be happy when he figures that out." She glanced at Leone, "or when he sees his box of toys was removed from his hideout."

Leone nodded, "things are going to get messy now."

Daxx frowned, "messy how?"

Bethany looked slowly from the image on the screen, "all powerful ancient mage throwing a temper tantrum kind of messy."

Daxx's shoulders slumped, "great, just what we need more magic crap."

I stood up and the whole room spun, my vision went blurry. The only time I'd ever felt like that before was after using too much energy to heal someone. "Quinton." I said softly.

He turned to look at me.

"I don't feel well." I whispered.

"Thought you never got sick." Autumn said.

I focused in on her, and blew out a breath, "I don't." I said, then braced myself by putting my hand on the desk.

"Did he touch you?" Bethany was right in front of my face now.

I closed my eyes, "he touched my arm to look at the porter."

"Get Romulus and Clairee here now." Quinton growled.

Chapter Twenty-Nine

The doctor nodded, "her body is fighting it."

I looked at Romulus, he was in agreement. "I've never seen a person remove something like that without using magic to counteract it."

"It is remarkable." The doctor said.

"So, her body is fighting it like it's a cold or something?" Alona sat down on the edge of the bed.

"Yes." The doctor closed his bag. "I imagine in an hour it will be like it never happened."

Troy turned to the mage, "you're certain he couldn't trace her here?"

Romulus gave a nervous nod, "no spell or tracker of any kind works inside the ward." He looked at Clairee, then back to him, "we've tested it extensively."

Troy crossed his arms over his chest and looked at Chase. "Question is why would he want to track a random person?"

"She just appeared in his little circle." Paisley said glancing up from her phone.

"I guess it's a good thing your body knew the mate's tattoo was meant to be there." Bethany said with a smirk.

I rolled my eyes. "I've never felt ill before, not like that." I looked around at the others, "I'll be quite happy to never feel it again."

Elder Nodin walked into the room carrying a thick book with him. It was old and worn. "Your majesties." He bowed his head and waited.

"You've found something?" Michael went over and looked in the book when the elder held it open. "That's him the man Reagan saw."

Romulus went over and looked at it as well. "He looked just like that?"

I got up off the bed, waving Quinton off when he gave me a look asking if I should get up. I went over and looked at the book. It was a sketch of three people, the middle one was the man from the circle. "That's him." I gave the elder a curious look, "how long ago was that done?"

"Before all of our time." He said quietly.

"It's Arwan." Romulus said. "He looked that young?" He turned to me.

I studied the picture, "close to that."

Romulus exhaled slowly. "We're lucky all of Alterealm isn't a wasteland."

Daxx frowned, "I don't get it. Why suck the life out of the realm you want to take over?"

"I don't think he wanted this one." Kara said. "I think he convinced Willis Hubert they could take over this one, but Arwan's sights were set on much more."

"Many more realms." Victor stated in a thoughtful tone.

"We need a camera inside his little hideout." Paisley said.

Arius looked at her for a moment, then turned to Troy, "she's right. We need to know when he's there and when he isn't."

Chase turned to Romulus. "Can you make your own trap? A portal or something to keep him in one place?"

Romulus stood motionless for a moment. "It will take many mages, and other magical abilities to do that—and with the amount of power he's stockpiled, I can't guarantee it would be effective."

"Can we do something like that so he doesn't sense it?" Clairee asked.

Romulus looked at Troy, then to Chase. "I will need time to research this." He nodded slowly, "done incorrectly and it could give Arwan a trail back to all those involved in its making."

The doctor, standing motionless to the side of the room, stepped to the end of the bed. "Good, that will give me time to perform the tests on Prince Quinton." He looked around at a few of the others, "as well as the rest of you." He nodded, "you've been too close to too many oddities and magical forces as of late," he inclined his head to Chase, "I would be remiss if I didn't ensure the health of our royals."

"Tests?" Daxx frowned.

Troy gave her a quick appraisal. "It can't hurt." He looked at Clairee, "to make sure we're all healthy with no trackers on us."

Clairee nodded. "I can have someone at the medical facility during the doctor's testing."

Crissy's head popped up from her notebook. "No needles."

The doctor gave Victor a careful look. "No needles, Princess." He said quietly.

Arius pointed at Romulus, "get in touch with Princess Aireese's people and make sure your casting is perfect."

Romulus inclined his head. "I will, my prince." He gave Clairee and nervous look, then walked quickly from the room.

"Twenty-four hours." Troy said in a commanding tone. "Get the doctor to check you out, then get some rest, we're taking a twenty-four-hour break, then we're going to get Arwan."

I leaned forward in the chair and glanced out the door. Troy stood there with his arms crossed, Chase in an identical pose. Arius paced a few feet in one direction, then stopped and looked at the door before pacing the other way. Rafael was perched on the desk, his leg jiggling constantly with impatience. I sat back and looked at Alona, "I think I know why he never told all of you."

Alona glanced around, "smothered in concern." She agreed quietly.

"I'm glad the rest of us checked out okay." Bethany said.

Paisley nodded, "I just want Quinton to be at one hundred percent so I can remind him for a few centuries that he's an idiot."

Daxx nodded, "at least a few." She frowned, "I can't believe I'm thinking in centuries now."

"Took you long enough." Leone smirked at her.

Emil leaned against the wall. He looked at his phone and shook his head, then put it in his pocket.

"Trouble?" Autumn asked.

"No," he tilted his head to the side, "parental woes." He grimaced. "Rena is dead set on coming over tomorrow, regardless of what's happening."

Autumn nodded, "she can't look at the same walls any longer." She shrugged, "I don't blame her, I would have lost it months ago."

Emil sighed again. "I know, I just—" he flicked his hand in the air, "worry."

"The palace and underground chambers are secure now." Rafael told him. "She'll be safe."

"And be able to wander much larger areas." Kara offered.

"I know, I just," he looked at Rafael, "did you know her guard was on that island with her?"

Rafael nodded. "We gave her options, she chose Kinsley, brother."

Emil straightened from the wall. "I don't like it." He frowned, "I know the guard risked her life being there, but she also didn't…"

"There was no way she could safely help each woman trapped there." Alona stated.

"I'm aware, it's just," He heaved another loud sigh, "won't it make it harder for her to be around another woman that was there? The constant reminder."

Autumn got up and stretched, "it's not like she'll ever forget it, Emil." She shook her head, "the baby growing inside her is a reminder every second."

Emil nodded. "I know." He rubbed his hand over his face. "I just worry."

Michael stepped into the doorway. "They placed a camera at the hideout and one by the stone portal as well as the wasteland circle…"

"How did they hide a camera in the middle of the wastelands?" Paisley asked.

Michael shrugged, "I didn't ask." He nodded to her, "but your tracker idea was a good one."

"Tracker?" Daxx glanced at the closed door, then to him.

"Yes, a microscopic electronic tracker." He looked at Bethany, "untraceable by magic, has been placed so that he will unknowingly be carrying it with him."

Bethany frowned, "did they put it in his underwear?"

Michael smirked, "I didn't ask. I was just assured that next trip to his hideout he'd leave with it."

Kara leaned back in her chair, "this is good, right?" She looked around at the rest of us, "that we can find him?" She turned to Bethany, "I doubt he'd check for modern electronics."

"Romulus was pretty sure he'd know any magic used, so hopefully he's not techy." She said giving the closed door an anxious look.

"I can't wait." Daxx stood up and crossed her arms over her chest. "Good twelve-hour nap, then we go track him down and end this."

"I'm all for that." Rafael said, then jumped to his feet when the doctor's office door opened.

Quinton came out, followed by the doctor. He lifted his hands slowly, a somber expression on his face. "Picture of health." He grinned.

There was several audible sighs and mumbled words of thanks.

"Had us worried." Leone grinned.

Quinton looked around, then waved his hands in a circle, "This, right here, is why I told none of you."

"We deduced as much while we sat here waiting." Alona stood up. She smiled at the doctor. "The entire royal family are fit as fiddles."

He smiled back. "May it always be so." He bowed his head.

"I'm starving." Leone nodded and held his hand out to Bethany. "I'm going to stuff my face then sleep for ten hours."

Bethany got up and took his hand. "That sounds wonderful."

They disappeared.

I stood slowly, watching Quinton, whose eyes were only for me in that moment. I felt like a giddy schoolgirl when he smiled at me, knowing full well how I was feeling.

He came over and put his arm around me. "Anyone bugs us before the twelve hours is up, does so at their own peril." He gave his brothers a quick grin and then we were no longer standing in the doctor's office.

Chapter Thirty

I looked around and realized we were in his room, and there was furniture in it. I turned slowly, "Is this the furniture Alona had me select for my room?" I went over and ran my hand over the plush royal blue chair and looked at the matching sofa.

"Yeah." He crossed his arms over his chest. "I didn't see much sense in having it hauled to your room, then moved up here." Despite his stance, the expression on his face was hesitant.

"Oh?" I wandered around the room, trying to appear as nonchalant as possible. Inside my heart was racing. The room was perfectly decorated. I stopped, unable to process when I spotted a portrait on the wall. It was my mother. With weak knees I went toward it. She was lovely, just as I remembered her before she was ill. Beneath the portrait was a decorative table and on it was my mother's pendant, now strung on a delicate silver chair. I touched it.

"It's okay if we keep my parents' room, isn't it?" He now stood behind me.

I nodded and inhaled a deep breath before turning. "Yes. I understand needing that connection to family."

His soft gaze moved over my face. "I had them duplicate a painting your grandmother has of her."

I blew out a breath, "grandmother." I whispered.

"She's still alive." He said, watching me with care. "Once we get Arwan and end it, you can meet everyone."

I nodded slowly, "I wouldn't want to put them at risk seeing them any sooner." I gave him a little smile, "until I came here, I never dreamt I'd be anything but alone."

He touched my shoulders and looked down at me. "Me either." He grimaced, "aside from too many annoying brothers."

I smiled back at him, then glanced around. "so, does all this mean we're shacking up together?"

His grin widened, "we *are* officially mated," he shrugged, "and I'm not dying anytime soon."

I nodded slowly as I pulled off my gloves. "Very true. It's funny how finding out you're not dying brings a new perspective." I looked at my left hand and the pattern that wove its way up under my sleeve. I smirked at him. "The other night, we both passed out."

He smirked, "Yeah, well, no sleep and miraculous healing was exhausting, and I had to—process."

"You're feeling refreshed now?"

He gave me a heated look. "Very refreshed."

I looked back down at my hands. "I've never been able to be with a man without wearing gloves," I gave him a brief look, "which makes most men not want to be with a woman wearing gloves."

Quinton smirked, "I'm good with wearing nothing."

"On my hands?"

He leaned down as he pulled me closer, "on all of you." He grinned, "and I'm healthier than I've ever been, so we don't have to worry about your touching me slowly killing you."

I ran my hands up his arms, feeling the warmth of his skin under my touch. "That's a plus."

Leaning down, he kissed my mouth softly. I expected more, but he lifted his head again, his gaze holding mine. "What is it?"

"I'm waiting for one of my brothers to interrupt."

I smirked, "you expect them to?"

"Always."

"I'm sure they're busy right now or catching up on some much-needed sleep."

"Maybe."

"You could ignore them and kiss me. Really kiss me." I watched as his eyes started to change color, it was the most sensual thing I'd ever seen in my life. It was just one more confirmation that told me this was where I was meant to be, and the supposed miraculous mix of my heritage was something I wasn't afraid of—for the first time in my life. I looked at him, really looked at him for a moment. Physical attributes were nice, there was no denying he was good looking, but for me, he was perfect. Perfect in that he wasn't thirty years old and could understand the atrocities that I'd lived through in the changing times. He'd understand living through the many decades I had, how there were things you just knew after that much time. Fate knew this all along. Although she could have let me know a hundred or so years ago, rather than have me wallow in doubt and self-pity from year to year.

"What are you thinking?" His voice was rough.

"That I'm not afraid of who I am." I played with the back of his hair, "I don't have to worry about others knowing either now." I noted how he listened to every syllable I uttered. I'd never had that. "How after so many years alone, I'll never be alone again," I smiled, "and I'm glad for it." I inhaled slowly, tilting my head to the side. "I want lots of children, Quinton." A dream I thought I'd pushed aside too many years ago.

His eyebrows went up, he leaned back and looked at me. "Define lots."

I smirked, "five at least, maybe six." I shrugged.

The look of shock didn't fade on his face, "that is a lot." He nodded slowly, "so when were you thinking of starting to build this horde?" He cocked one eyebrow at me, "I feel like

I should remind you that we could live a thousand more years."

I chuckled, "yes we could, I don't want to space hundreds of years between them. I want them all close to each other."

Without releasing me, he looked around, "we're going to need a bigger room, or a whole floor of rooms."

"At least." I whispered.

He looked down at me, so many emotions going through his eyes, none were fear or panic. "Okay, a horde it is." he nodded slowly, "but I'd like to end Arwan's insanity and a least have six months with just you before our lives are overrun by loud, demanding..."

"Adorable children." I finished for him. "Deal. After Arwan and a six-month honeymoon."

He grinned, "I can handle that."

"It's never going to happen at this rate, though." I said with a sigh.

His expression became serious, "we're going to get the bastard..."

"Not him." I said trying not to smile.

"Then what?" He had such concern on his face it made my heart ache.

"We'll never have the honeymoon or the horde of children if you don't shut up and..." Quinton grasped me around the waist and lifted me up until our faces were level. I barely had time to notice his eyes were red before he attacked my mouth. Several heartbeats later, I caught up and was kissing him back with all the pent-up passion and loneliness I had.

He tore his mouth away. "We may kill each other with years of abstinence..." His mouth was on my neck as he started walking toward the bed.

"I'll heal us." I gasped as he bit into my neck. I sucked in a breath, "as many times as I have to." I finished breathlessly.

When my legs hit the back of the bed, he gave me a gentle shove until I sat down. Kneeling in front of me, he undid my boots and pulled them from my feet. My socks were next.

The whole time his red eyes held my own captive, and I was drowning in lust by the time he tossed my shirt over his shoulder. He made a deep sound in the back of this throat as he pushed me to lie back and undid my pants. My whole body was vibrating with when he finally pulled the denim past my feet. I raised up on my elbows and looked at him, still fully clothed. I licked my lips and slowly got up onto my knees on the bed. He pulled his shirt over his head, then reached to undo his belt. Too slow, was all I could think. "Faster." I said in a husky voice I barely recognized. I was rewarded with a fanged grin as he kicked off his boots and stripped his body free of the rest of his clothes.

Quinton crawled up me in what felt like slow motion, his gaze never leaving my eyes. "We have the rest of our lives." He said softly.

I swallowed, trying to find my voice. "Yes, but we have about thirty seconds before I burst into flames."

We were face to face now, close enough I could now feel the heat from his body. "I'm not afraid to get burned." He whispered as his mouth covered mine.

I watched him walk to the small refrigerator across the room. I sighed and closed my eyes for a second. Even after the nap, my whole body was still buzzing from some very vigorous loving. "I don't know how you're walking." I grinned, "I feel like I'm floating."

He chuckled as he opened it. "I need sustenance and something to drink." He turned and the smile faded off his face. "Reagan?" His eyes were huge as he walked toward me, glancing to his left, then right?

I sat up, "what is it?"

He froze, a horrified look on his face. "How are you doing that?"

I pulled the sheet up and looked around, "doing what?"

He held his hands out from his body. "I can't *see* you." He said slowly.

I jolted and looked down at my body, I could see myself. "I—I..."

"Oh, thank the gods." He rushed toward me and pulled me off the bed and hugged me tight. "What the hell was that?"

I was shaking, not understanding. "I don't know."

Sitting, he kept me in his lap. "Shit." He said softly. "Kara said Bastian just appeared in front of her once."

I looked at him, my eyes felt like they were bulging from the sockets. "What? I can be invisible?"

"You've never done it before?" His eyes held such concern for me.

I shook my head. "Not that I know of."

Kissing me hard on the mouth, he shifted and got up. He lifted his shirt, then went over and picked up his pants. "Better get dressed." He pulled his phone out of his pocket and taped the screen. "I'm putting it on speaker."

"This better be really important, brother." Arius said.

"It is." Quinton set the phone down on the table and started to pull his pants on.

"What's happened?" That was Victor.

"I've been awakened from my wonderful slumber." Chase mumbled.

"It's Reagan." Quinton did up his pants and tossed me my shirt.

"What wrong?" That was Autumn.

"She went invisible." Quinton looked at me, his gaze moving the length of my body.

"What?" Leone sounded amused.

"Like Prince Bastian." Kara said in a hushed tone.

"Yeah." Quinton nodded and sat down to put on his socks and boots.

"I'd love to be invisible." Crissy said.

"Has it ever happened before?" Troy asked in a serious tone.

"This is a game changer." Paisley whispered.

Quinton shook his head. "No. I need Bastian here. Now." He gave me a concerned look, "if she can't control it, then we've got a problem."

"I'll reach out to him." Victor was all business.

"I don't even know what time it is." Emil mumbled. "Where are we meeting?"

Quinton stood up and watched me put on my shoes. "Meeting room. Ten minutes." He leaned over and tapped the phone then turned back to me.

I was completely shell-shocked. I stood up and I secured my porter around my wrist. "These have trackers in them?"

He nodded. "We'll figure this out." He held out his hand to me.

I took it, my own hand was shaking. "I hope so, or your brother is going to give me some lame nickname."

KEEP READING FOR AN EXCERPT OF

The Kinetic

Alterealm Series

Book 9

By J. Risk

Prologue

She looked over her shoulder to be sure the guards weren't paying any attention to her. They didn't bother with her; she kept her head down and never gave them a hard time. A few of the others wore the same color wrist band, and were sitting close enough to see. She gnawed on her lip, not sure if she should trust them. If she was caught—well, she didn't want to think of what could happen.

Kinsley looked at the band around her wrist. As far as she could tell it was only for sorting purposes. In her case it was because her eyes changed color. Little did they know she was a full blood Alterealm resident. She glanced to the other women again, wondering how much Alterealm DNA they had. Some of the women that slept on the main floor wore bands as well, but those were ability blockers. That brought her thought cycle back to the reason she was thinking about all of this in the first place. They couldn't find out she had an ability. And most definitely couldn't find out she was working undercover for the Alterealm royal family.

She watched a woman wander close to the barrier and stand there. That one was going to get all of them in trouble. None of them wanted to be on this island, but that one was making her escape attempts too obvious. She turned to see if the guard was watching her and blew out a breath of relief to see he wasn't.

Her gaze landed on another woman, or more specifically, the bruising on her face. Kinsley's heartbeat sped up, she felt like she was failing. There was only so much interference she could create to keep them men away from them. She was just as much at risk with the number of men that came and went from this hunk of land in the middle of the water. Twice now, she'd had to fend for herself to prevent unwanted advances. Her heart was pained knowing that she couldn't do that for the rest of the women. She'd barely slept since agreeing to be here, the crying at night that echoed through the building wouldn't allow her to attempt sleep. She didn't know what the royal family had done on their end, but security and more frequent visits from the higher-ups in this crazy place had increased tenfold.

Okay, she put her hand out and touched the tall weeds growing beside where she stood, *now or never. You can't get caught with this phone.* With her other hand she reached into her top and pulled the small phone out. With a quick glance, she opened the message and hit send. *Hurry, hurry,* she chanted in her mind. It vanished from the screen. *Check your messages, Justice.* Clutching the phone against her chest, she turned and scanned the nearby people to be certain no one was looking her way. Taking a quick breath, she backed up a few steps so she could see the rotted-out knot of the tree. Taking a deep breath, she held out her hand and watched the phone levitate above it, with careful movement, she sent the phone toward the tree and didn't take another breath until it was inside the resting place of the tree.

"Hey."

She started and turned to see one of the guards scowling at her. With a faked yawn, she stretched her arms over her head and gave him a sweet smile. He watched her for a moment more, then turned away.

Let the cavalry come soon. She thought as she slowly wandered back to the others.

Chapter One

I stood there looking at all the things I'd tossed on the bed. There was no way all of that was going to fit into one duffle bag. I had no idea what I would or wouldn't need from this point on. Did royal guards even get days off? I didn't know. They had to, right? The other personal guards spent a lot of time at the yard, so they must have free time.

I looked at my new porter. It had three locations programmed in, the underground chambers, the palace and the guard's yard. I smirked, only the high ranking and personal royal guards had this elite porter, so I shouldn't complain that home was a long way away. I had no idea when I'd be back to even visit.

With a dramatic sigh, I went back over to my closet and dug around for another bag. Finding an old one, I tossed it on the bed. I needed to pick up the pace. I didn't want to keep Captain Rafael waiting downstairs with my family too long.

My family. They were exhausting. Of course, my father understood the honor of getting the placement I had. He'd been a royal guard for over a hundred years. His father and my great-grandfather before him. My mother was not understanding. I often wondered if it was due to the fact that my brother had dropped out of the training yet her daughter had passed. To her a daughter should be delicate and spend all her time in a dress, doing womanly things. I didn't exactly fit into her fantasy of what a daughter was. I was petite, a whole five foot three, but delicate was not my forte. I could take down three quarters of the other guards in a practice skirmish, without using my ability. For the others I did need the odd assist from my ability, but Captain Rafael and Prince Michael laughed as I did it, so as far as I was concerned it was more than acceptable to use it to defend myself.

Stuffing the last of it into the smaller bag, I did it up quickly and went to the door. I paused and looked around my room. Truth be told, I wouldn't be heartbroken if I never had to sleep here again.

I walked back into the kitchen and cringed. My mother was hovering over the captain with that look on her face. The one that meant she was trashing my profession again.

"...her best friend's father died on that island rescue." My mother's tone was hostile.

Rafael glanced at me and stood up. "I'm aware, Mrs. Hinton." He inclined his head, "we are doing everything possible to help his family."

My mother made a noise of discontent. "That won't bring him back." She pointed to me, "I don't want my daughter to end up the same way."

Rafael cleared his throat. "Kinsley is a *very* skilled warrior. You should be proud of her."

I watched my mother's shoulders rise and fall. I glanced at my father; his expression mirrored my thoughts. I needed to get out of here. "I hope this isn't too much to port back."

Rafael gave me a quick look. "As long as it's not a car, I can manage."

My father chuckled. "I wouldn't say that, Captain, she'll be running back up to get her weights."

Rafael grinned. "She has access to the family's gym now, so hopefully they won't be needed."

"Who is she guarding?" My mother blurted out.

I wanted to melt into an invisible puddle.

"My niece." Rafael said calmly.

I watched my mother process that. "So, she won't be in fights anymore? Will just be spending her time hanging around the palace? You know she hurt her arm not long ago doing *something* for the guard?"

My father interrupted before Rafael could answer. "It's an honor for her to get this posting."

I picked up the duffle bag. "We should get going. I want to be there before Rena arrives."

Rafael came over and took the duffle bag from my hand. "It's going to be an adventure." He smirked.

When we stepped outside, I glanced to make sure my mother hadn't followed. "I'm so sorry." I whispered.

"Don't be." He stopped and looked down at me. "It's not the first time as a royal, or captain of the guard, I've dealt with hostile mothers." He grinned.

I blew out a breath. "I like to think any other mother in this realm would be thrilled her daughter was selected out of several hundreds of guards to be a part of the royal guard." I shrugged, "but no, she'd rather I'd be in a frilly dress drinking tea."

He laughed. "If you prefer, we can get you a frilly uniform to wear."

I cringed. "No. Thanks." I smiled. Hopefully the rest of the family was as easygoing as he seemed to be.

KEEP READING FOR AN EXCERPT OF

After
the
Silence
Volume 1

BREE

By Jacqueline Paige

Chapter One

I was nineteen when the world went crazy, nothing that was would ever be again.

Remnants of a familiar world remained, but not enough to instill those warm, fuzzy feelings you get when life is comfortable and predictable.

I'm Bree Taylor. This is an account of what I remember, how things happened when life changed forever and I managed to survive. There is so much to tell, a thousand pages wouldn't be enough to explain it all, but someone has to tell it. There needs to be a record so if we, as a planet survive, others will have the history. If we don't, then the next species to invade earth will know what we did wrong.

It is now just a few days after my twenty-second birthday, I'm standing looking out the window and wishing my brother, Shawn, well in the afterlife. A seemingly small laceration on his leg became so much more and took him away from me, leaving me to figure out this world on my own. If I have relatives left living, I wouldn't know. All that I cared for are now ashes spread over the dirt and just memories inside my head.

I am alone.

"Bree?"

I turned towards Darren, one of my adopted brothers, and gave him a look to tell him we were done discussing my decision. He didn't heed the warning.

"Are you sure this is what you want to do?"

His voice was filled with grief and worry. *Was I? Yes, at least eighty percent certain.* "Darren, I can't stay here. Being in the city is dangerous enough as a family, never mind a single girl."

A desperate look appeared in his eyes. He was probably wishing at this point that some of the other brothers were still alive, but only Bobby and Darren were left out of my six older brothers.

"We'll move you closer to us, keep you safe."

We, being his very old mother and wheelchair bound brother. I gave him my most stern look. "I think you have enough to worry about, you don't need me to add to that list."

Darren's eyes strayed to the picture I still held. The one of my family and me before life was forever altered.

"Shawn would have wanted me to. I feel like I'm letting him down."

I offered him a smile that said I had accepted it, even though I really didn't. "Shawn is gone and I have to go and try to find my own place now. You guys did all you could to prepare and teach me to fend for myself, your job is done.'

He stuffed his hands in his pockets and leaned back against the wall. "Where will you go?"

I turned and looked out the window. "I think the mountains."

A sound came from him that told me he thought I was too much of a girl to survive that. "The crazies hide there."

I chuckled and slowly turned back, rolling my eyes at him. "And they don't in the city?" His expression pleaded with me. "Darren, I know you have always been close to my family, you're like family. So I know that Shawn probably told you I changed after the virus." The fear in his eyes confirmed my suspicions. He knew the truth. "I have to find out what I've become, before others do. I need to know if I'm a good thing or a bad thing. And I need space and solitude to discover this."

"Bree, you could never be bad."

My heart warmed from his words. "I hope you're right."

He sighed loudly. "Fine, but you're taking Tremor and Shawn's weapons – otherwise I'm going with you."

I knew he wouldn't, we both knew it, but it was his way of feeling like he had done all he could. "I don't have to take Tremor. I can walk."

He shook his head sending his black hair scattering around his face. "We have LadyBell and her colt; we don't need any more than that. Tremor's fast and loyal and he'll get you through the bad times."

I was hoping the bad times would be few, naive I know, but I could hope. My heart strained as I fought to keep my resolve. He loved his horse and to know he was sending him out there with me meant more than I could express. "Thank you." I wanted to hug him, I really did, who knew when I'd have any friendly human contact again. If I hugged him now I knew I would fall apart, and I needed to keep my head out of the emotional whirl that was already threatening to suck me in. "I should get ready. I want to leave early enough so I can be out of the city before darkness falls."

Darren nodded, even though his entire face told me he didn't agree. "I'll go get Tremor. You get your stuff packed up." He looked at me for a long silent moment before he rushed back out the door.

I stood there looking at the door long after he'd gone. In my head I wasn't at all sure this was a good plan. I was following my heart and it was telling me to get out of town and find out where I was meant to be. Of course my head was saying that was a load of crap, but I was still going to do it. I couldn't explain why I needed to be outside and away from all the buildings and people, it just felt right.

Darren didn't know I was already packed. When I knew Shawn wasn't going to recover I started to gather up what I would need. Before Shawn was too far away from me, we had discussed my plan. He agreed I needed to leave. He had also said he was coming with me as soon as he was on his feet. I think by that point we both knew he would never recover.

I swore to follow the least traveled path. I promised to stay away from crowded places. I vowed to him I would survive and then I tucked the blanket around him and went off to cry by myself until my eyes felt like they were going to split in half.

I'm done with the crying and ready to take on what's left of this planet and the series of trials I know it will throw in my path. Tale of a colony of peaceful people live high in the mountains, it's my plan to find them. I hope the stories of the crazies that live between here and there are just that, a farfetched creation of some idiot's imagination.

Going into my room, I quickly headed to the closet to pull out the packs that had been sitting ready for me. I didn't need a lot. I could live off the land if needed, but one entire bag contained dehydrated food, just to be safe. As I swung the largest pack up onto my shoulder I caught a glimpse of myself in the mirror. Would this be the last time I saw the woman looking back at me? I looked into my now green eyes, a leftover from the virus. I stared until I saw it; determination, hidden just under the surface. Sighing, I ran a hand through my choppy red hair and debated, very briefly, if I should dye it a dull brown and tone it down. I knew that would never happen. I wouldn't trade in my brilliant hair for anything. It was a statement and if I couldn't do anything else I was definitely going to make one.

Closing my eyes, I prayed for my spirit to stay strong. When I opened them I didn't look at the mirror again, just picked up the other two bags and walked out of my home for the very last time

Darren stood outside holding the reins and crooning softly to Tremor. I couldn't see his face, which was a blessing, I didn't have to see his eyes begging me not to go again. The large horse's ears flicked as he listened attentively. No doubt he was receiving instructions to keep me safe and out of harm's way. Darren lifted his face away from the animal and looked over at me. "He's quite happy you're getting him the hell out of this city." A halfhearted grin appeared on his face. With a tilt of his head he motioned to the other side of the porch. "We're going to walk with you until you're outside the city limits."

I turned and looked to see Bobby leaning against the side of the house. I couldn't help but smile when he wiggled his eyebrows at me. Bobby was the clown of the group that grew up together. I often wondered if anyone else ever sensed he was too serious inside and that was why he joked around as much as he did. Bobby was my first crush when I was thirteen. It never went anywhere, for obvious reasons, but I still had a secret place for him in my heart. I was grateful he was coming along; it would prevent Darren from pleading with me to change my mind, again. "Hey, Bobby." He pushed away from the wall and sauntered in his easy way towards me, his long leather jacket making him look like he floated.

"Hey, Brat. You didn't think you were going to sneak off without saying bye did you?"

"Wouldn't dream of it."

He pulled the bag from my shoulder. "Good to know."

Darren came over and took the bags, taking them to secure to Tremor's saddle. "I think you should walk with us for a while and then he won't be too tired to haul ass when you need him to later." He didn't look at me when he spoke.

"She'll be fine, Dare, we taught her." Bobby's tone sounded annoyed.

Silently I hoped he was right.

Stepping in front of me, he looked me over. Without a word he moved and took off the coat that I couldn't ever remember him not having. "You're going to need something to keep you dry and warm." He held the coat out to me.

I opened my mouth to say something, but nothing came out. Pulling my hands out of my pockets I took the jacket and looked up at him. Bobby was a good six inches taller than my five foot five making me wonder if the leather was going to drag on the ground when I put it on. He continued to stand there and say nothing so I put my arms quickly into the sleeves. It hung about three inches off the ground. He gave me a triumphant grin and then moved around behind me, pulling at the material muttering about straps as he did. When he was finished, the coat didn't gape away from my body as much as it had.

"There's a nice custom pocket on the inside left." Leaning around me, he flipped the coat open to point to it. "And this…" Bending down to the cuff of his jeans, he pulled up the material to reveal a knife handle sticking out of his boot. "Fits in it perfectly." I knew my eyes were wide as he slipped the knife into the pocket.

He stepped back quickly and jammed his hands into his pockets like he was afraid of grabbing me if he didn't. As he looked down, just before his shaggy blonde hair covered his eyes, I thought I saw a tear running down his cheek. "Find a better place, Bree," he whispered, so softly I almost missed it.

I swallowed the lump that lodged in my throat and nodded. "Thanks."

"Let's go." Darren urged from where he stood. "I want you to have more than enough time to find somewhere to stay when it gets dark.

I wanted to take a huge breath and build the courage to take this final and first step, but I couldn't bring myself to do it in front of them.

"Mom sent a bag of things." Darren patted the small one tied to the back of the saddle. He didn't elaborate what kind of things. Running his hand to the front of it, he flipped open the small pack. "Shawn's hand-gun is in here and there's enough ammo on the other side to last a long time." He looked down at the ground and said nothing further.

I moved around to the front of Tremor and looked up into his big eyes. "We're going to be just fine aren't we?" I ran my hand down the blackness of his coat over his neck and picked up the reins. His ears flicked and he brought his mouth down to nibble at my shoulder. As far as encouraging signs went, that one worked for me.

I couldn't stand the looks Bobby and Darren were giving each other, so without prolonging this any further, I turned and started to lead the way down the street, thankful we weren't far from the nearest border.

I kept Tremor at an easy trot until we were far enough away that I wouldn't be tempted to go back. Stopping, I turned him and looked back to the two men that stood exactly where I'd left them a few minutes earlier. I waved my arm at them, silently thanked them and wished them well. Turning the animal in the opposite direction, I prodded him with my heels to get us out of here. He complied without hesitation and carried us quickly away from the city that was filled with nothing but heartache that I could no longer face.

About the Author

J. Risk is a pseudonym used by Jacqueline Paige

I wanted to write a story that would fit into new adult levels as well as adult. Something that was serious with fun elements--paranormal / fantasy that everyone could read and enjoy.

I've decided to use J. Risk as the pen name for this to separate this series from my other writing which is definitely adult reading material.

Jacqueline Paige lives in Ontario in a small town that's part of the popular Georgian Triangle area.

She began her writing career in 2006 and since her first published works in 2009 she hasn't stopped. Jacqueline describes her writing as *all things paranormal*, which she has proven is her niche with stories of witches, ghosts, physics and shifters now on the shelves.

When Jacqueline isn't lost in her writing, she spends time with her five children, most of whom are finally able to look after her instead of the other way around. Together they do random road trips, that usually end up with them lost, shopping trips where they push every button in the toy aisle, hiking when there's enough time to escape and bizarre things like creating new daring recipes in the kitchen. She's a grandmother to six (so far) and looks forward to corrupting many more in the years to come.

Jacqueline loves to hear from her readers, you can find her at

http://jacquelinepaige.com/

Author note:

Did you enjoy reading one of my books?

If so, PLEASE help spread the word on social media. You can help by sharing on Facebook, tweet about it, post something on Instagram, Pinterest. Posting a review on your favorite book sites go a long way to help authors. With your help in keeping my books "out there", I can continue writing to keep those stories coming.

Writing and promoting can be very time consuming. I love talking to readers, but the hours spent on keeping so many social media outlets current can become overwhelming and time for writing pays the price. If you can take a few minutes to help, that would be awesome. Thank you!